THE GIRL IN CABIN 13

A.J. RIVERS

PROLOGUE

I slide to the edge of the couch cushion and lean forward. My elbows resting on my thighs, I clasp my hands and force myself to maintain eye contact with the crystal blue gaze in front of me. Those shouldn't be the eyes of the man sitting in the stiff-backed chair. He's less than two feet across from the sagging brown and beige plaid couch where I'm perched. Less than two feet and dingy green shag carpeting separate me from hands I know in my gut are soaked in blood. Clear, wide blue eyes like that shouldn't have seen the things this man has done.

It's a struggle not to let my expression give away any of the thoughts or emotions swirling in my brain. I can't let on anything. The men on either side of me are calm and collected; their faces almost blank. They're hearing the same things I am, but it's not having the same effect. The words hit me like bullets, searing through my skin, and burning the edges of my mind until I only see red. It's only worse that I know they're lies. At the very least, he's not telling the whole truth.

"Cut the bullshit," I snap.

Some part of me is aware the man beside me is talking, but I don't hear what he's saying before cutting him off. He shoots me a glare through the corner of his eye, his shoulders tightening.

"What do you mean?" the man in front of me says.

His name is Jeffrey, but we've been referring to him as Snake. The sheer cliché value of it makes me shudder. No one with that astounding of a lack of creativity should be responsible for the atrocities he's confessing to. And should have even less to do with the ones he's keeping tucked close to the vest. Those are what we really need to hear. I don't want to hear them. I know it will make me sicker. But if he doesn't, everything else he's already said won't matter.

"Give it up. That's all the same shit you've been spouting since the day we scraped your sorry ass off the asphalt," I say.

"Brittany," the man to my side, Tank, says. The hint of warning in his voice goes completely ignored. At this point, I don't care.

"I'm telling you everything," Snake insists. Again.

"The fuck you are. Do you think we're stupid? Do you think *I'm* stupid? I told you, my connections can get you off on some of these petty charges and get you a shorter sentence in a good pen for the bigger ones. But you have to be straight up with us. I'm not going to put my skin on the line for someone who's too chicken shit to man up to what he did. You're the one who did it. I'm not going to pretend you didn't, and neither are the cops. They will rope you up and drag your ass without a second thought. You think they care for a minute what you have to say?"

"Brittany," Gage, the man to my other side, hisses.

"No. I don't care. This guy is pissing me off. Where would you be right now without us? If we hadn't found you and took you in, you think you'd have even half a chance? If you do, you're fucking fooling yourself. By now, you'd have been passed around the cell block for a phone call home and three packets of ramen. And where do you think you'll be without us when you get yanked up on these charges? You think you're smart enough to wriggle your way out of them? Without our help, you don't have a chance. People like you have a really good habit of ending up as scum at the bottom of the shower drain. So, unless you want the last thing you see to be a pair of hairy legs and mildewed tile, you're going to cut the shit, stop flapping your jaws, and tell us the truth."

"I did," Snake argues.

"You told us about some convenience store clerk you shot, the drugs you stole, and the cop you ran over. You think any of those things mean anything to us? You think we're impressed?" My throat aches with the tension of the words slicing through it, and my temples throb. "I've heard all that before. That's stuff I pulled off before high school. Tell me about the little girls."

Gage shifts beside me, his knuckle's digging painfully into the small of my back. He's trying to shut me up, but the words have already started tumbling out, and there's no stopping them. It's taken everything out of me to make this man part of my life. Befriending him and earning his trust has been harder than anything else I've ever had to do.

It will be worth it if he gives me what I want. But if he doesn't, I've wasted this time and opened myself up to filth I'll never be able to wash away. Worse than that, he might keep going.

"What little girls?" Snake asks.

"Ignore her," Tank says. "She's messed up. Partied too hard last night. Probably doesn't even know where we are or who she's talking to. Just talk to me. Look, you know why we're here. You've got some pretty serious shit hanging over you, but you're one of us. We're not going to let one of our brothers go down. But our brothers don't lie to us. The only way we can hook you up with our guys is to know everything we're dealing with. We need the details. You can't hold anything back from us and still expect us to help."

"Stop babying him," I nudge him angrily. "We know what he did. He just needs to spit it out."

Snake stands up and shakes his head, holding his hands up. "Look, I don't know what's going on here, but I didn't agree to any of this."

"Yes, you did," I say, standing up and taking a step toward him to block his way. "When we initiated you in, you knew you had to be straight up with us. Now it's time to give it up."

"Whatever you're on, it's nasty. You need to have a word with whoever you got it from. I'm leaving."

"You're not going anywhere," I say.

Snake pushes me out of the way, using me like a weapon to knock Gage and Tank off balance. He runs for the door and bursts out before we get a chance to get back to our feet. The men try to keep me in the house, but I don't listen to them. Chasing after Snake, I reach under my shirt and wrap my hand around the handle of my gun. He doesn't have a car, but that's not going to stop the slimy piece of shit from trying to get away from me. After jangling a few handles, he finds an unlocked door and dives behind the wheel. My shot obliterates the back window, but it doesn't stop him from cranking the engine.

Ignoring the screams of my name behind me, I run down the crumbling sidewalk to where he's already working the car out of its tight parking spot. Wrenching the passenger door open, I throw myself into the car.

My fist makes contact with Snake's jaw. He slams on the gas. The car lurches forward and smashes into the back of the car in front of it. I fall forward and land across him but manage to pull my knee up at just the right moment to dig into his belly.

He lets out an infuriated grunt and punches me in the side, knocking the wind out of me. Pain radiates along the side of my body. In the few seconds it takes to recover, he slings me back over into the passenger seat, and lights burst in front of my eyes as my head cracks against the window.

I don't let it stop me. I jam my foot out, smacking him in the side of his face. His sharp turn of the wheel makes the car spin to the side. Holding the wheel tightly, he leans over to search me and the area around me. I know he's looking for my gun. The wind whistles through the back window, reminding him of the shots I took at him. Him getting his hands on my weapon and being able to turn it on me is the last thing I need right now. At least for the moment, I'm on my own.

Hitting the control with my elbow, I lower the window and toss my gun out over my shoulder. It scatters somewhere on the pavement outside.

Snake drives faster, sending the car swinging back and forth as he struggles with me.

"What the fuck is wrong with you?" he demands. "Get off me!"

"No. Not until you pry your balls out of your belly and admit what you did."

"Do you get off on this stuff or something? You want to hear all the details?" He backhands me across the face, and I fall back. "You want to bring that back to bed with you tonight? Cozy up with all the images in your head of what I did to those little girls? I bet you didn't know there were boys, too. It's the most fun when they are so little and young; they don't know what's going on. They think we're going to play a game. One thought I was her babysitter. She didn't know I robbed her father and left him dead in the landfill. They still haven't found his body."

He laughs, but I don't hear it. The blind rage takes over. His voice is still around me, but the words aren't registering. The next thing I'm aware of is my hands around his neck and my knee buried in his stomach as he struggles to drive around me. Suddenly, the rumble of the engine stops, and the car slows to a stop. He shoves me away, spewing profanity as he tries to start the car again. It's pointless. He'd have to hot-wire it again.

Seconds later, the door behind me opens, and a hand grabs me by the back of my shirt, yanking me out onto the pavement. The slam of another door tells me he's gotten out. I struggle to get to my feet so I can chase him. But the man holding me isn't about to give me that chance. He's already tearing into me, and I know it's just going to get worse.

———

It started raining right after Bruno dragged me out of the car. I'm soaked to the bone by the time he stuffs me into one of the unmarked black cars parked behind the disabled sedan. I haven't gotten to change, and two hours of sitting in the frigid air conditioning of the office has my dirty blonde hair stuck to my head and my cutoff t-shirt clinging like ice to my skin. It's penance for the mess I just made of the operation. It's a little much. The least they could do is let me change into my real clothes.

Finally, the door opens, and Bruno sticks his head in.

"Griffin, get in here."

I let out a sigh and follow him to the office at the end of the hall. Creagan sits behind the desk, hunched over a file as he scribbles something. Bruno gestures me into the room and leaves as fast as he can. That's not a good sign. I sit down and watch him. The seconds tick past, and he doesn't acknowledge me. His office is even colder than the rest of the building, and my skin might start flaking off at any second. When ten minutes have passed, I lean forward.

"Creagan?"

"What's your name?" he asks.

Considering I've been working under him for the entirety of my career, that's not the question I'm anticipating.

"Excuse me?" I ask.

"Your name. What is your name?"

"Um. Emma."

That's me. Not Brittany, like I told Snake. Not Sugar, like a couple of the guys called me before I could stop them.

"Emma Griffin?" he asks.

He still hasn't looked at me. I have the strange feeling I've somehow transported backwards through time and am back at my initial interview.

"Yes," I tell him.

"Special Agent Emma Griffin, FBI?"

I'm not sure how much longer this is going to go and how many more pieces of identifying information he's going to tack onto the end of the title, so I try to flash-forward to the end.

"That's me. What's this all about?"

He finally looks at me.

"So, you're not Brittany, also known as Sugar, street runner, and gang member?"

I narrow my eyes slightly.

"Not at this particular moment."

Red dots appear on Creagan's cheeks just before he explodes.

"Then do you want to explain to me why the fuck you're acting like her?"

Oh, shit.

"Look, I know that didn't go ..."

"No. *You* look. Do you have any idea what you did out there? You could have compromised the entire operation," he fumes.

"Could have?"

"Somehow, even in the middle of your meltdown, you managed to get him to admit to everything before he crushed the recorder in your bra. He took off running after we disabled the car, but a couple of the guys caught up with him, and he's been arrested."

"So, everything worked out."

"Don't even try that. It's an absolute fluke this ended with us getting the information we needed, and the only reason that happened is because of the foundation laid out over the last few months. That saved your ass. What the hell happened to you out there? It's like your brain just stopped working."

"Did you hear the things he admitted to?" I asked.

"Yes. And I've heard worse before, and I'll hear worse again. It comes with the job, Griffin. Your job was to get him to admit to what he did so we could nail him. You couldn't control yourself out there, and it could have gone south real quick. You could have gotten yourself killed, or worse, gotten one of the guys killed."

"Wow. Thanks for that," I mutter.

"What is it you want me to say? You went completely off the handle. I'm going to leave my concern with the men who were actually doing what they were supposed to and maintained the professionalism during this operation."

My face burns, and I cross my arms over my chest.

"I've never had my professionalism questioned."

"You've also never given up so much information to a suspect, chased the suspect down, and tried to beat the living fuck out of him while he was driving a car. You could have ruined the entire operation!"

"He could have gotten away."

"It was a bait car, Griffin! It was put there in case something like this happened. We had control over that car. You know that. You're the one who begged and finagled your way into this operation, to begin with."

"I want more serious responsibilities. And my injuries are fine, thanks for asking," I spit.

It's petty, but I'm getting angry and don't want him to know just how far under my skin he's managed to crawl.

"You wouldn't have been injured at all if you didn't lose trust in the team and go bat-shit insane. If you weren't a lucky son of a bitch, that guy wouldn't have said a single usable word, and you would have been smashed and smeared across the street. Then he would have been free to find more children to play with. Is that what you wanted?" he asks.

"Of course, it isn't," I snap.

"Then you should have had your shit together."

I've had enough. I stand up.

"You've made your point. I'm sorry I went off script. It won't happen again," I say.

"No, it won't. Not any time soon, anyway," Creagan growls.

"What's that supposed to mean?"

"Until further notice, you're out of the field. Turn in your gun and find a cushion. You're riding the desk from now on."

CHAPTER ONE

SIX MONTHS LATER

The feeling of riding a train has always put me to sleep. I'm far from unique in that. No matter what time of day it is, every train crisscrossing around the country is dotted with sleeping passengers. Some try to be subtle about it and pretend they aren't really sleeping, crossing their hands over their stomachs and closing their eyes as they maintain as perfect of posture as they can. Others have no shame and dive into it full-bore, slapping on their sleep masks, and curling up under blankets to hide from the trip. I have a far deeper knowledge of that phenomenon now after spending the last sixteen hours in this seat.

Right now, I'm fighting the urge to join the latter group. I have a giant cardigan in the bag at my feet, and I want to wrap myself in it and just block out the rest of the ride. Unfortunately, that's not an option for me. My stop is coming up soon, and for the last seven hours, I've been on strict orders to stay awake. I am officially on duty even if the messy bun on top of my head and my shoes sitting discarded to the side say different. Paying attention to my surroundings is crucial, and I can't do that sleeping.

This is the first time I've been allowed out in the field since the unfortunate incident during my last operation. I'm not entirely clear on why Creagan sprung me from desk duty to put me on this one, but it doesn't matter. I'm tired of shuffling papers and never want to see another highlighter in my life. I can't afford to mess this up.

If that means not letting myself sleep so I can be vigilant about what's happening around me, even when I'm on the train, that's what I'm going to do. And I will read the same newspaper for the tenth time to keep my brain going even though it's creeping well past sundown. Fortunately for this particular mission, the section of paper tucked in my bag when I got on the train has just the bloody, disturbing story to keep my mind from wanting to relax.

Unfortunately for me, that bloody, disturbing story is the exact reason I'm on this train headed to a tiny town in the middle of nowhere. Or more precisely, to a train station, a forty-five-minute drive from the tiny town in the middle of nowhere. There I'll pick up the car left for me by another agent. It all feeds into the narrative, the persona I'm taking on for this investigation.

Going undercover isn't new to me. My foray into being Brittany was just the latest in a long line of operations that had me slipping in and out of the life of people who didn't really exist. It's all with the goal of wedging myself into a situation in just the right way to make it crack open. This assignment is different. I don't have my team beside me. There are no other agents planted strategically on the train, and I won't have to pretend not to know them when they show up in town. Creagan sent me alone. There's no backup to help in case things start to go wrong.

Which means I sure as hell better keep them from going wrong.

And that brings me to the hours I've been keeping myself awake, paying attention to every face that walks past. The trip didn't actually have to be this long. I could have driven straight from my neighborhood right outside of Quantico in less than seven hours. But the direct path would have been too easy to track. Instead, I've been on a roundabout adventure, changing trains and following a few different routes to get me on this final leg. After every stop, I get up and stroll through the cars, taking note of passengers who got on and off. I can only hope each of them gets to their destination and none end up dead along the tracks.

My eyes sweep over the newspaper in my hands again. Ten sets of eyes in stark black and white stare back at me. For at least two of them, this train was the last thing they saw. For the other eight... well, they'll have to be found before anyone will know that.

These ten are why I'm going undercover in Feathered Nest, Virginia. With a name like that, the population of the town can't be high, making the number of victims all the more staggering. Eight of the ten are still missing. According to the information Creagan gave me during my briefing, the amount of blood found at the scene of each disappearance, along with there being no sign of any of them since, give credence to the theory they are all dead. The two found mangled by the railroad tracks offers a glimpse into the possibility of what might have happened to them.

It's the interesting positioning of the tracks that brought me into this. Though the two bodies were found in locations within a few hundred yards of each other, the curve of the track meant one, the young woman, was actually in North Carolina. Once the blood starts spattering over state lines, we tend to get involved.

Personally, I think creating a collection of eight missing person posters on the utility pole of such a small town is a bit extreme of a distance to go before calling in help. But I'm here now. And I'm going to figure out what's happening to these people and stop the son of a bitch doing it before it happens again.

A few minutes before pulling into the station, the sleepy-eyed conductor makes his way down the aisle, letting us know we'll arrive soon. Neon note cards tucked above each pair of seats contain abbreviations indicating our destination. It's no surprise I'm the only one getting off at my station. It's the closest one to Feathered Nest, which is hidden somewhere in the woods we rumbled past several minutes ago and consists of a single platform. A small booth takes on the responsibilities of a station building.

By the time I toss my bag over my shoulder, gather up my small suitcase, and head out of the train, my larger luggage is already leaning against the booth. I don't know how it managed to get there so fast, but the train isn't playing around. I haven't even picked up my bigger suitcase before the train lets out a loud whistle and chugs away. It seems just as suspicious of the surroundings as everyone else has gotten.

Just as Creagan promised, a car sits in one of the four parking spots behind the booth. It's just old and nondescript enough not to get noticed. It is the oatmeal of sensible cars. My phone rings in my pocket as I fish the hidden key out of the wheel well and unlock the trunk to haul my luggage inside.

"Are you there yet?" Bellamy whispers loudly through the line.

I chuckle and shut the back door before slipping behind the wheel.

"You don't have to whisper, Bells. There's no one around here to hear you. I just got to my car."

I grab the rearview mirror and tilt it to reflect the entirety of the backseat.

"What about hidden people? You just checked your mirror for someone balled up in front of your backseat, didn't you?" she asks.

I've been called out. As one of my two best friends, and the person in my life who has known me the longest, Bellamy might very well have too much insight into me.

"You would, too, if you saw this place. I didn't know there was this much dark in the world."

She gasps. "Oh, no. What happened? Did you already see something horrible happen?"

"No," I tell her, pulling out of the parking space and onto the road behind the platform. "I mean actual dark. Like lack of light. There are two light posts on the platform, and I'm currently driving away from them. Speaking of which, I need my GPS to get to the house, so I've got to go."

"Okay. Well, stay safe. Keep me updated."

"I will."

I hang up and plug the address of the house where I'll be staying for the duration of the job into my phone. It pulls up a twisty path through the woods, and I set to it. The quiet outside the car is incredible. I can't decide if it's better to have music on or not. It makes the quiet inside the car less oppressive, but at the same time, seems to make the tangible silence outside more unnerving. The music means I can't catch any sounds beyond the car. I'm even more isolated.

The music situation goes back and forth a few times before I finally pull up in front of the house. Cabin is a more appropriate term. I find it at the end of a long driveway barely visible under a thick layer of leaves and pine needles, the log and river rock house is totally dark and facing a lake. Creagan arranged the rental, and I know the owner is expecting me. But apparently, that doesn't translate into making sure the house is welcoming for when I actually get here.

I park to the side, with my headlights shining on the door and go up onto the porch. A key hangs from a piece of twine off a nail in the middle of the door. I assume it used to be the seasonal home of a wreath. Just above it are the slightly rusty, dingy house number digits.

13. Well, that's not ominous at all.

Unlocking the door, I feel around for a switch. When the room fills with hazy yellow light, I make my way back to the car and unload everything before turning the car off. I step inside, closing and locking the door behind me.

Here I am. Officially a temporary resident of Feathered Nest.

I should want to crawl into bed right now, but the exhaustion from the train is gone. I change into stretchy pants and ward off the chill of the night with a baggy sweatshirt. Twisting my hair up onto my head, I make my way into the living room to look through the files I brought with me. Reading through the stories of the people who have gone missing sends chills along my spine and makes my skin prick. But it isn't just their eyes haunting me.

Looking at them makes thoughts I try to keep pushed to the back of my mind rush forward. In the dark-haired man laughing from a lawn chair as fireworks reflect just in the bottom corner of his sunglasses, I see my father. The corners of my eyes sting just thinking of him. In the nine years since he disappeared, I haven't stopped wondering what happened to him. I won't stop looking for him.

My throat tightens more when my eyes move over to the picture of a younger man sitting astride a motorcycle at the edge of a dirt road. Greg would never have ridden a motorcycle. I cringe at the thought. I'm thinking of him in past tense again. I can't do that. He's out there somewhere. I have to tell myself that and really believe it. There's a reason he went missing. Just like there's a reason our last conversation, just three weeks before he disappeared, was a breakup that came out of nowhere.

Forcing both men out of my mind, I replaced their images with the details about the case. I'm trying to lay them out to coordinate with a map of the town and surrounding areas so I can visualize the places where they disappeared. It doesn't make any sense. There aren't any patterns or obvious meaning to any of the locations. My phone rings, and I pick it up from the corner of the table where I set it, glancing at the screen before answering.

"Hey, Eric."

"Did you get into the deep, dark woods okay?" my other best friend asks.

I can almost see the laughter in his light brown eyes.

"You were in on this, weren't you?" I ask. "You knew what they were sending me into."

"I thought you wanted to be back out in the field."

"Of course I do. That doesn't mean I love the circumstances. Especially since I know what the Boys' Club has been saying about it."

"What do you mean?" he asks.

"You know exactly what I mean. Every guy on the team has been muttering and griping about Creagan sending me here rather than any of them. They think I can't possibly handle something like this, and he only chose me because I'm a woman and will be able to manipulate the people of the town more easily."

"I don't think that's really what they think," Eric says.

"One of them called the case the Mayonnaise Jar," I tell him.

"The what?"

"The Mayonnaise Jar. Like when a girl can't open a jar of mayonnaise and a guy does it, but she says she loosened the lid? Yep. That's what they think of me. Van Drossen came up to me right before I left and told me not to worry. All I needed to do was a little snooping and see if I can get a lead or two, then you boys would swoop in and finish it up for me. I wasn't going to have any trouble."

"He said that to you?" Eric asks incredulously.

"With his arm wrapped around me," I say, shifting a few of the pictures.

I put the phone on speaker and set it down, so I have both hands to work with.

"And he still has all of his appendages?"

"He's lucky as hell I'm still on a short leash after the Mr. Big incident. But it's fine. It will just make him look all the worse when I figure this out myself and don't need any knights in shining FBI badges to come rescue me," I mutter.

"You're going to solve the case yourself?" Eric asks.

"Was that a note of disbelief I heard in your voice?" I ask.

"No. Just keeping up on the news."

I laugh. "Well, that's the news. I'm tired of having these guys look at me like I'm not good enough or that they're better agents than me. Even worse are the ones who are treating me like glass since Greg."

I swallow hard to rid my throat of the sudden tightness.

"We're going to find him, Emma," Eric tells me gently.

I nod even though he can't see me. "I know. But I can't really think about that right now. I have to concentrate on this and how I'm going to figure it out."

"Have you made any progress?"

"Not really. I've been looking over the files for the last week, and nothing has fallen into place. I can understand why the local police didn't immediately link the disappearances. They don't seem to have anything to do with each other. There's no pattern other than the people being gone and there being blood. They all come from this same tiny town, but that's about it. No other real connection. I can't really imagine a police force in a place like this has a tremendous amount of experience with murder cases, much less mass disappearances."

"Are you sure you don't want me to come out there to help? I could take a backseat and just give you a hand when you need it."

"No. Thanks, but I really need to do this on my own. This is my chance to get back into the Bureau's good graces, and it really is a fascinating case. I'm looking forward to trying to unravel it. Besides, it would be more suspicious if there were two strangers who suddenly showed up in town and started poking around."

"Well, the offer stands," he says. "You let me know, and I'm on the first covered wagon out to you."

My laugh almost drowns out the sound of the two slow knocks on the front door of the cabin. I scoop up my phone to carry it with me.

"Hold on. I think the owner of the cabin where I'm staying just showed up. Give me just a second."

I cross to the door and pull it open. The man outside stares at me with widened eyes, then collapses onto the porch with a heavy thud.

"Emma?" Eric says.

"I'm going to have to call you back," I tell him, my eyes locked on the blood soaking through the man's shirt.

I shove the phone in my pocket and crouch down over the massive form. He's gripping something in his hand, and I pull it out. The folded piece of paper feels hot and damp from his palm despite the chill of the night. I unfold it slowly, with trembling hands.

My heart wedges in my throat. Scrawled across the paper, in heavy writing, is my name.

CHAPTER TWO

THEN

She cowered behind the banister, gripping a spindle in each hand as she watched what was going on in the landing beneath her. She was too old to be hiding this way, she knew it, but that didn't take away any of the fear that kept her locked in place on the steps. All the men in dark suits shuffling around on the shiny polished floor made her think of ants in the summertime.

No matter what they did, the tiny little sugar ants made their way through the windows and gathered on the kitchen counters and in the bathroom sinks. They were so tiny they looked like specks; their legs invisible until you were right up on them. They always looked so busy, so determined to do whatever they needed to do. Sometimes she would put her finger down right in the middle of their line just to see what would happen. The ones ahead of her fingertip marched forward, unbothered by the sudden appearance of an obstacle behind them. Those she blocked scrambled back and forth, trying to decide which way to go. When they finally did, the line fell into place, and they just continued on their way.

Nothing would stop them. Nothing deterred them.

Carry on; she would giggle to herself.

That's what the men down in the landing were doing. They called each other and scrambled in place, moving around quickly. She knew something terrible had happened. You could feel it in the air. Every breath was harder to take, and it seemed like the pressure in the atmosphere was pushing down around her until she might be crushed. She needed somebody to talk to her. Somebody needed to come up onto the steps and tell her what was going on so she would be able to let the air go and move. But they didn't. Nobody did. Not even her father.

She saw him once. Among the men in the dark suits scrambling around the foyer. He was there, just for a second, a bright spot in pale blue striped pajamas among all the unfamiliar darkness. All the men spoke to him with respect and dignity, like they didn't notice he was in his pajamas. She couldn't tell what they were saying, but the way they held their bodies and leaned into him when he spoke said he was in charge, if only for those seconds when he was there. And then he was gone.

She didn't see him again until much later. Long after the strange metal bed draped in white wheeled out of the back room and through the foyer out of the house. She knew what it was. She was old enough to have seen a stretcher before. She even rode on one when she fell and broke her wrist during a game of kickball. But the blankets weren't pulled up over her then. They didn't even make her lie all the way down. Half the bed sat upright, propping her tiny frame up while a woman in blue clothes far too tight for her body and a smile just wide enough for all her bright white teeth talked to her and took her blood pressure.

But she knew what it was. She knew why it was covered all the way up and why no one was hurrying to get it outside. They only didn't hurry when there was nothing they could do. Even when she broke her wrist, they hurried. They hurried her onto the stretcher, and they hurried her into the ambulance. They even hurried her through the emergency room and to the little cup of liquid Tylenol the nurse gave her to lessen the pain.

But they weren't hurrying this time. Which meant the stretcher was holding someone who didn't need help anymore.

Her mother. Her mother didn't need help anymore.

Later that night, her father came back home. He didn't leave her alone. One of his friends stayed there with her, but she didn't talk to him. She didn't even see him. He was just downstairs in the living room with the TV sending up the sounds of a game show and commercials for Easter candy and Spring Break. She didn't move. She stayed right on the step, gripping the spindles, and watching the door for her father to come back in.

When he finally did, he didn't notice her. The door closed behind him, and he pressed against it, his head falling back as he slid down to sit on the floor with his knees pulled up high to his chest. His elbows rested on his thighs, and he combed his fingers back through his hair, holding it so tight it looked like he was trying to pull it out of his head. He wasn't wearing his blue striped pajamas anymore. She didn't know when or where he changed his clothes, but he was suddenly in one of the dark suits like the ant-men who roamed around before the stretcher was wheeled out of the house. She wished he was still in his pajamas. She had never seen her father cry, and she wanted to wrap her arms around him and bring him to bed, to tuck him in and give him something warm to drink.

She would get her mother. Her mother would know what to do to make him feel better. She almost got to her feet before she remembered. She couldn't get her mother. Her mother wasn't there anymore and was never going to be again. She wasn't a little child, but she felt like one. There was no other way to feel. She walked down the steps and sat on the floor to cry next to her father.

She didn't know she fell asleep until she woke up the next morning in a bed she didn't recognize. This wasn't home. This wasn't where she slept just the night before. Sunlight streaming through the window told her it wasn't really morning anymore, and the smell of a grilled cheese sandwich and tomato soup said she missed breakfast but was getting her favorite lunch. She hated getting out of bed and not knowing where to walk. This wasn't the first time it happened to her, and deep inside, she knew it wasn't going to be the last. There was no permanence. There was nothing she could hold onto long enough for it to really feel like hers.

Even the sunlight changed. From place to place, wherever they went, the sun wasn't the same. Sometimes it was hot and strong, stinging on her skin and warming the ground beneath her feet. Sometimes it was weak and milky, seeming to barely even get all the way down to the ground before fading out. And sometimes it was a trick, looking bright and vibrant, but giving no warmth when she walked outside.

All she had was her family. And now she knew that changed, too.

CHAPTER THREE

NOW

"No, I don't know him. No, I don't know who he is and have never seen him before. Yes, I'm sure."

I have answered the exact same questions over and over and over and over again. Not that it's a surprise. I've been the one to ask this question so many times before. But I've never stopped to think of just how obnoxious it could be to have someone staring me right in the face and demanding me tell them information I couldn't possibly give them because I don't know it. I've been standing in the doorway to the rental cabin for over an hour now, watching what amounts to a police department in this tiny little town shift around the front porch and try to make sense out of the body still lying on the wood. The heat from inside keeps the back half of me at least partially warm, but the chill outside keeps getting sharper, and I'm quickly losing patience.

But at least I'm getting the opportunity to see these men at work. This department is why I was sent to Feathered Nest in the first place. They aren't handling the investigation into the disappearances and murders as they should be and refusing to accept help from any of the agencies and departments in surrounding areas.

"I'm gonna have to ask you to come down to the station with us and answer a few more questions," one of the officers tells me.

He never introduced himself, so I have nothing to call him. His coat covers up his nametag and badge, so for all I know, I'm letting the local chimney sweep investigate the body on my porch. I reach into the cabin to grab my bag and close the door behind me. It feels strange just walking away with the body still there. The paper with my name on it is inside, hidden out of view, and I have no intention of telling the police about it until and unless the right time comes up.

I follow the officer to his car and climb inside with him. We make our way through the town, and I take the opportunity to look around and try to get a little more familiar with it. Everything seems fairly quiet, like the entire place has already gone to bed, except for one stretch of the main street. Cars fill most of the space for at least a block, and lights pour out onto the sidewalk. I lean forward and point through the driver's side window at it.

"What's that?" I ask.

The officer looks at me like he's shocked I would dare speak to him, then remembers I'm not actually a suspect, and he didn't arrest me. He swallows and adjusts his grip on the steering wheel.

"That's Teddy's. Some people around here call it a bar. Some call it a tavern. It's a place to go get a bite to eat and a drink at the end of the day. See friends. Maybe even do a little bit of dancing," he tells me. "It's owned by a guy named Jake Logan. You'll always see him up there. He doesn't trust even a day to go by without overseeing the bar himself for most of the time. Pretty good man, all considering."

"All considering?" I ask.

The officer laughs. "Just something folks say. Doesn't just about everybody have an 'all considering' in their past?"

"I guess they do," I muse.

A few moments later, we turn into the small parking lot of the police station. He goes along to the side of the building and parks next to one other police car. I get out, and he walks me around to the front of the building so we can go in the main door. An elderly woman looks up from the desk when we walk in.

"Evening, Esther," the officer nods.

"Nicolas, if you're bringing this lady in, use the side door. You know how the chief doesn't like you to bring them through the lobby," she says.

"I'm not bringing her in," the officer, whose name is apparently Nicolas, replies. "Not exactly. She's here to have an interview with the chief."

"Well, go on back. He's in his office."

I follow the officer through a door behind the desk and along a hallway. He gets to a closed door and raps on it twice before turning the knob and glancing inside.

"Chief, I have her here."

"Come on in," a gruff voice says.

Nicolas pushes the door the rest of the way open and steps out of the way so I can go into the office. A large man sits at a desk sipping from a can of soda. He shoves his hand into a bag of potato chips but pulls it out empty and stares at it unhappily. I walk up to the desk, and he stands, brushing off his hands and extending one to me.

"Chief LaRoche," he says.

I take his hand and shake it. He gives the kind of unnecessarily firm handshake men tend to give when they want to exert some sort of dominance. I don't hesitate to give it right back. If there's one thing this man isn't going to do, it's intimidate me. He has no idea I'm here to save his ass, but that doesn't give him an excuse to act like he hung his fucking belt buckle in the sky and called it the moon.

"Emma... Monroe."

I struggle over the name slightly. It's still strange to have my last name different but keep my first name. Sometimes I don't understand Creagan's decisions. *A lot of times,* I don't understand Creagan's decisions. But he's who determines if I stay in the Bureau or not, so I'll keep following along with them.

"Nice to meet you, Ms. Monroe. Why don't you go ahead and have a seat?" He gestures to the chair across the desk from him. I settle in, and he folds his fingers together, placing them on the desk and staring at me for a few silent seconds. "Why don't you tell me what's going on?"

I suddenly have a feeling like I've come in to talk about a sore throat.

"I'm not sure what you're asking me," I tell him.

"My officers tell me there was an incident out at the house you're renting," he says.

"I guess you could call it an incident. I didn't see what actually happened, so I don't know how exactly to describe it."

"You didn't see anything? Nothing at all?"

"Nothing at all. Not until I opened my door and saw the man fall on the porch."

"How long have you been in town?" he asks.

"I got here less than half an hour before his body showed up on my porch," I tell the chief.

"Is that so? And what are you doing in Feathered Nest?"

Now's the time to start weaving my story, to lay the foundation of who I am and why I'm here so I can better slip into the atmosphere and learn more about it. With a little town like this, it shouldn't come as a surprise for people to be a little suspicious of a new person showing up. Places like this are well-established. Everyone who lives here built their lives with the resources and opportunities created on the backs of their mothers and fathers, and their mothers and fathers before them, and before them. Things stay close here, and new faces are always few and far between.

"I'm looking to start a new life," I tell him. "I just got out of a bad situation and need to take some time for myself and decide what I'm going to do next. I have a cousin who lives not too far from here, and she's told me stories of driving through your sweet town, and it sounded exactly like what I'm looking for. Somewhere peaceful and quiet, where I'll have the time to think and where I can feel safe."

With the exception of the serial killer running around, I think to myself.

LaRoche seems to contemplate what I said, then something like a smile bends his lips. The expression doesn't quite get into his watery green eyes. I don't like the feeling he's giving off. It's like the shimmer on top of a pool of oil. Tenuous and morphing. Like every time I look at him, there's something slightly different about the way he's looking back at me or the thoughts going through his mind.

"Well, it doesn't seem like you're off to a great start, does it?" he asks with an uncomfortable, inappropriate laugh.

"Am I just about done here?" I ask. "It's been a long trip, and as you can imagine, tonight has been stressful. I'd like to get some sleep."

"I have just a few more questions for you," he says. "You say you don't know the man on the porch."

It's not a question, but I shake my head anyway.

"I don't. Like I said, I just got into town a few minutes before he knocked on my door. I have no idea who he is."

"He knocked on your door? I thought you said he was dead when you opened it." LaRoche says it like he thinks he's caught me up in some sort of lie.

I narrow my eyes at him slightly.

"I was inside my cabin checking in with a friend who wanted to make sure I arrived alright. Someone knocked on the door. Since the owner of the cabin wasn't there when I got there, and I didn't meet anyone in town, I figured it was probably them there to welcome me and give me information about the place. I opened the door, and the man fell forward onto the porch."

"Dead?" LaRoche asks.

"Yes," I tell him.

"And how did you know that?" he asks.

I resist the urge to roll my eyes.

"He had no pulse," I say.

"How did you know to check his pulse?"

"In the cupcake baking seminar I attended last summer, a sweet old lady had a heart attack while making caramel filling. She just laid there for the next twenty minutes because no one knew what to do with her. Finally, someone thought to check her pulse and called 9-1-1 when she didn't have one. The paramedics came for her, and that very night the organizers of the seminar stopped all cupcake baking to teach everyone how to properly check a pulse," I answer, straight-faced.

LaRoche stares at me like he's trying to figure out if I'm being genuine. When I don't say anything else, he looks down at the paper on his desk.

"And when you realized he was dead, did you notice anything else about him?"

"He appeared to be bleeding," I say.

"Did you see who did it?" he asks.

I look at him strangely.

"I didn't say anyone did anything to him."

"Well, if he was bleeding, don't you assume someone did something?" he asks.

"Not necessarily. The cabin is out in the woods. He could just have easily been attacked by an animal. Or been in an accident."

"And you didn't come to any conclusions?"

"No."

He stares at me for a few long seconds, then stands again, offering me another handshake.

"I appreciate your time. I'll let you know if there's anything else I need from you. Welcome to Feathered Nest. Nicolas?" The door to the office opens, and the younger officer looks in. "Bring Ms. Monroe here somewhere to wait."

"To wait?" I ask. "For what?"

"Until the body has been properly processed and removed from the porch, you can't return to the cabin. I'm sure you understand that. The officer will bring you somewhere comfortable to wait, and I'll let you know when you can return."

I'm frustrated as we head out of the station and get back in the officer's car.

"Bring me to Teddy's," I tell him.

"There's a diner that might be a calmer place," he suggests.

"That's fine, I'd rather go to Teddy's."

I have no interest in sitting around a quiet, empty diner for whoever knows how long it's going to be until they let me go back to the cabin. At least at the bar I have the chance of learning something about the town and the people in it.

And have a drink. Could definitely use one of those.

CHAPTER FOUR

S tepping into the dimly lit interior tells me everything I need to know about why people in town would call this place a tavern. It has the feeling of a place a traveler would like to stop and rest. Whether there are actually places to sleep here or not, it's a comfortable place to find yourself when you need a break from the rest of the world.

Until everyone else there notices you. Dozens of eyes turn to look at me from around the room. The crowd in the bar is far from huge, but their scrutinizing eyes make it seem like I'm out on a stadium stage. I stop just inside the door and look back at them. Unsure of exactly what to do next. A man sitting at a nearby table stands up and comes towards me with a swagger in his walk. I can't tell if the swagger is purposeful or alcohol induced. Possibly a little of both.

"Well," he says, hiking up his pants and sucking his front teeth. "Aren't you a pretty one. You must be new around here."

"And you must not be," I retort.

"Why don't you let me show you around?" he asks, trying to sling an arm around my shoulders.

I duck out of the way, shaking my head.

"No thank you. It seems to me you need just about all the guidance you have to get back to your table over there."

Some of the other men scattered throughout the bar let out whoops and hollers of delight. The man in front of me goes red in the face. He looks like he's going to say something else, which I'm sure won't be nearly as friendly. A younger man comes up behind him and smacks him hard on the back.

"That sounds like a good idea, and I'm sure Randy here appreciates the suggestion. Don't you, Randy?" the younger man says jovially.

The older man blinks at him a few times like the words are having a hard time getting all the way into his head, then he nods.

"Sure, Jake. I was just trying to welcome her to town."

"I know, friendly as you are. But why don't you go on back to your table and I'll take it from here. The missus will probably be sending along your usual ride soon, so I would think you want to make sure you finish up that beer."

Randy looks embarrassed and downtrodden as he maneuvers his way back over to his table and plops down into the seat, pulling his beer over to him and nursing it. I look over at the younger man and smile.

"Thanks," I say.

"Not a problem. I wouldn't want Randy giving you the wrong idea about our town."

He starts walking over to the dark wood bar up against the wall at the side of the room. I fall into step behind him. He walks behind the bar, and I slide onto one of the stools still available at the very corner.

"And what would the wrong idea about your town be?" I ask.

"That all the men around here are like Randy, who won't even give you two seconds to breathe when you walk into a room," he shrugs.

"Then I am glad I don't have that idea," I chuckle. "So, Jake. Does that make you Jake Logan, the owner of this place?"

He looks at me in surprise. "My reputation precedes me. I'm not sure if that's a good thing or not."

"Don't worry. The police officer I rode over with told me."

He laughs. "Police officer, huh? Maybe your reputation should be the one we're worried about. Quite a way to make a first impression in town."

"You have no idea."

"Well, why don't I get you a drink, and you can tell me about it. Then I'll decide for myself what kind of rumors I'm going to spread about you among all the townsfolk."

"Make it a good beer, and you've got yourself a deal."

He takes a glass from the rows lined up on the counter and fills it at one of the taps. The thick, dark brew fills the glass and ends in a perfect head. He slides the glass toward me, and I smile.

"I'm impressed," I tell him. "Looks like you might have poured a beer once or twice in your life."

"Once or twice," he echoes with a grin. "I think I was pouring beer before I poured my own milk at breakfast."

I take a sip and lick the foam from my lips. "Is that legal?"

"It is when it's the police you're pouring for," he shrugs.

I nod. "Funny how laws are flexible like that."

Jake tilts his head toward the glass. "You like it?"

"It's really good. So, why is it you've been skipping nursery school to pull beer?"

"Well, this was my father's bar before it was mine. And his father's before it was his."

"Was he Teddy?" I ask, taking another sip.

"Nope. Teddy was the man my grandfather won it off of in a game of poker," Jake tells me.

I laugh. "You're kidding."

Jake shrugs. "Feathered Nest has all kinds of stories."

"So, you've been here your whole life?" I ask.

"Oh, no. You're not going down that path anymore. You can't avoid it all night. I want to hear about your brush with the law."

"I wouldn't exactly call it a brush with the law. Just an incident involving the law."

"Go ahead," he nods.

I wait for him to laugh and wave off the story, but when he doesn't, I let out a sigh.

"Alright. So, I just got into town. Literally. I was at the place I'm renting for less than half an hour when someone knocked on the door. I assumed it was just the owner of the house because no one had left me information or stayed to meet me or anything. So, I opened the door, and it was definitely not the owner of the house."

"Who was it?" he asks.

"Well, that's kind of the problem. I don't know. He collapsed when I opened the door and died on the porch. That's how I ended up getting picked up by the police and brought to the station to meet the delightful Chief LaRoche."

He fills his own cup of beer and holds it up to me in a toast.

"Now that is an entrance," he says.

I hold my glass up toward his and bow my head slightly. "Thank you. I try my best."

"Did you find out what happened to him?" he asks. "Was it a heart attack or something?"

"I don't know. I'm sure I'll find out more when they do the examination on him, but I highly doubt it was a heart attack. He was bleeding."

Jake's face darkens slightly.

"Bleeding?" he asks. "Did the police seem concerned about that? Did they mention anything about it?"

He seems suddenly aggressive, like the idea of this stranger being hurt is seriously upsetting him.

"Not specifically. They were obviously worried about someone being dead on the porch, and they asked me a lot of questions, but they didn't say anything directly about it," I tell him.

He's looking down at his feet like he's trying to get his thoughts together, but then suddenly lifts his head to look at me.

"I'm sorry. I just didn't expect you to say that."

"Is something wrong?" I gently prod, seeing how much he'll reveal to me.

"Don't know if it's something you really want to be hearing about on your first night here," he says.

"It's alright. I can handle it," I offer.

He shakes his head again, tipping his glass to gently tap the rim against mine.

"On to better things. Where are you staying?" he asks.

I don't show my disappointment, but keep up the conversation, hoping to guide it back to the situation in the town.

"A cabin by the lake in the woods," I say with a laugh. "Out near Rattlesnake Point."

"I know where that is. It's a cute little place from what I've seen of it."

"Well, that brings me to a very important question... are there actually rattlesnakes around here?" I ask.

Jake laughs and shakes his head. "No. You don't have to worry about that. I don't know exactly why it has that name, but those cabins up there are nice and quiet, even if they're usually empty. It's nice to know someone is giving the place some life. How long are you planning on being here? Or are you just passing through?"

"I'm not sure exactly how long. I don't have a specific end date in mind. Coming here is kind of a fresh start for me. I'm looking for a re-do in life, I guess you could say. I want somewhere a bit calmer and more peaceful, so I can have some time to think."

"I hope it's nothing too terrible you're getting away from," he says.

I shake my head. "No. Nothing too bad. Just a relationship that went on longer than it should have and didn't end on good terms, a dead-end job I hated but hung onto because I didn't know any better, and a general feeling of not knowing who I am and what I should be doing with my life."

"I know a little bit about that feeling," he commiserates. "Frustrating, isn't it?"

"It definitely is. So, I sold a bunch of things, stuffed everything else in storage, took my savings, and left. I came here on a recommendation, and I'll see where the wind takes me."

"Hopefully, it won't take you very far," he says.

An unexpected blush warms my cheeks, and I turn to look over my shoulder, pretending to be taking in my surroundings while I wait for my face to cool. When I turn back, Jake is talking to a guy sitting on the other side of the bar, giving me a chance to look him over. His brown hair is long, brushing his shoulders, and his frame is tall and strong, but not overly big. The guy he's talking to says something, and Jake drops his head back to let out a laugh. The sound is full and round, untethered as he lets it pour out rather than measuring and controlling it the way Greg often did.

I shouldn't be thinking about Greg right now. Being distracted by his disappearance has already cost me enough. Creagan made it very clear I'm not to try to inject myself into the investigation and to stay back and out of the way of the team already on it. I'm too close to the situation to be an appropriate and valuable part of the force and need to trust the others to do their job. It's hard but being here should be a way for me to step away from it. Back in the field, I have something to concentrate on and can let my rapid thoughts be productive rather than just filled with questions and worry.

Jake comes back to me. "Hungry?"

"A little," I nod.

"Savory or sweet?" he asks.

"Sweet," I tell him.

He winks at me and heads into the kitchen. The wink makes my cheeks burn again, and I down the rest of the beer to chase the feeling away. A few seconds later, the door to the bar opens, and the officer who was working with Nicolas comes in. He glances around, and when we make eye contact, he crosses to me.

"Emma Monroe?" he asks.

The name still sounds strange. I'll have to talk to Creagan about my undercover names from now on. But I nod.

"Yes. You saw me at the cabin not two hours ago," I point out.

"I've come to tell you it's safe to go back to the cabin now," he says, ignoring the comment.

Jake has come out of the kitchen, and out of the corner of my eye, I notice him staring at the officer.

"Safe to go back? What's going on?" he asks.

"It's nothing," I assure him. "Chief LaRoche didn't want me to go back while they were still processing the scene. But they've apparently removed the body."

A woman eavesdropping on the interaction gasps, and we all look her way.

"Body?" she sputters. "Did you just say body? Someone else has died? Who was it?"

"Did you just say someone else died?" a man asks from the next table.

"It's happening again?" comes another voice.

"Dear god. No," says a fourth.

The situation is quickly getting out of hand, and the officer holds up his hands to try to stop them. When they don't respond, Jake climbs up on a step ladder and lets out a loud, piercing whistle.

"Everybody be quiet. Listen to Barry here."

A hush falls over the bar, and the officer nods at Jake.

"Thank you, Jake. Now, folks, I don't want anybody to panic. This isn't what it sounds like. Yes, there has been a death." Just the word starts another ripple of reaction moving through the crowd, and he raises his voice slightly. "But we have no reason to believe it has any connection to the others. There is no sign of any link, and according to findings from processing the scene and the medical examiner giving an initial look at the body, it does not seem to have any relation. Everyone is safe. Please, just relax and go back to enjoying your evening."

The message appeases the crowd, and they dissipate back to their tables and booths. The officer turns back to me.

"I'll be bringing you back to the cabin now," he says.

"Actually, I'll just stay here for a while longer. Thank you, though," I reply.

"Chief LaRoche gave me clear instructions to find you, make sure you knew it was safe to return to your cabin and bring you back there," he insists.

"Well, you have found me and made sure I knew. But I don't need you to bring me. There's really no reason I need to be doing what he tells me, so I'll just thank you for the offer, and you can tell him you tried so he knows you were trying to follow his orders," I tell him.

He looks like he's about to say something else, but Jake puts his hand on the bar and leans slightly toward him.

"Hey, Barry. Two out of three ain't bad, buddy. Alright?" he says.

The officer gives a single nod and walks out of the bar. I turn back to Jake and smile at him.

"Thank you, again," I say. "You are certainly very good at swooping into uncomfortable situations."

"It's a gift," he shrugs. "Actually, it's a life skill for a bartender. But I'm happy to use it for you anytime you need it."

He puts a plate down in front of me. A scoop of vanilla bean ice cream melting between two massive chocolate chip cookies, all topped with a mound of whipped cream and just enough of a drizzle of hot fudge. It's amazing. I can't stop myself from swirling my finger in it and licking it off.

"This looks incredible," I marvel.

"Enjoy," he says.

A few minutes later, Jake comes back up to me and leans to the side, so he rests on his elbow against the bar.

"Things seem to be quieting down," I tell him.

"Can I take you home?" he offers.

"Look, Jake. I really appreciate you being so welcoming and everything, but…"

"Hey, Jake. Have space to take me home tonight?" a man calls from several feet away.

"Sure thing, Conrad," he calls back.

"Drop me off on the way?" another asks.

"If you can both fit in my car. Don't have my truck with me today," he teases, then looks back at me. "I give rides to people who have been hanging out here and need a way to get home, or who might have had one too many."

I cover my face with my hands.

"I am so sorry," I say. "I sound like a lunatic. I thought you were flirting with me. Um, if you could bring me my check, I'm just going to slink out into the darkness and try to disappear."

He laughs. "You don't sound like a lunatic. I'm sure you've had your fair share of indecent proposals at bars. I don't blame you for being a little bit cautious. There's no check."

He ducks his head slightly closer to mine as he takes my empty dessert plate. "And that is me flirting with you."

CHAPTER FIVE

I hang around the bar with the bartenders and the lingering customers as Jake starts his rounds of bringing people home. I agreed to his ride, but I'll be the last of the night. I don't mind. Sitting here looking out over the people gives me the opportunity to start getting a feel for Feathered Nest and those who live here.

I was fully anticipating the uncertainty at my arrival. People always think of the inhabitants of small Southern towns being hospitable and welcoming. But there's a tremendous difference between hospitality toward guests and visitors, and openly trusting and welcoming those who may linger around. Especially for people who have grown up in very small, isolated towns like this one, new people are reason to be suspicious. If you can't connect at least a few dots and prove some sort of link to the area, you don't belong.

The backstory I rambled out to the police chief and to Jake gave me a fake relative in a nearby town, but that's enough to give me credibility. I'm going to have to ease into their existence and earn their trust. That starts with learning about them and the way of life in the town. I'm drawn into watching the conversations unfolding and the slivers of life happening in all corners of the bar. Couples stare at each other, seeming to have lost all awareness of the rest of the world around them. New couples are at the brink of forming between people paired up on the dance floor swaying, even though the music volume has been turned down to nearly inaudible in preparation for closing. People sit alone, decompressing from their day, longing for someone, or enjoying time on their own, thinking of what to do next. Friends carry on like they have the rest of the night even though last call was half an hour ago, and soon the bar will close.

I'm so drawn into watching them I barely even notice when that Jake gets back. He steps up beside me, and I jump slightly.

"Sorry," he says. "I didn't mean to startle you."

"It's fine. I'm not usually so jumpy," I tell him.

"Nobody can blame you. When your welcoming committee to a new town consists of a dead body, people are going to give you a little bit of leeway when it comes to jangly nerves. Are you ready to get going?"

"Absolutely."

Jake reaches out, so his hand hovers a few inches away from my back as I get down from the stool. He uses the presence of that hand, not touching me, but right there, close enough that I can sense it, to guide me out of the bar and to a car waiting at the curb. He walks around the front of the car to the passenger seat with me. He opens the door, holding it for me as I climb inside. The sharply cold air coming from outside follows me into the car, and I shiver.

"Don't worry," he says as he gets behind the wheel and notices my shaking. "The heat gets going fast."

"Thank you," I tell him as he turns the engine over, and we start toward the cabin. "I really appreciate this."

"Not a problem. It'll make me feel better to know you got back safely. You've only been here a day so you can't know the town well, yet. Rattlesnake Point is a little bit out there. It would be easy to get lost trying to make your way through those woods at night."

"I'm sure it would be," I agree. We fall silent for a few seconds before I speak again. "So, giving people rides home is a normal thing for you?"

He nods without looking at me. "I've always given the occasional ride here and there to people who needed it, but over the last few months, it's become a much more regular thing."

"Why is that?" I ask.

That makes him glance my way for a few seconds before he looks back through the windshield.

"You mean, you don't know?"

"I don't know what?"

"I thought everybody knew about Feathered Nest and what's been going on around here. But I guess that only makes sense. Why would you agree to come out here when you're looking for something calm if you did know?" he asks, almost to himself.

"You lost me somewhere," I frown. Of course I know, I just need to keep up the act.

"Oh, I'm sorry. Now I'm the one who sounds like a lunatic. It's just... Feathered Nest has built up its own reputation recently."

"Why?"

He hesitates, not seeming to want to go any further.

"Because of the disappearances," he tells me.

"What disappearances?" I ask, readying myself to absorb as much information as he'll give me.

"I don't want to talk about them tonight. You're about to go into a cabin in just about the middle of nowhere completely by yourself. I don't want to scare you."

"But I want to know," I insist.

He looks at me again, and a hint of a smile plays at his lips.

"You sure are persistent. You know that?" he asks.

"I might have been told a time or two," I grin.

"Well, I'll tell you what. I'm not going to get into it tonight before you go to bed. But if you'll meet me for breakfast in the morning, I'll tell you everything."

"Is this another one of those deals like me drinking a beer and telling you about my brush with the law?" I ask.

"That worked out well for me," he shrugs. "I figured I might as well try it again."

"Where should we meet?"

"Mary Belle's. It's a little place on Main Street. Can't miss it. Has the best breakfast in town."

"I'll meet you there at 7:30," I say.

"Sounds good to me," Jake nods. The car crunches along the drive up the road. There are several cabins out here, but each one is so remote from one another that mine might as well be the only one around for miles. The cabin I'm in is the closest one to the lake.

"Which one are you?" Jake asks, keeping his eyes peeled in the darkness as we continue on.

"Number 13," I say. "Very last one."

Finally, we get to the very end of the road. He stops in the glow of the light at the side of the porch.

"Thank you, again. I'll see you in the morning," I tell him.

I climb out of the car and walk up the steps onto the porch. Ice gleams on the wooden boards where someone rinsed away the signs of blood. Jake is still sitting in his car watching me, waiting for me to get inside, so I don't hesitate long. Unlocking the cabin door, I step inside and turn back to wave goodbye to him. He waves and starts backing out of the driveway as I shut the door and lock it.

What a day. Despite everything running through my brain, I can't stay awake for one more minute. I try my best to put it all aside and collapse onto the bed.

The next morning I'm up before the sun doing a final read-through of the notes Creagan gave me before I came here. When the disappearances first started, the police department tried to launch an investigation and look into it. But they weren't really prepared for a case like that. People around here don't just disappear. There's the occasional runaway or someone who gets mad at their spouse and stalks out for a few days, but they always come back. This is the first time in recent memory people were vanishing and just not returning. The more people who disappeared, the harder it was for the department. They didn't know what to do or how to follow the clues left in each circumstance.

In my opinion, it took far too long for them to make the connections between the disappearances. While most of the time, people don't want to think of strings of events or occurrences having to do with one another, it's important to find these links. The sooner you make the connections between individual cases, the faster you'll be able to find the right path to solving it.

In looking over the cases, something that stands out to me immediately is the crime scenes from each disappearance. Often when a person disappears, it goes unnoticed. Even if it's for just a short time, there's a stretch when nobody realizes they're gone because nothing has gone amiss. Nothing looks strange or different, and the only way they realize that person is missing is because they don't show up somewhere they're supposed to be. It's not the same with these cases. Instead, there's a distinct crime scene associated with almost all of them. In the last place these people were, police noted blood and signs of a struggle.

The most recent disappearance was only a short time before the Bureau was called in, and the fresh reality of that girl being missing hangs over the town. On the way down Main Street last night, I noticed a missing poster attached to a light post. It hasn't even had time to get faded by the sun.

I suddenly realize the time has gotten away from me. I need to hurry if I don't want to be late to breakfast. As it is, Jake's already waiting for me at a table when I get to the tiny restaurant. He smiles at me and waves as if I'm going to miss him among the six other tables. But I smile and wave in return.

"How did you sleep?" he asks when I slip into the booth across from him.

"Very well, thank you. How are you this morning?"

It should be the uncomfortable small talk of people who don't know each other and are trying to get accustomed to sharing the same space. But it's not. For some reason, I feel at ease with Jake, like I've always known him. In a way, that puts me on edge even more than the discomfort would. I didn't come here to form connections, and the immediate draw of this man surprises me. Maybe it's because he's so different. From the shine in his eyes to the ponytail tied loosely at the back of his neck to the playful energy around him, he's nothing like any man I've ever dated. It might be the sheer novelty of him and the way he looks at me like I'm the only thing he notices in the room that keeps me fascinated. That stops me from ending this now and staying locked away with nothing but my work.

A waitress comes by and hands us menus. I order a cup of coffee before she walks away, and Jake laughs.

"Are you one of those people who believes they aren't capable of any sort of functioning before they have the right saturation of coffee in their blood in the morning?" he asks.

"Without a shadow of a doubt," I respond without hesitation.

He laughs again. "Me, too." The waitress returns and sets mugs in front of both of us. He lifts his to show me. "See?"

She takes our breakfast orders and leaves. I stare at Jake expectantly.

"Well?" I ask.

"What?" he asks.

"I believe we had a deal," I say. "You're supposed to tell me about these disappearances."

"The agreement was we'd meet for breakfast, and I'd tell you. We haven't had breakfast yet, so technically, the terms haven't been met," he points out.

"You drive a hard bargain. Are you just trying to stretch this out?"

He picks up his coffee and puts it to his lips for a long sip. Gazing at me over the mug, he winks like he did the night before. It has the same effect.

"You see that man over there?" he asks when he's finished with his sip.

I look where he's pointing and see a man in a red and black plaid golf hat sitting by himself in the corner of a booth.

"Yes," I say.

"That's Elliot. He comes here every single morning and has the exact same breakfast. Coffee, orange juice, a bowl of grits with butter, two over-easy eggs, and a piece of white toast, heavily buttered."

"Just one piece of toast with two eggs?" I ask.

He gives a slow single nod, still watching the older man. "It's cut in half, and he uses the points of the triangles to poke open the yolks of each egg. He's been doing it for twenty-five years," Jake says.

I scoff at him. "How could you possibly know that? You aren't old enough."

He straightens up. "I'm thirty-four."

"Seriously?" I start.

He looks at me strangely. "Why is that so unbelievable?"

"You just seem younger," I tell him.

"Well, if you want to talk about young, look over to the booth under the window."

I do, and see a pretty brunette woman around my age, maybe a couple years older, feeding a baby sitting in a highchair at the end of the table.

"Okay," I nod.

"That's her grandson," he says.

"What?" I ask, my voice climbing so loud and sharp, nearly everyone at the restaurant turns to look at me. "Sorry," I whisper meekly, then look back at Jake. "What?"

He nods, chuckling. "Yep. Her family is known for their... let's say, consistency. For the last four generations, the women have gotten married and had their first baby at fifteen. That's Ella. She followed right along in her mother, grandmother, and great-grandmother's footsteps. She has a sister, Fanny, who just turned fourteen and says she isn't speaking to anyone male until she turns twenty."

I laugh. "Smart girl."

Our breakfasts come, and we eat for a few moments in silence. Finally, Jake takes a sip of coffee to wash down a bite of his omelet.

"You sure you want to hear all this?" he asks, forking a piece of his food.

"Yes," I tell him.

I settle into the bowl of yogurt and granola in front of me and listen as he tells me about the disappearances. He doesn't give me any information I don't already have from the case files, but there are emotion and insight those clippings and printouts didn't give me. The emotion of living through the discovery of each disappearance and the horror of the two bodies is evident in his voice. This has had a major impact on the people of this town, and it's seeping deeper. Every day without a resolution is stirring suspicions and turning people who were once content to never lock a lock and stroll everywhere in town at night into those who hide behind deadbolts and keep to their homes.

"I started escorting people home when it got obvious the police weren't going to find whoever was doing this and make them stop. I hate the thought of anyone coming to my place to relax and enjoy themselves, only to have something happen to them when they leave. Keeping them safe became a top priority for me. I want to protect them and do whatever I can to make this town as secure as possible. Watching people change their lives because of this is heartbreaking. No one should have to live in fear all the time and not be able to just live their lives."

"I agree."

CHAPTER SIX

"No, no, you don't understand. It was everywhere. In his ears. In his hair. It was the most ridiculous thing I've ever seen."

Jake's laughing almost as hard as I am, making it difficult to understand exactly what he's saying. We're walking through snow that fell heavily over the town three days ago but has started to melt in the slightly warmer temperatures. Those warmer temperatures are still keeping me chilled to the bone most of the day, but the time I get to spend with Jake is very effective at distracting me.

We've seen each other every day since I arrived in Feathered Nest, and the closer we get, the more I feel like he's infiltrating me into the real version of this town. Showing me around and introducing me to people gives me an in with them, automatically giving me more credibility. It lets me have conversations with them without the cocked eyebrows and hesitant speech, or at least with less of it. Gradually, I'm getting more comfortable. When he goes into the bar in the evenings, I bury myself in the case, filling pages with notes and making every link and connection I can.

Yesterday I got the opportunity to talk to the mother of one of the missing people. Even a year after the last time she saw her daughter, she gets emotional just saying her name. It was hard to watch her struggle with herself to talk without dissolving into tears. I comforted her, telling her it was alright to cry, but part of me felt fake offering the comfort. I'm the one who still buries my face in my pillow to cry over my parents. And it has been much longer than a year.

There was something about the conversation that struck me. Though she fully accepted her daughter was gone, abducted by someone, and very likely killed, she couldn't wrap her mind around the way it happened. Her blood was found strewn across the alley behind where she worked, but her mother said she would never have gone back there alone in the dark. It just didn't make any sense. Her daughter hated the dark and didn't even like to walk through her own home by herself without turning on all the lights. She just couldn't imagine her going out into the alley to bring out the trash without someone being there with her.

I'm still tumbling that around in my head as I walk along beside Jake, listening to him tell me stories about his childhood here in Feathered Nest. His mother, father, brother, and sister ensured he rarely had a dull moment. And when he did need something new to spark his imagination, or he was on overload and wanted a break, his grandmother's house was within walking distance, set on sprawling grounds filled with hiding spots and secret rooms and forts he crafted with his siblings. It sounds idyllic, and a pang goes through me at the thought of my own hectic, never truly settled childhood.

"Alright. So, now you know the story of what happens to a peanut butter and marshmallow sandwich when it's put into the microwave for five minutes," he says.

"Important life lessons learned," I smile.

"Yes. So, now it's your turn. Tell me something about yourself. I know you're an only child."

"Yep. Just me. My mother was a ballerina in Russia when she was young but came to the United States after an injury ended her career."

"That's terrible," Jake says sympathetically.

I shake my head and take a sip of the steaming hot apple cider I've been carrying mostly to keep my hands warm as we walk along one of the smaller streets in town.

"Not really. She enjoyed dancing, but it wasn't really her passion. She didn't live or die by it by any means. When it was over, it was simply over, and that was it. She was ready to move on to the next part of her life, and that meant my father."

"And you," he says.

"And me," I confirm with a smile.

"What about your father?"

"He was not a ballerina in Russia." Jake gives an exasperated laugh, and I giggle. "He worked for the government."

I don't go into any details. I learned early on in my life not to offer more than was asked of me, and most of the time, not even that much. Especially, when it came to my father.

"Worked? Past tense?"

I nod. "Both are gone."

Despite everything else I'm fabricating as I tell him, that answer seems to burn on my tongue. I can't tell him everything. I can't tell him my mother was murdered when I was young and my father, a top CIA agent, disappeared. I have to protect myself, my identity, and my motivations, but not telling Jake almost feels like a betrayal.

"I'm so sorry to hear that," he tells me. "Mine are, too."

I nod, and a few seconds of silence fall between us as we commiserate in the pain and emptiness of being without our parents.

"I'm sorry," I say.

He looks directly into my eyes with an intensity that makes something inside me ache, but I don't know why.

"Emma, there's something I need to tell you."

"Alright," I say, gingerly.

Jake looks away, then back to me.

"It isn't just my parents who are gone. I wasn't always alone here. I was married."

"You were?"

He nods. "It was a long time ago. We were both young, but it didn't matter to us. We wanted to be together, and there wasn't anything that was going to stop us. Fortunately, no one tried. We only got three months together before she died."

A lump forms in my throat at the sound of pain in his voice.

"What happened to her?" I ask.

"She was hit by a drunk driver," he sighs. "The only thing that got me through it was knowing it happened instantly. She had no idea." He lets out a long breath, and his eyes meet mine again. "Does it bother you?"

I shake my head. "Of course not."

Jake leans forward, touching his forehead against mine. I've only known him for a few days, but I'm slipping deep into him, and I'm afraid of what might happen when this is all over.

Finally, I break the silence by turning to him.

"Favorite family vacation," I ask.

"Hmmm," he muses, leaning his head back slightly as he thinks. "That's a tough one. We did a lot. My mother was the family adventure type. I'm going to have to say Disney Animal Kingdom. I was seven years old, and I remember seeing the elephants and thinking about how incredibly big they were. That seems so silly now, but when I was that age, I didn't really think about an animal being that big in real life. When I got to see them fairly up close, it was just mind-blowing."

We walk a little farther, and Jake looks like he's about to say something when shouts ring out through the cold air. I look at him, and his eyes widen.

"That's coming from the park," he says. "Come on."

We toss our cups into a nearby trashcan and run as fast as we can through the snow. He leads me toward a small park several streets away from the main shopping area of the town. As we approach, we see a crowd starting to form.

"Get off me!" I hear someone shouting. "Get your hands off me!"

"What did you do to her?" another man demands. "Where is she?"

A few voices from the crowd shout at the two men, split over which side they are supporting. Jake and I rush into the fray, and he forces people out of the way to reveal a man dragging another by what looks like a rope around his neck. The man thrashing on the ground has his hands shoved between the rope and his neck, desperately trying to keep it from choking him.

"What's going on here?" Jake asks.

The man with the other end of the rope drags the man on the ground a few more feet toward a low-hanging branch of a nearby tree, and my heart jumps into my throat as I realize his intentions.

"He took my daughter," he says.

"I didn't do anything with his daughter," the other begs. "Please."

Jake grabs onto the rope and looks the first man directly in the eye. "Let go. You need to put down the rope."

"She's gone," the man says, his voice cracking. "My little girl is gone, and he's the last one I saw her with."

"That doesn't mean he did anything to her," Jake says.

"There's blood in his car. I saw it."

"I went hunting. Like I told you. I put my knife down, and some blood got on my seat," the other man insists.

"You don't just put down a hunting knife without realizing it has blood on it. He had to have done something to her. And since he won't tell me where she is, I'm going to make sure he's gone, too."

"Stop," Jake says sternly, tugging the rope again. "That's enough. Don't you think enough has happened in this town? We can't be turning against each other. We need to pull together right now and try to help each other through this, not lose control of ourselves."

As Jake talks, I drop down to my knees beside the man on the ground and release the rope from around his neck. He rubs at the red, raw skin left behind, but at least he's still breathing and not dangling from the tree like an homage to the vigilante justice of the Old West.

"Thank you, Jake. I can take this from here."

Chief LaRoche walks through the crowd and stares at the two men. Jake hands over the rope and comes over to me, wrapping his arm around my shoulders to guide me away. I'm shaking, my hands trembling so hard I can barely keep them down.

"I'm sorry you had to see that," he sighs.

"I can't believe someone would go that far," I mutter. "He was ready to kill that guy."

Jake nods. "He was. The people around here are getting pushed too far. They want the police to find out who's been doing this and stop them before more people are lost."

I shiver as we walk away from the park. In those few moments, everything got so much more intense. There's a darkness over this town. Secrets it's holding onto. If I don't bring an end to them, it will only get worse.

A n emergency in the kitchen meant Jake had to go in early. It leaves me with the afternoon to do something I've been planning since I arrived. Taking a bag of supplies and equipment with me, I pile into the car and start the long drive back in the direction I came. When I'm certain I'm close, I pull the car onto the gravel beside the train track and park. Climbing out of the car, I look around.

A few feet away, the end of a wooden post sticks out of the remaining traces of snow. Bright pink plastic tattered by the wind and rain marks where the body of the woman, Cristela Jordan, lay months ago. It's one of the realities of crime scenes that often shocks people. Most people hope scenes like this are cleaned up when the police are finished with the initial investigations, so no traces of the horror are left behind. They want not just the body gone, but anything that might remind passers-by of what happened there.

That doesn't always happen. In fact, it's rare for scenes to be totally broken down, even when cases are closed. It's too easy for investigators to just walk away and leave behind traces. Some linger for years after.

I'm glad for this one. The marker matches the pictures given to me by Creagan. It's as clear in my mind now as if I'm holding the image in my hand. The gravel looks clean, but I'm sure if I dug down past the first few layers of rocks, I'd find traces of the blood that was spread across the entire area when they found her. Standing beside the marker, I orient myself and look down the tracks. I can't see it, but in the distance, there is likely another marker where the body of the man was found weeks later.

In both cases, the bodies were badly damaged. The man was dissected, and several body parts were missing, while the woman appeared to have been hit by an oncoming train after death. Examining the body as much as they could showed she had marks on her like she was strangled and suffered various cuts and blunt force trauma, but the train mangled her, making it harder to determine what actually happened.

The initial investigation into Cristela Jordan's death considered the possibility that she and her killer had hopped one of the commercial trains that come down this line several times per week. They theorized she was murdered after an altercation and tossed onto the tracks. That doesn't make sense. If she was thrown from the train, she would land directly on the gravel, not on the track to be hit. Later there were examinations of the trains that passed this way for several days before the body was found. None of them were covered in blood. That didn't surprise me much when I heard it. The high-pressure water used to wash the trains would remove any signs of blood before they knew to preserve anything. There was really no way of knowing what train hit her or when.

It makes me wonder why she was dropped on the tracks to be ground up by a train, but the man was relieved of several of his limbs and then what was left was deposited by the tracks. One in Virginia; one in North Carolina. The line that separated the two states wasn't extremely obvious, but that made me even more curious if whoever did this realized what they were doing by disposing of the bodies where they did. The only thing that linked the two bodies to the rest of the disappearances was that all ten victims were from Feathered Nest or the next town over. It seems strange for ten people to go missing in small-town Virginia, only for one to be found brutally murdered a few yards over the state line.

But that's what brought in the Bureau. Whoever did this, made a serious mistake with those few feet. They brought me here.

"I just don't want to think too much of it," I say into the phone later that night, after I finish examining the site and return to the cabin.

"Why not?" Bellamy asks. "He sounds just about perfect."

I pull open the top drawer of the dresser and take out a pair of thick, fluffy socks.

"He's not perfect. He's good looking and has an amazing smile. He's sweet and attentive. He's funny. He wants to take care of the people around him..."

"You're not really making your case here, Emma."

"He's a great guy, but it doesn't feel right."

I go to shut the drawer, but something stops it. I jiggle the handle of the drawer and try to force it back, but it won't move.

"What's going on?" she asks, obviously hearing me fight with the drawer.

"There's something stuck in the drawer. I can't get it to close." I reach into the drawer and to the very back so I can feel along it. My fingers hit something, and I pull it out. "Got it."

"What was it?" she asks.

"A thimble," I tell her, looking it over carefully before setting it on top of the dresser.

"That place is full of all kinds of surprises, isn't it?" she asks.

"I guess you could say that," I tell her.

"Which is exactly why you need to be more open about Jake."

"I'm not sure I see the connection between a thimble and Jake," I say.

"Not the thimble," she insists. "The surprise. Maybe he showed up in your life to help you through everything. He's a bright spot for you when you really need it. Now's the time for you to realize there are more hearts out there, more men. If there's anyone in this world who deserves to just stop thinking and start enjoying a connection with someone else, it's you."

I hear someone knocking on the front door and head into the living room.

"Someone's at the door," I tell her. I peer through the window and can't believe what I'm seeing. "Bellamy, I'm going to have to call you back. Jake is at my door with takeout."

"Then open it!"

"This isn't me, Bellamy. I don't fall for people like this," I say.

"No, it isn't you! It's Emma Monroe! This could be exactly what you need. You're undercover, right? Let that version enjoy being in control for a little while."

CHAPTER SEVEN

I am trying to shower off the foggy effects of another night with no more than two hours of sleep as I work on the case, but the sound of my phone ringing incessantly drives me out from under the water. After hearing about the near-hanging, and another woman going missing a few towns over that isn't confirmed but might be linked to these cases, Bellamy and Eric have reached epic proportions of worry in the last few days.

But I'm not going to let it stop me. I'm going to figure this out. I can feel it. There are just a few pieces missing, and once I find them, this will all be over. But in order to do that, these two need to leave me alone and let me breathe for ten minutes.

Getting out of the shower, I snatch my towel off the hook on the back of the door and wrap it around me. My last call was from Bellamy, so I expect it's Eric's turn now. But when I grab the phone off the counter, it's neither of their names on the screen. Unless I've been standing in the shower for several hours, it's still before dawn, so I'm shocked by the call. Holding my towel in place with one hand, I push the button to connect.

"Jake?"

"I've been calling you for the last twenty minutes," he starts, almost accusingly.

"I was in the shower. But it's also not even daylight yet. What's going on?" I ask.

Knowing I'm not going to be able to make it back into the shower, I release my towel and reach in to turn off the water. Within seconds the temperature in the bathroom drops. My wet skin intensifies the cold, which at least helps to wake me up.

"I need you," he says.

That's a sentence a lot of women long to hear murmured to them in the dark of night. But not in that tone.

"Jake, what is going on?" I ask again.

"Something horrible happened. Can you meet me at the bar? Please, Emma."

Emotion cracks in his voice. He sounds like he's right on the edge, and my training to diffuse tense situations kicks in.

"Alright, Jake. I just got out of the shower, so it will take me a few minutes to get ready. But I'll be there as soon as I can. Is there anything I can bring you?" I ask in a slow, calming voice.

"No. Just you. Please, hurry."

The call disconnects, and a chill runs through me. Forgoing the stretch pants and sweatshirt I initially brought with me into the bathroom, I rush out of the dissipating steam and into the bedroom. I dress in layers to ward off the biting cold of the early morning air and blast my hair with a blow dryer before rushing out of the cabin.

The drive into town feels longer than it should. The curving driveway and twisting road unfurls in front of me but never seems to get any shorter. Jake's voice was frightening, and my mind is jumbled with different scenarios of what could be happening. Halfway there, icy snowflakes drift down and land on the windshield.

When I finally get onto the main street, I notice Jake standing outside of the bar. He's leaning against his car with his arms folded tightly over his chest, staring down at his scuffed boots like he's lost to the rest of the world. I pull up in front of his car, and when I'm within a few steps of him, he looks up. As soon as he realizes it's me, Jake rushes toward me, gathering me tightly in his arms and burying his head in my neck. I'm startled but wrap my arms around him and run my hand over strands of long, glossy hair chilled by standing outside in the ice.

"My father's grave," he whispers, struggling to get the words out. "They destroyed my father's grave."

"What? Who?"

I take his shoulders and guide him back away from me so I can look into his face. Bloodshot eyes flash back and forth like they can't find anything to rest on. His hands still clench around me. He seems afraid to let go. Snowflakes cling to the tips of his eyelashes and brush his cheeks like they did the first time we stood in the snow. He was gorgeous then. Now he looks drawn and about to crack.

"I don't know. The police just called me. They got a report and went to the cemetery. I want to go see what happened. Will you come with me?" he asks.

"Come with you? To the cemetery?"

"Yes. The police are there, and I want to know what's going on."

"Maybe that isn't the best idea," I tell him. "They're investigating."

"Which is exactly why I should be there. That's my father, Emma. I'm the only one to speak for him. I want to make sure they're respecting him. I need you there with me," he pleads.

It feels strange, uncomfortable in its disruptive intimacy, but there's so much desperation in his voice I nod.

"Of course. I'll go."

"Thank you."

He takes my hand and rushes me around to the passenger door. His hands wrap so tightly around the wheel as he drives that his knuckles turn white. The tendons along the sides of his neck are taut, pressing against his skin so hard they look like they might snap. I want to say something, but don't know what. I'm still not entirely sure what's going on, and I don't want to push Jake any further.

After a few minutes, we leave the main part of town and head into the outskirts. A massive black iron gate looms ahead. With pointed tips and closely arranged bars, the gate is a cemetery cliché I wasn't expecting. Feathered Nest is so small I was expecting a tiny graveyard behind the church or even a family plot tucked in a field somewhere. Instead, the cemetery looks like it contains the final resting places of every citizen who has ever lived within the town.

Set on a gently sloping hill, hundreds of stones, from ancient crumbling monoliths to humble flat markers, fill the grass. But it's hard to focus on any of them with the red and blue lights flashing from the police car parked at the edge of the road.

Jake doesn't even bother to pull up behind the car. He stops his car haphazardly with the nose pointed toward the cemetery gate and the back still hanging in the road before throwing off his seatbelt and tumbling out onto the frozen grass.

As I move to follow him, something tugs on the cuff of my pants. I reach down and feel a piece of metal sticking out from the bottom of the seat that had snagged the fabric. As I release it, my hand hits something under the seat, and an umbrella rolls out. The snow is falling harder, so I grab the umbrella before climbing out of the car to follow Jake.

He's already through the gate and stumbling through the stones. I try to rush to catch up with him, but the ice-glazed grass is slick beneath my feet, and I struggle to stay upright. As I make my way through the grave markers, I notice the yard doesn't seem arranged like others, in sections designated by time. Instead, the graves are interspersed, so the eras of the town mingle with each other. Stones of people from a century ago are right against those only there for a matter of months.

It's why I find Jake leaned against a Celtic cross-shaped stone weathered smooth and sinking into the dirt. His hand grips the side of the stone, but his knees look like they're going to buckle under him. Ahead of him, three men move slowly around the tattered ground. Clods of dirt and torn-up grass scatter the plots around the gaping grave. The stone that stood at the head of the grave lies in three pieces.

Everything in me wants to walk up to the officers meandering around and ask what's happening. But I have to remember they don't know me as a federal agent. They've already made it clear they don't want anyone interfering with the happenings in their town, and I don't think they'd respond kindly to me sticking myself into this. I have to force myself to stand back and glean what I can from the distance.

I slide my hand along Jake's back. "I'm so sorry."

"Who would do something like this?" he asks. "Why would they do this to my father?"

I shake my head. "It might just be stupid kids. Teenagers like to pull stupid pranks and destroy things because they think it makes them seem cool, or some stupid shit like that. For some reason, they really like to target graves, but..."

"They took his body."

The words send a chill down my spine.

"What?"

"His body, Emma. It's gone. My father isn't in his grave. Whoever desecrated it took his body."

Somehow his voice sounds stronger like his shock has reached an intensity that forced his brain to shut down. I've seen it happen many times before. Jake's here. But he's not processing it anymore. I open the umbrella and tuck it into his hand before walking over to the nearest officer. I don't care what they think anymore.

"This is a crime scene," the thin man says. He turns to me. I remember his name is Nicolas. "You can't be here."

"What happened here?" I ask, ignoring his warning.

"That's what we're trying to figure out, Ms. Monroe. Now, if you'll step aside."

I do, but not in the direction he wants. Instead, I move closer to the dug-up grave.

"I'm here for Jake. If you haven't noticed, no one is talking to him. Don't you think he has the right to know who did this to his father's grave?"

I hazard a glance down. Frozen grass and clumps of dirt lay on the splintered casket. Moisture from years below ground has discolored the satin lining and made it pull away from the corners of the lid. But in some places, there are still signs of where the body crushed down into the casket and left its permanent impression.

"Like I said, we are trying to figure that out right now. Until we know something, there's nothing for us to tell him. But this really shouldn't surprise him."

Nicolas turns away, but I step up to him and grab his shoulder to stop him.

"What's that supposed to mean?" I ask.

"You can't touch me like that," he frowns.

"Yes, I can. You're a police officer, not the pope. As long as I don't assault you, I can touch you. What was that crack supposed to mean?"

"Ask your boyfriend. The two of you need to get out of here. We'll get in touch with Jake if we need to."

He turns away, and I walk back to Jake.

"Come on. Let's get you home. You look like you need a shower and something to eat," I say.

"No. I'm not leaving until they know who did this and where my father is," he says back through gritted teeth.

"Jake, we need to go. This is an investigation now, and we're just going to be in the way."

"I'm not in the way. My father needs me."

"They are doing everything they can. You're not going to be any good if you don't take care of yourself. Let me take you home. I'll make you some food and tuck you into bed. You'll feel better after you get some sleep."

Jake looks up at me like he's going to argue, but in an instant, the ferocity drains out of his eyes, and he nods. Just before we head out of the cemetery, I have a thought.

Pulling my phone out of my pocket, I quickly snap a few pictures of the grave. Two of the officers catch me and start to say something, but I steer Jake around, and we head back to his car. The keys are still in the ignition, and I climb behind the wheel to drive him back to his house.

CHAPTER EIGHT

I'm most of the way through my second cup of coffee, and the shower is still running down the hallway. Jake didn't say anything to me when we got to the house. He got out of the car and walked inside like he almost forgot I was there. The only sign of acknowledgement that I was still with him was the door standing open. By the time I got inside and locked it behind me, he was already in the bathroom, and I could hear the water. I take the last swallow of my coffee as I stare through the kitchen window at the snippets of the horizon visible through the trees. The vibrant colors of the sun coming up illuminate those spaces, creating patchwork against the sky.

It reminds me of the quilt my grandmother kept draped over the back of her couch when I was a little girl. It's a distant memory. Like I told Jake, I didn't get much time to spend with my grandparents when I was younger. But even with my memories of my grandmother few and far between, that quilt stands out in my mind. She called it a crazy quilt. It wasn't until I was an adult that I realized that was actually the name of the pattern. Or lack of pattern. It basically just meant she kept a bag stuffed full of all the scraps and remnants of fabric from every sewing project she did. Sometimes when a dress or shirt of hers got worn out or stained, she'd cut that up and add it to the bag, too. When it was full enough, she took all those scraps and pieced them together in whatever order they came out of the bag when she reached inside. Those turned into her crazy quilts.

By the time I figured that out, she was gone, and I never got to ask her what happened to all the other quilts magically born from that scrap-stuffed bag. I only ever remember seeing that one. Most of the scraps must have come from the same project or recycled garment. Bright shades of orange and yellow interspersed with a few pale blues and white all stitched together and backed in plain black.

Thinking about the quilt makes me feel chilly. My outer layer of clothing got damp in the snow, so it's tumbling around in the dryer to warm back up. This leaves me in only the leggings and tight shirt I had on beneath. I sit my mug down, shuffling over to the closet door in the middle of the hallway. Inside I find a stack of blankets and take one out to wrap around my shoulders. Down the hallway, I hear something along with the sound of the water. I think its Jake's voice. He definitely strikes me as the type to sing in the shower in good circumstances. But these aren't good circumstances. And the voice doesn't sound like it's singing. It's more muttering, mumbling just beneath the sound of the stream coming down from the showerhead.

I take a few steps closer to the bathroom to try to see if I can understand what he's saying, then turn sharply away. He's going through a hard enough time right now without me being nosy. If that is him in the shower talking to himself, I can't really blame him. If there's anything I know, it's having to try to wrap my brain around something that seems so nonsensical, and at the same time, so horrible.

Back in the kitchen, I refill my mug and carry it with me into the living room so I can curl up on the couch. The warm recesses of the blanket take away the chill on my skin quickly, but I can't shake the feeling from what Nicolas said in the cemetery. No one in town seems to have any ill will toward Jake. In fact, he's adored. There hasn't been a single day I've spent with him when he hasn't had a dozen or more people want to stop and talk to him. It's hard to reconcile that with the horrifying desecration of his father's grave. And the way they could have talked about it as if it was somehow expected, or even justified.

A thick book with a dark green leather cover catches my eye where it's sitting on the bottom shelf of a small bookcase. Picking it up, I take it with me back to the couch and open it across my folded legs. It's a picture album, one of the old-fashioned style ones, with each picture tucked carefully into little black paper corners. Much of the open space on each page is filled with delicate gray ink. Captions and notes in ornate, tightly spaced handwriting. It makes me think of mosquitoes spread out across the paper.

"My family."

I'm several pages into the album when Jake comes into the room. I'm so absorbed in the pictures I didn't hear the shower stop. He smiles faintly at me when I look up. The shower seems to have taken the tension out of his muscles, but there's still a dense swirl of emotions behind his eyes.

And he's only wearing a pair of gray sweatpants. No shirt at all and the morning light reflects off the muscles in his body.

"I'm sorry. I don't mean to pry. I just noticed it and was curious," I say.

Jake shakes his head. "It's fine. Photo albums are to be looked at, right? If people don't look at them and share the memories, maybe they don't exist at all."

It's a strange sentiment, but I think I understand what he's trying to say.

"Let me bring you something to eat. I'll be right back."

He leans forward and kisses me softly as I stand. There's sadness in the kiss, and a bitter sense of searching, like he's trying desperately to find some sort of answer in me. Our eyes meet for a fleeting second, and I walk away into the kitchen. The sheet of biscuits I put into the oven has just finished, and I quickly cook some eggs. Piling them onto the biscuit with a slice of cheese, I fill a glass with orange juice and bring it to him.

Jake is sitting on the couch, staring down at a page of the photo album. His fingers run around the edge of a picture, and I feel awkward approaching him like I'm intruding on an extremely private moment. I hover uncomfortably, the plate extended toward him, for a few seconds before he notices me. A faint smile crosses his face.

"Thank you." He takes the plate from my hand and looks down at the cushion beside him in invitation. When I sit, he gestures at the picture. "That's my grandmother. She loved that dress."

The simple pale purple and blue floral print is a quintessential grandmother pattern. It's the kind of dress that makes me think of the smell of cookies and long hugs. The close-up image only shows a sliver of wood beneath her feet and nothing else about her surroundings.

"Where is she?" I ask.

"That's her house. I remember when this picture was taken. It was Easter. She always made a huge lunch, and we spent the afternoon hunting for eggs around her yard. She didn't want any of us siblings or cousins to not get enough eggs or for one of the older ones to find all of them before the little ones could, so she used a different color egg for each of us. We could only keep our color, and we weren't allowed to open any of them until everyone had found all of them, so we helped each other."

I try to decipher the caption, but the handwriting is too wispy, and I can't catch it before he turns the page and shows me a snap of a young girl. It's washed out with a flare of bright sunlight, but I can make out pale blonde hair. She squints and leans toward the head of a large dog she has in what could either be a hug or a headlock.

"Is this your sister?" I ask.

Jake nods as he takes a bite of the sandwich I brought him. "That's Mocha. She was obsessed with that dog."

"He doesn't look so happy about it," I point out.

"He didn't particularly like anyone. But he was best with her. My father found him as a puppy out in the woods, and I think he was just used to being on his own. He didn't really want anyone to mess with him and didn't necessarily want to be domesticated. One day he just ran off. I never saw him again."

"I'm sorry."

Jake shrugs. "Better to have your good memories than someone around who doesn't want to make any more of them."

He closes the album and holds it on his lap as he finishes the biscuit. Early morning sunlight filters through the curtains, and there's an odd sense of anticipation sparking in the air around us. We're waiting for something to happen, but I'm not sure what. When he finishes eating, Jake leans back and rests his head on the couch. His eyes flutter closed, and I take his hand.

"Come on. Let's get you into bed for a little while. I know you haven't gotten enough sleep," I say.

He shakes his head but doesn't lift it. "I'll wait right here. They might call me."

"You'll be so much more comfortable in your bed, and you'll get better sleep. It's not going to make a difference if you're in there or in here if the police call."

He finally relents and lets me guide him into the bedroom. I pull back the blankets, and he climbs under them, letting out a breath as his head sinks into the pillow. Tugging the blankets up over his shoulder, I lean down and kiss his forehead. As I turn to walk away, he reaches out and grabs onto my wrist.

"Stay," he whispers. I look into his eyes and see more of the searching. "Please. I don't want to be alone right now."

I nod. I was probably just going to go back to the cabin and go to sleep anyway. If it will comfort him, I might as well stay here.

The sheets are cold when I slip into them, and I tuck up close to Jake to find some of his warmth. He already seems more relaxed. The clean smell of him starts to soothe me. I wish I knew something to say to him. I can't even imagine what he's going through right now. Part of me can understand, but not fully. When my father disappeared, it was a shock and left me dangling. I'm still dangling. But I still have the hope of him being alive. I know what it's like to lose a parent, and I can't imagine what it would feel like to have someone disrespect my mother's grave and take her body away. It would feel like so much of an intrusion, a violation.

I try to will myself to fall asleep, but the situation hangs heavily over me, and I can't make my eyes close. I'm not sure how much time has passed when Jake rolls over and looks at me. He lets out a soft groan and runs his fingers through my hair.

"What's wrong?" he asks.

I shake my head. "Nothing."

He cocks his head at me, and I let out a sigh.

"There's just something bothering me, but I don't want to talk about it. You don't need anything else on you."

"What's going on? Tell me," he says.

"When we were in the cemetery, and I went to talk to the officers, Nicolas said something to me," I admit.

"What did he say?" Jake asks suspiciously, propping himself up on his elbow and looking down at me.

I feel strange with him hovering over me, and I force myself to push away memories I haven't been able to shake, memories that make me suspicious any time someone comes too close.

"He said... about your father's grave... that you shouldn't be surprised."

Jake's expression falls, and he turns around to lie on his back again, staring up at the ceiling. "I'm sorry. I shouldn't have said anything to you."

"No. I'm glad you did. Truth is, he's not the only person in this town to think that. There's some bad blood here. Grudges some of the old-timers haven't been able to let go of. There are families in this town who blame my father for things that happened a long time ago, things he didn't have anything to do with. It looks like with every-thing else that's going on; they want to bring it up again. I don't understand why they won't just leave well enough alone. It's hard enough that he's dead. They don't have to torture his ghost, too."

CHAPTER NINE

"That's it?" Bellamy asks.

"What do you mean?"

I open the trunk at the foot of the bed and pull out one of the folded quilts. They smelled damp and musty when I first came, but I washed them all during my first week so I could use them if I needed them. The temperature has dropped significantly, and I can never seem to get warm enough. I sit down on the couch and sling the blanket around my shoulders.

"He tells you there's bad blood against his father in town, and you don't ask him about it? The man's grave was desecrated, and his bones dug up. Don't you think that's worth poking into a bit?"

"What is it that I should have asked him? Like you just said, his father's grave was desecrated. He wasn't exactly in the best place. I didn't think that was a great opportunity for me to start prying into obviously sensitive things about his past," I explain. "It just strikes me as so strange. Everything Jake has told me about his family has been idyllic. Almost perfect. He tells me these stories about things they did together and how much he looked up to his father. Now I find out there was enough bad feeling in town for people to not be surprised somebody dug him out of his grave? Doesn't that seem a little extreme to you?"

"I mean, it's not something I would do. I've had my fair share of disagreements with people, but it's never crossed my mind to dig them up out of the ground," she notes.

"Me, neither. It's just so creepy. Somebody is keeping secrets in this town, and unless I start figuring out who and what, I have a feeling this is all just going to get worse."

"Do you think this could have anything to do with the other disappearances?" Bellamy asks.

I take a long sip of coffee. "I really don't think so. It wouldn't make any sense."

"Why not?"

"Well, to start with, everybody else was alive when they disappeared. Jake's father very distinctly wasn't. It's like the town is starting to unravel. People are remembering feuds and trying to settle old scores. I'm afraid it's just going to get worse."

"Where's Jake now?"

"He went to the bar. I thought he should stay home and try to get some rest, but he's too worked up. He says being at the bar makes him feel more secure and in control. I guess I can understand that. Working is his normal. He needs that right now."

"That's definitely the way it was with you when Greg..."

Her voice drifts off, but that doesn't cover up the rest of the sentence.

"Disappeared?" I ask. "It's alright. You can say it. That's what happened. And, you're right. I did the exact same thing. When I found out he was gone, I buried myself in work and did everything I could to not even come up for air. It made it easier to deal with when I didn't have the time or space in my brain to think about what was really going on. I'm sure that's what Jake is feeling right now. He just wants to go about his daily life and try not to dwell. There's really nothing he can do until the police figure out what happened."

"What about you? What are you going to do? Do you have any other leads to follow?"

"That would imply I had any, to begin with." I let out a breath and sift through the pictures spread out across the table again. "I'm starting to feel like this is the real reason Creagan picked me to do this job. It's not that he had any faith in me or even that he wanted me to lay the foundation before he sent in the rest of the team. He sent me here because he knows this case is impossible."

"It's not impossible. Not for you," Bellamy reassures me. "You're going to figure this out. Just do what you always do."

"Freak out and try to beat up a suspect in a moving bait vehicle?" I ask with a laugh.

"That was one time. I mean, what you've done since you first started working for the Bureau. Go back to the beginning. See how far you've come, then go from there. I'm sure you've found out a lot more than you think."

I pick up a picture that's been at the bottom of the stack and stare at it for a few seconds. "You know, Bell, sometimes you really know what you're talking about."

"What did you figure out?" she asks.

"Nothing. But I have a place to start," I tell her, standing from the couch and shucking off the blanket.

"Good. Be careful."

"I will. Call you later."

I end the call and head into the bedroom to add a layer of clothes on top of what I'm wearing, then stuff my feet into my boots. I send a quick text to Jake, letting him know I might be out of range so he doesn't worry if he can't reach me and promise to drop by the bar later that evening. Using the information jotted on the back of the picture, I pull up a map on my phone, throw on my coat and gloves, and head out.

It's just as cold as it was when I got back from Jake's earlier, but I hope tromping through the woods will warm me up. I could drive. That would be the most time-effective option. But to do that would mean going on the same road I've followed countless times during the investigation. Instead, I'm going to walk along the edge of the woods and dip back through the corner of town to the train tracks. Maybe I'll notice something I haven't seen or thought of before.

The drive from the train station took forty-five minutes, but that was because of the strange way the road turned and curved, making the train go well past the town before dropping me off. Using the overhead view of the area on my phone, I trace the most direct way to the spot where the first of the two bodies was found. It takes me a few minutes to get to where my self-designed path begins, and I carefully begin to pick my way through the thickly overgrown woods.

I'm thankful for my thick pants and layers as I delve into the trees. Branches and thorns scrape and cling to my clothes, and I pull my hood tighter to prevent my hair from getting snagged. I've been walking for about fifteen minutes when the trees in front of me thin slightly, and I notice a change in their pattern to one side. I climb through a covering of bushes and vines, finding myself on what looks like an old path. It's neglected and overgrown, but the thick carpeting of pine needles and leaves creates a path several feet wide between the trees.

My instincts keep my feet on it, and I watch my surroundings carefully as I step forward. I strain my neck this way and that, trying to see where the path leads in the opposite direction. I'm tempted to head back in that way, but I decide to turn around and keep going toward the train tracks.

It isn't too much longer that my instincts are proven right. I step out of the trees and onto the gravel barrier before the tracks. I take out my phone and snap a few pictures of the area, including the spot where I emerged from the trees. It isn't a clear mouth to the path. Instead, the trail itself closed in and became less distinct for a few hundred yards, then opened out through an arch between narrow trees. It would be easy to miss for anyone not looking for it or not very familiar with the area.

I'm only a few feet away from the pink marker I found the first time I visited the tracks. Looking to the other side, I note where I parked my car that afternoon. I didn't even notice this path that day. I walked right past it, stood only feet from it, and had no idea it was here. Making my way back to that spot, I look over to the marker.

Out of the corner of my eye, the woods look even and unbroken. Even as I walk up to the marker, I barely notice anything different about the trees. The only reason I can perceive the opening of the path as much as I do is because I know it's there. If I was coming on it for the first time, absorbed in the gruesome sight of a mangled body in front of me, there's no way I would know it was there.

I think back to the notes from the local police's examination of the crime scene. There was nothing about the path or anything related to it. Of course, not having access to the full investigation notes because of their refusal to cooperate with the Bureau means I don't know everything they found out or are looking into. But I would think if they knew about the path that led into the outskirts of town, they would still have this area marked and under scrutiny.

Unless they already tossed it out as being meaningless. I only found it by chance, and it doesn't seem to be used with any sort of regularity. It wasn't even visible on the map I used to find my way from the cabin. Dipping back through the narrow entrance, I find the path again and follow it back in the direction I came. A chill settles down the length of my spine with each step further down the path, like eyes watching me. I stop suddenly and listen for the sound of anything moving in the trees. The ice on the ground and tightly tangled branches and twigs would make it next to impossible to navigate the area without making some sound. But it's eerily quiet around me.

A sound behind me makes me turn sharply. My own breath creates a white gust in the air, and for a moment, I can't see. The vibrant splash of red in front of me is out of place, but the flutter of the cardinal's wings make it settle into its surroundings. It doesn't move from where it's sitting on the ground, and I walk up to it cautiously. Another frantic flutter of its wings combines with a shrill cry. It's hurt.

Taking off my gloves, I crouch down and carefully scoop the small bird into my palm. As I lift it, I see its foot stuck in something embedded in the leaves. The dirty, rusted buckle comes up slightly when I release the foot, then settles back to the ground. I touch the bird's foot, and it continues to struggle against me holding it but doesn't seem seriously hurt. When I place it back down, the vibrant crimson bird immediately hops away, then flutters into the air. I watch it for a few seconds before turning back to the buckle on the ground.

I brush the leaves away and finally get a look at what caught the bird. The buckle must have been in just the right position for it to slip its foot under the edge while looking for food. I move enough leaves to reveal the buckle is attached to something. A piece of thick brown leather looks almost like a tiny belt, but as I move it further, I realize it's a dog collar attached to a metal chain. Tugging it up, I find the end of the chain. It's wrapped around a nearby tree.

A chill creeps along my spine again, and I bury the chain back where I found it. It's still only mid-afternoon, but the wind is picking up and the temperature getting sharper. I feel ice in the air, just waiting to fall. This is going to be one of those years I spend longing for palm trees and the blistering heat of water park concrete on my feet right up until I can go outside without even thinking about a jacket.

My feet move faster along the path until I reach the spot where I first stepped onto it. I start further down it but stop when I realize it's curving away from the direction of the cabin. Just as I expected, the service on my phone is spotty at best out here, so I decide to turn back. Now is not the time for me to get lost out in the woods. Not that there's really ever a time for that to be a good idea. But I'd rather it happens when I'm better prepared.

I climb off the path and head back through the woods how I came. My hands are numb, and my feet feel heavy in my boots when I make it back to the cabin. Thoughts of a huge bowl of soup and a cup of tea beckon me, but that promise disappears the instant I get to the porch.

Letting out a heavy sigh, I take the small white notecard out from where it's sticking out of the doorframe.

"I need to speak with you. Please come to the station when you get this."

There's no signature on the note, but there's also no question about who wrote it. The only person in town who would both want to speak with me and would have enough of an ego not to give his name or offer even a hint of respect to my schedule.

Chief LaRoche.

CHAPTER TEN

Conceivably speaking, I could just pretend I didn't get the note. Just having the corner of the note stuck in between the door and the frame is a tenuous connection at best. It very easily could have gotten swept up by the wind and fluttered off into the woods. I could release it into the wild and let it return to its tree ancestors while I hibernate for the rest of the day.

Or I could acknowledge my sleep deprivation is getting to me and will only get worse when the Chief comes storming to the cabin when I don't respond to his beckoning. As much as I hate the thought of following orders when the man snaps his fingers at me, I hate even more the thought of him banging on the door and dragging me out of the cocoon I have every intention of hiding in if I spend more than five minutes inside.

I groan and let myself into the cabin only long enough to shuck my outer layer of clothes and grab my keys. What the hell does he want with me? It's an unfortunate reality that there are several different options for what the police chief might want to drag me in to talk about. I'm used to juggling a variety of tangled webs being my reality, but this man throws me off balance. He doesn't know who I am or why I'm in his town, and I feel like I'm at a disadvantage because I have no idea what he wants to talk about. Being undercover is about staying a step ahead, and I can't do that when I don't even know what I'm walking into. But I have my suspicions.

I walk up to the reception desk when I get to the police station and wait for Esther to look up at me.

"Hi. I'm here to see Chief…"

"Come back to my office," LaRoche calls from the doorway to the back of the station.

"And there he is. Chipper as ever. Thank you, Esther."

I follow Chief LaRoche down the hall to his office and drop down into the hard, wooden chair at his desk.

"Where were you?" he asks, coming around the desk to sit in his own thickly cushioned chair.

"Excuse me?" I ask.

He leans back, and his eyes rove up and down me. I might feel offended if I thought there was anything behind the look other than disdain. And maybe a healthy dose of suspicion. The longer I look at him, the more the suspicion and offense both creep up the back of my neck.

"I don't think it's that challenging a question, Ms. Monroe. I went to the cabin where you are staying, and you weren't there. Where were you?"

There's a lilt to the way he says the name, and I narrow my eyes slightly. He seems unsure, the suspicion shifting from what I did to who I am. My body tenses. Could he have found out why I'm here? It's not like Creagan's choice for name and backstory are all that creative. Not that it matters much. It's not illegal to be FBI in public. But the way he says it makes the hair on the back of my neck stand up.

"I don't think that's any of your business," I state flatly.

"It is my business when I'm trying to protect the people of my town from what could be a serial killer."

"That was a very compelling assertion. Throw in a ten-gallon hat and I might even believe it. But here's the thing. Didn't you in not so flattering terms tell me I'm not one of the people of your town? Just someone passing through?" I ask.

He leans back further in his chair and folds his hands over his stomach as he stares at me. The smirk on his face makes me dislike him even more.

"You're right. Which makes me want the answer to my question even more. I don't much like a stranger lurking around and not being honest about what she's been up to."

"I don't have to tell you anything," I say.

He draws in a breath through his nose, his nostrils flaring. When he lets it out, he gives a single nod.

"I've been looking into the dead man on your porch," he says.

"You dragged me down here to grill me about something I've already told you I know nothing about?"

"I didn't drag you…"

"He wasn't there the last time I checked," I snap, cutting him off before he can spiral into a self-important speech. "Unless you put him back, I don't think it really has anything more to do with me than it did the last time we spoke."

I hope my voice is convincing. He can't know about the note hidden in the drawer of the nightstand in the cabin or the name scrawled across it. He can't know I need the information about that man even more than he does, or why. But I need every word LaRoche might have about him.

"I would really like to think that, Ms. Monroe, but you have to understand what this looks like."

"No, Chief. What does it look like? As far as I can tell, this man doesn't fit in with the other disappearances or the murders. The last time we spoke, you said you didn't even know who he is."

The chief opened the top drawer of his desk and pulled out a slip of paper. He slid it across the desk toward me.

"Does this name mean anything to you?"

I look down at the paper.

"Ron Murdock?" I shake my head. "No. I've never heard it."

"Seems nobody else has, either. At least, not when it comes to him. Which leaves me wondering why that's the name he used for the hotel room he rented three towns over."

"How do you know he rented a hotel room?" I raise an eyebrow in doubt.

"Surveillance video." He tips his face down to look at me through lowered lids and licks his lips in a slimy way that makes me cringe. "I guess we know a little bit more about the investigation than you want to give us credit for."

"Is that all you wanted to ask me?" I ask.

I start to stand up, but Chief LaRoche leans toward me.

"Do you know anyone in Florida?" he asks.

My breath catches in my throat, but I won't let it show on my face. Letting the breath out slowly, I keep my eyes locked on him.

"Why?"

"Do you?" he asks.

"Is this some sort of game we're playing?"

"The address he gave when he registered for the hotel room is in Iowa but his license says he's from Florida."

"What does that have to do with me?"

He throws his hands up in the air and gives a disingenuous smile. "Probably nothing. Just thought I'd run it past you and see if you had any ideas."

"I was in that cabin for less than an hour when he came to the door. Why would I have any ideas about who he is?"

My mind wanders back to the note in the drawer. Part of me wonders if I should tell LaRoche what I know. There are details I could give him, insight I could offer. That man is dead, lying somewhere waiting for someone to know who he is. But I stop myself. His face hasn't shown up on any missing person's reports. The news hasn't shown a desperate woman pleading for the return of her husband. No one is looking for him, but he was looking for me. I need to know why, and I'm not going to compromise the link he has to my past.

"Be careful where you go around here, Ms. Monroe. It's easy to get lost when you don't know what you're dealing with."

My eyes narrow.

"I don't think this is something we should call him about. He should know in person."

The chief's eyes lift up toward the voice going by the open door to his office.

"I tried, anyway. He's not answering. We should just go find him," another voice answers.

The two voices are close, which means the men likely stopped in the break room just to the side of the chief's office. LaRoche doesn't look happy about me hearing them, which means I want even more to know what they're talking about.

"Is he up at the bar at this time of day?" the first voice asks.

"Thank you for coming up here to talk to me," Chief LaRoche harrumphs, clearing his throat and making his voice a little louder like he's trying to cover up the sound of the other men. "I appreciate your help."

"They're talking about Jake," I say. "What's going on?"

"I don't know what they're talking about. But I promise I will keep you updated on the man on your porch if there are any further developments."

I point behind me toward the door. "They're talking about Jake. I want to know what's going on."

He stares back at me, his watery eyes daring me to challenge his authority. I stand up and walk out of the room. The sound of his chair scraping across the floor as he pushes back to chase me would be amusing if I wasn't so interested in finding out why they were talking about Jake. Nicolas and an officer whose name I never caught look over at me from the coffee machine as I walk into the break room.

"Are you looking for Chief LaRoche?" Nicolas asks.

"What's going on with Jake?" I answer.

"Ms. Monroe, this area is not open to the public," the chief says, coming up behind me. "If you'll come with me, I'll walk you out."

But I stay still, staring at Nicolas. His gaze flickers from me to the chief and back. "This is an active investigation, and until we've spoken to Jake, we can't talk about anything."

He's not going to budge. But I'm not going to back down. I walk out of the police station and get into my car, but don't leave the parking lot. Several minutes later, Nicolas and the other officer come out of the side door and get into the marked car parked in one of the few spots. I wait until they pull out of the lot, and then drive up behind them. They might not tell me what's going on, but there's nothing they can do about me driving through town and happening to go to the bar. Maybe I want a snack. I definitely need a drink.

Nicolas glares at me when he sees me parked across the street from the bar.

"I thought I told you this was an active investigation," he says.

"You did. You didn't say anything about me not being able to go to a public place."

I step in front of them and walk into the dimly lit building. Jake is leaned against the bar, staring down at something in front of him. There are only two people sitting in one of the tables in the far corner, and the rest of the room is silent. He looks up when he hears the door, and a look of relief softens his face. He crosses to me and gathers me in his arms.

"The police are here," I manage to tell him in the second before the door opens.

I step away, but Jake takes my hand and keeps me close beside him.

"Nicolas, Brent. What is it? Did you find out something about my father's grave?"

"Is there somewhere we can talk, Jake? In private."

His eyes slide to me, but Jake's hand tightens around mine. "I want Emma with me."

"Fine. Can we go in the back?" Nicolas asks.

Jake looks over at the one occupied table. "Burke. Keep an eye on things for me. Cissy should be in soon to cover the bar."

One of the men lifts his hand above his head in acknowledgment. Jake leads us behind the bar and through a door leading into the back of the building.

CHAPTER ELEVEN

THEN

There wasn't really a water park season in Florida. That's one of the reasons she loved living there so much. There were a few months during the year when the temperatures would drop low enough to keep her out of her bathing suit, but that didn't stop the parks from being open. Some might shut down briefly and others would have long refurbishments, but seeing the slides churning out water when they drove past, even if she was in a jacket, made the lonely days less dark.

They didn't get to go to them nearly as often as she would have wanted to. If she had her choice, she would check in to one of the parks sometime in February and not leave again until the Christmas lights went up. She longed for the peaceful weightlessness of floating in the lazy river. Hours could slip by under the bright sun, nothing but the flowing water and inner tube beneath her, and she barely noticed. There was no worry in the water. It held her up and guided her along. She didn't even have to think. There were no decisions to make, no reason to have to feel on edge.

When she wasn't in the lazy river, she went for the slides. The bigger and faster, the better. She remembered being younger and staring up at the biggest slides. They towered over her, the sound of the water rushing down them almost deafening. People screamed as they shot down them and bounced across the surface of the pool at the bottom. Some children even sobbed as they dragged themselves out after toppling beneath the water. It didn't deter her. She wanted to experience it. She wanted to feel what it was like for gravity and water to take over completely and send her shooting along the brightly colored tubes.

She was too small then. Her head hovered a few inches beneath the wooden arrow that marked the height requirement, not even letting her straighten her spine or puff up her hair and steal a bit of extra height. She would have to wait.

Then they were gone. They went somewhere without water slides or pools, where a park was little more than a sandbox and swings. It was cold and gray a lot of the year. That's when she started to long for the palm trees and ache for the sting of the hot concrete. By the time they went back, and she stood on that concrete again, staring up at the slides, they didn't look as big. The rush was still there. The people were still screaming. But she didn't want to know what it was like to give over her control. Instead, she wanted to push back.

She refused to close her eyes when she crossed her arms over her chest and slung herself down into the slide. The vibrant orange tube glowed with sunlight and echoed with the movement of the water and her own gasping breaths. She watched every instant, refusing to close her eyes or completely relinquish control.

There was only one slide she wouldn't ride that day. As much as she didn't want to admit it, the dizzying, almost vertical slide at the very end of the complex seemed insurmountable. People stepped into a small clear chamber on a floor that acted as a trapdoor. With little more warning than the flash of a light, the person operating the slide released a lever, and the floor went out from under the rider. In an instant, they were gone, dropping into a black tube that finally ended in a large rectangular pool. It made her heart beat in her temples, and her throat run dry. As much as she tried to cross to it and step up onto the narrow, steep steps leading up to the top, she couldn't make herself.

She went to the concession stand instead.

In other areas of the country, in the town they just left, people were still cowering beneath hooded sweatshirts and jackets. It was that time of year when the weather was untrustworthy. The sunlight could seem bright and intense, promising warmth, but the air felt thin and fragile. A hint of a breeze or a wayward cloud would tip the temperature over into chilly territory again. So people hid themselves in layers and didn't tempt fate.

Not here. Here the breeze was soft and warm, and the sunlight evaporated droplets of water from her skin almost as soon as she got out of the water. She craved sno-cones and salt-coated French fries so hot the oil burned the tips of her fingers. She took cash from the waterproof container hanging from a bungee on her wrist and carried the food back to the chairs she and her parents claimed when they first came in early that morning.

It wasn't too hard to get seats at that time. As soon as the summer months officially rolled in and more tourists flocked the parks, claiming a spot beneath an umbrella became survival of the fittest. Her father tossed himself down onto the chair beside her moments after she sat and immediately dipped his hand into her fries. He laughed at her protest, and she smiled at him. She liked how he looked in the sunlight. She preferred the touch of gold that showed up on his skin when they were in Florida. Her mother never got that glow. Her milk-white skin was a gift of her Russian bloodline, and it stayed that way no matter where they traveled. It was consistent. Reliable. She thought her mother was the most beautiful woman in the world.

The rainbow slush froze her lips and tingled on her tongue. She chased it with the heat of the fries. Her father lay back against the chair and rested his head on a rolled-up blue and white striped towel. Round black lenses covered his eyes, but she could see his head move when he looked across the small pool at the edge of the collection of chairs. She turned her eyes like his. Looked past the white rubber lounges and multi-colored scatter of pool bags and towels. Saw beyond the sun-drunk adults and water-hyper children.

Found the man staring back at them. A tall man with dark hair and sunglasses that reflected the people staring back. Dark jeans and a light-colored button-up shirt with rolled up sleeves didn't fit in with the rest of the park. But as out of place as he looked, he seemed completely at ease.

In the back of her mind, he looked familiar. Not in a way she could really put her finger on. Not in a way that she was even fully sure about. But it sparked something small that made her fingers twitch like she wanted to wave. She didn't.

The next day her father left before the sun came up and didn't come back until tourist season. But her mother wasn't afraid. So she wasn't afraid. At least, not when anyone was looking. When he came back, the gold was gone from his skin.

CHAPTER TWELVE

NOW

The basket of fresh French fries the cook brings into the office is a clear ploy to find out why the police came to talk to Jake. He doesn't get anything out of it. Jake's intense eyes chase him out of the room before the officers say anything. But I can't resist the salt glistening on the sheen of oil and the way the smell reminds me I haven't had anything to eat since before the sun was fully in the sky. I eat one of the fries and offer another to Jake, but he turns his head away.

"What are you doing here?" he asks Nicolas. "You've got me back here. What is it you came to tell me?"

"What can you tell me about your father's death?" Nicolas asks.

Jake's shoulders square off, and his hand clenches around mine. The fries are forgotten. Heat stretches across my chest. I know what that question means. I've heard it asked so many times before. I've asked it even more times. It's never really what it sounds like. Jake's father didn't die recently, and that only makes the question even more ominous.

"What the hell kind of question is that?" Jake demands. "Do you think that's funny?"

He starts forward, and I press my hand against his chest to hold him back.

"Jake," I murmur under my breath. "He doesn't mean anything by it."

"I'm not trying to start anything, Jake. We're just trying to get to the bottom of what happened, and that means starting from the beginning."

"There is no beginning," Jake says through gritted teeth. "This was all over with a long time ago. Why are you bringing it up again?"

My attention piques. A secret simmers just beneath the surface of this conversation, and I'm aching to hear it. It's something everyone else in the room knows, and I feel on the outside, separated by years and space.

"We're just trying to figure things out. This isn't anything official. Just us talking."

I tilt my head at him; my eyes narrowed as I silently send back what he just said. The officer avoids looking at me. He knows he's being a hypocrite, talking out of his ass to try to get Jake to come down from the angry, roiling place he's quickly climbing into and talk with him.

"If it isn't anything official, maybe you could stop talking in circles and just tell him why you came," I say.

"My father died from natural causes," Jake bites off. "At least, that's what his file says."

"Has there been any sign of vandalism or interference with his grave before now?" Nicolas asks, sounding relieved Jake is talking.

"No."

"And have you experienced any threats recently? Anything that might indicate someone was planning this?"

"No." A breath snorts through his flaring nostrils.

"How about the date? Is there anything significant about the date?"

"What do you mean?" I ask.

Nicolas looks at me like he shoved acknowledging my existence out of his thoughts and isn't happy to have to bring it back to the forefront.

"Sometimes, in situations like this, the date is not chosen randomly. A person will pick a certain day because it has something to do with the person or their death."

I bite down on my tongue to stop the retort that quickly forms there. I scrape the words back down my throat and take a breath to clear them away.

"I understand the concept. I meant, why would you ask him that?"

Jake shifts with built-up energy. "You think this is personal. It's not just something random."

The second officer looks at Nicolas with a heavy expression in his eyes. "What are you doing?"

Nicolas doesn't take his eyes away from Jake.

"No," Jake says, his voice becoming low and gravelly.

"And is there any reason to believe there's someone who might want to hurt you? Or to upset you like this?" Nicolas asks.

Brent rocks back and forth uncomfortably. He's lower in rank than Nicolas and won't argue with him, but there's something building up inside him. His eyes keep flickering to the door, and his hands clench on the sides of his belt. Thin lips press together as he leans forward, wanting to say something but holding back the words.

"What is this about, Nicolas?" Jake asks.

"Just doing my job."

"Seems like you're just trying to open up old wounds and drag up old shit for fun. Why did you really come out here and make such a fuss about talking to me?"

"We're following up on some new information," Nicolas says.

Brent's eyes close briefly, but the gesture isn't lost on Jake. He looks at the younger officer, then back at Nicolas. His eyes widen.

"You found him, didn't you? You found my father's bones. Where?" Neither of the officers answer, and Jake takes a threatening step toward them. "Where did you find him?"

Before either officer can say anything, Jake's expression shifts, and realization crosses through his eyes. He storms out of the office, dragging me along with him by my hand.

"What are you doing?" I ask. "Where are you going?"

"Jake, you need to stay here," Nicolas commands as he follows us.

The order is futile. Jake isn't going to do anything either of them tell him. They lost him very soon after the beginning of the conversation. He brings me to his car and opens the passenger door. Part of me expects him to stuff me inside like a piece of luggage, but he resists and just lets go of my hand so I can get in myself. As I'm hooking my seatbelt, he storms around the front of his car and gets in. I can hear Nicolas shouting after Jake as they come out of the bar. Brent is on his radio, and Nicolas has his hands planted on his hips, watching us. When they realize we aren't stopping, they run for their police car.

"Where are we going?" I ask again, trying to keep my voice as steady as possible in hopes of calming him down.

I don't know if that's possible. If I was in his situation, I don't think I could be calm, either. But I don't love the frantic look on his face and the way his knuckles look like they're going to snap under the tension of their grip on the steering wheel. He's not fully in control, and the winding, narrow streets of Feathered Nest aren't the place to test muscle memory.

"Look, Jake, I know you're upset. That's perfectly understandable considering what you're going through. But I think you need to take a second and think through this," I say.

"I don't need to think through it."

Holding tightly to the door handle beside me, I keep watching his face. I'm waiting for the expression to change, for the crazy to drain from his eyes and the laughter to come back. Then I'll know he's in there somewhere.

It doesn't happen. But I'm relieved when he pulls the car into a gravel driveway studded with grass and shrubbery growing up through the jagged rocks. I don't know where we are, but at least we've stopped. He didn't bother to put on his seatbelt, which puts me at a disadvantage getting out of the car. By the time I wrench myself out of mine and climb out, he's disappearing around the side of the squat blue house.

Overhead, the cloud cover has moved back in. A white sky streaked with smoky wisps of gray promises more snow, or at least the sharp, almost violent needles of freezing rain that cover everything with a glittering glaze. The atmosphere is too still. It amplifies the voices coming from the backyard of the house, and my boots crunching over the rocks.

They aren't casual voices. They're low and measured, controlled to a rhythm I know. Before I even see him, I know Chief LaRoche is back there. He's talking to the other officers, the ones who weren't sent to talk to Jake and instead are investigating the gruesome desecration.

I run to the side of the house and see Jake nose to nose with LaRoche.

"Back up, Jake," the chief growls.

"Get out of my way."

"I'm not letting you back there. This is nothing you should be seeing."

"I don't need you to tell me what I should be seeing," Jake says back through gritted teeth. "I'm a grown man. You have my father back there, and I have the right to know about it."

LaRoche holds up his hands, playing the innocent again, and shakes his head.

"Now, Jake, we don't know what we have back there. And I'm not giving out details. What we might have found is part of an ongoing investigation, and I have to guard my information closely," he says condescendingly.

Jake stabs a finger angrily over LaRoche's head toward the backyard.

"You know damn well what you have back there. That's my father. All that's left of him. And if the man who did this to him is here, he needs to have a word with me."

"If you keep acting like this, I'm going to have to arrest you for interference."

"I'll take my chances," Jake fires back, his voice lowering.

He steps around LaRoche, and I rush after him. I stumble over a rotting piece of lumber positioned at the end of the driveway that made its way from the front of the house around to the side. I reach out and grab Jake's hand just as we get to the backyard. All I see are blue tarps hanging from trees with white nylon rope. It's clunky and unwieldy, but it does the job. We can't see anything beyond a few steps away from the driveway and the cramped cinderblock patio built at the back of the house. Jake looks at each of the tarps like he hopes to see through them and find out what's going on beyond them.

From my angle, I can see piercing yellow tape set up in a perimeter a few feet away from a small shed. What looks like the sum of the rest of the police force mills around snapping pictures, taking notes, and setting down markers. One officer walks to the edge of a well and peers down into the gap created by the lid sitting off-kilter by several inches. A wheelbarrow sits a few yards from the shed, mounded with dirt, and supporting the handle of a large shovel. The darkness of the ground behind it tells me that dirt came from being dug out of the ground fairly recently.

"Get off me!"

I turn to the sound of the shout and see Jake with his hands wrapped around the shirt of a man standing on the patio. His hands are already handcuffed behind him, but Jake tries to yank him away from the officer leading him down the steps.

"What did you do?" he screams.

I rush up to him and pull him back by his waist. The man sagging from the handcuffs is white-haired, his face etched with deep lines. His shirt is well-worn and hanging over the waist of jeans broken in by years of wear, not the machines that are so trendy now. He looks old and broken. Jake doesn't care.

"What did you do?" Jake screams again.

He struggles against my arms, trying to get to the man, but I hold him back.

"You need to stop. You don't want to get yourself arrested," I say.

"You were his best friend," Jake shouts at the man, completely ignoring me. "He trusted you. And this is how you repaid him? Don't you think you already did enough?"

"Jake," LaRoche says, coming up to us.

I hold up a hand to stop him. "I've got it. Come on. We're getting you away from here."

Jake lets me pull him away from the man, but his eyes stay welded to him until the last second. I take Jake by the shoulder and walk him around the house until he's finally forced to break eye contact. I guide him into the passenger seat of the car and get in beside him. He's silent for the first few moments of the ride, but his seething creates tension I'm just waiting to cause the windows to explode.

"I'm sorry," I finally say, just to break the silence.

It's not the right thing to say. Not really. Of course, it very rarely is. It's one of those phrases people have tucked into their vocabulary to stuff into situations that feel like they need something. One thing that grates on me to the point of physically shuddering when I hear it is people who attach 'I'm sorry' to the beginning of questions or to sentences that don't need them. *I'm sorry, but what time is it? I'm sorry, can you tell me where you got your shoes? I'm sorry, but her wearing white at her wedding is a joke.*

This isn't one of those times. I have an ache inside me for Jake and what he's going through and want him to know I'm here. But those words just aren't enough.

"How could he do that?" Jake mutters. "After all these years, why couldn't he just let well enough alone? With everything else this town is going through, what could he possibly get out of digging my father up and leaving him in that shed? He helped *build* that shed."

I reach over with one hand to rub his back. No other words come to mind. All I can think of is the fragile-looking old man and try to understand how he could do something so grisly.

CHAPTER THIRTEEN

I drive past the turn to Jake's house and then down the main road, not stopping at the bar. He doesn't need to try to go back to work right now and being home won't do him any good. The familiar surroundings will only keep his mind spiraling. Instead, I drive back to the cabin. He sits with his head hanging, staring at his hands pressed between his knees even as I get out and walk around the front of the car.

"Come on inside," I tell him.

He looks up for a second before climbing out and following me up onto the porch. His eyes sweep over the wood planks, and my stomach twists a little. Maybe walking him across an unsolved murder scene wasn't the most compassionate choice in this moment. But he doesn't seem bothered by it. He walks inside without a word and immediately drops down onto the couch. Quickly scooping the pictures off the table and tucking them in the compartment under it, I take off my shoes and curl up onto the cushion beside him.

"Can I make you a cup of coffee?" I ask a few silent seconds later

He nods, and I head into the kitchen. Beyond the window, the sky looks angry again. Within a few seconds, a mixture of cold rain and snowflakes starts coming down. The coffee pot gurgles and fills the room with the warm, reassuring scent. While it fills, I peek into a few of the cabinets to see if there's anything I can bring out with the coffee. I know there aren't any cookies or pastries sitting around, yet I still look. Maybe one of these times, it will spontaneously appear.

Settling for a few foil-wrapped truffles from a bowl on the counter, I carry everything back into the living room and offer a mug to him. Jake takes it and holds it between his strong hands but doesn't take a sip. I breathe in the warmth of the steam coming up off the dark surface of the brew, imagining the caffeine somehow traveling through the air and getting a head start by seeping into my lungs.

"My father was a very good businessman," Jake suddenly says. "Maybe too good."

"What do you mean?" I ask.

Setting my mug of coffee on the table, I unwrap one of the truffles.

"He was driven to succeed and worked extremely hard to make sure he always did what he set himself out to do. But he didn't take shortcuts. He wouldn't settle for anything less than excellence. No matter what element of the business he was handling, he did it with every bit of him. He took pride in treating customers well, being honest, and making sure they always got the best experience from him. That didn't always sit well with other people."

"Why?"

"Small towns aren't always as sweet and innocent as people want to think they are. There are people in Feathered Nest who didn't have the same thoughts about business as my father. They thought only about themselves. They cut corners, did what they could to save money, and didn't care about the customers on the other end of their deals. Sometimes it was just unethical. Sometimes it was illegal. My father stood up for what he believed in, and it didn't matter who he had to cross to do it. A few people ended up in hot water because of it. Businesses closed or were forced to change their practices and make less money. Jail time."

I shake my head. "I don't understand."

"I don't know all the details of it, and a lot has been hushed up and brushed aside over the years. But I do know there were some suspicious deaths of farmhands and a lot of money rolling through the town. People were paying far more for their goods than they needed to, and nobody was saying anything about it."

"Money laundering? Did the police get involved?" I ask.

"The Chief at the time was LaRoche's father," Jake admits. "But he didn't seem surprised by any of it if you catch my drift."

"He was in on it."

"That's what some people around here think. But other people blamed my father for everything. They thought he should have left well enough alone and kept his nose out of things that didn't concern him. The tension remained for the rest of his life."

"What about that man? His best friend? What would he have to do with any of this?" I ask.

"Cole Barnes was my father's best friend from way back. They were just kids together. When I was young, he was a fixture at our house and at family events. They did everything together, and if one needed something, anything, then the other was there to do anything he could," Jake tells me. "But then that changed. Things started getting tense between them. Cole accused my father of betraying him."

"Betraying him? What did he do?" I ask.

Cupping my mug in my palms, I let the warmth of the coffee seep through me. What Jake's telling me stirs up suspicions and unsteady feelings that have been growing inside me since arriving in Feathered Nest. I don't want to push too hard or ask too many questions and possibly reveal the real reason I'm here. Instead, I tuck away the little bits of information, so I'll be able to take them out and tumble them around later, figuring out what they could mean and where they fit in the puzzle I'm trying to solve.

"I don't know all the details. Secrets are secrets for a reason. My father didn't want to air other people's dirty laundry if he didn't have to. All I know is they had a falling out. A serious one, from the way the town talked about the two of them after that. Then, my father died."

"How did he die?"

Jake shrugs and stares down into his mug like the coffee is going to reveal all the answers of the universe for him.

"That's a good question, isn't it?" he asks.

"What do you mean?"

"He was always the healthiest person I knew. Never sick a day in his life. Everyone else would get colds or stomach bugs, and it never once got him. He'd take care of all of us and keep going right about his life. Then, all of a sudden, he was sick as a dog. Just out of nowhere. One day he was perfectly fine like any other day, and the next, he was so sick he couldn't get out of bed. Stayed that way for three more days before we finally convinced him to go to the doctor. They couldn't help him, and he ended up in the hospital, where he died the next day. One of the doctors said it was the strangest thing he ever saw. They tested for a bunch of things, but couldn't find anything," Jake tells me.

"Tested for a bunch of things? Like poison?"

"Apparently some of his symptoms lined up with poisoning, but when they tested him, nothing came up. They ended up filling out his death certificate as natural causes, but I've never really believed that. Healthy men don't just die like that," he says.

"Do you think Cole could have murdered your father?"

"He acted a little shady in the days after the death. Cleaned out his shed. Piled his truck high with stuff to throw away but didn't bring it to the convenience center. Drove out of town with it and came back late that night without anything. My father's favorite cup went missing the day before he got sick. We didn't think a whole lot of it at the time. We were worried about other things. But once we did notice, it was all we could think about. He drank out of that cup every single day of his life. Then it just up and disappeared right as he's getting sent into his deathbed? Seems like too much of a coincidence to me." He shrugs again. "But LaRoche Senior didn't put any man-hours into it. He said it was just a cup, nothing that mattered. My father probably left it behind somewhere, or it got broken. We were putting too much thought and emphasis on it. He slammed that case shut just as fast as he possibly could."

Everything happening around me since I got here swirls around in fractured thoughts and ideas in my head. They're trying to fall into place. One stands out to me.

"Jake, does Chief LaRoche have a dog?" I ask.

He looks for me strangely as he reaches for one of the truffles piled on the coffee table. I'm still holding the one I chose, the foil half-twisted out of place. My fingers go back to it like they need something to do to aid my mind in processing the thoughts.

"A dog?" he asks. "Yeah. He has a big hound dog. Used to be a tracker for the force but has retired. Sometimes he takes her up through the woods for walks. Why?"

I shake my head and pop the chocolate into my mouth. My teeth have just cracked through the shiny shell when the lights in the cabin flicker.

"Oh, no," I sigh.

"Nothing to worry about," Jake soothes me. "It's just a flicker. The weather has been hard on the wires the last few days. Just give it a second." An instant later, the cabin descends into pitch blackness. "See, what did I tell you? It just needed a second."

I laugh. "Yeah, this is perfect. Nothing like the power going out in the freezing cold weather."

"It happens all the time out here. That's why most people around town have a generator. Rain, wind, snow, ice, heat wave. Power goes out, and those things automatically kick on. Anything can happen, and they just go right on with their football games and cooking chili."

"Speaking from personal experience?" I ask.

"I might have delayed jumping on the generator bandwagon for a while and ended up huddling around a half-ass fire eating partially cooked chili."

"Sounds like fun times."

"Good memories. The thing to remember is sometimes these old places have the power kick off just because. The power isn't actually out; the circuit just gets tripped for one reason or another. Give me a second, and I'll just flip the breaker," he says.

Using the glow of his phone screen for light, Jake makes his way toward the back of the cabin. He's gone for a couple of minutes, and the lights suddenly burst back on. Relief washes over me, and he gives me a smile as he comes back into the room.

"See? I told you it was nothing to be worried about," he tells me.

"Thank you. I was really not looking forward to the possibility of spending the night in the dark and cold," I say.

"Don't worry," Jake says. "I wouldn't have let you be out here all by yourself."

"I appreciate it."

He leans toward me across the couch, and I shift forward enough to meet his lips. His forehead rests against mine when the kiss breaks, and he lets out a long breath.

"Thank you for being here for me through all this. I know you came here to get some rest and relaxation and got swept up into this insanity," he murmurs.

"I don't mind," I tell him.

"That's hard to believe. On the other hand, most people would have gotten out of town as fast as they could after finding a dead guy on their porch the first night they came. But you didn't. Maybe I'm underestimating you."

There's flirtation in his voice, but for some reason, the words send a chill down my spine.

"Maybe," I say.

He kisses me again and leans back against the couch. "Is it weird that I'm almost relieved?"

"Relieved about what?"

"Cole. He stayed under the radar all these years, kept out of suspicion, and just lived his life. But he couldn't stay away. He just had to torment my father a little bit more. I'm sure he thought he would get away with it. No one has put any thought into my father's death in so many years. Cole thought he could add one more humiliation, one more horror, to my father's death, and no one would ever think of him. But now he's going to finally have to answer for what he did. And I feel… relieved. It was horrible to see that, and I hate him for doing it, but maybe I'll finally get some closure."

CHAPTER FOURTEEN

THEN

Where are you from?

It's one of the first questions people tend to ask each other. When they're in that wispy, tenuous period of trying to make connections that might solidify a link between them, people go back to the most basic elements of each other. Finding out origins provides structure and context. That one detail can give a glimpse into a person's culture and life experiences. It helps make the other person real.

She never had a real answer to that question. Not that there was ever a time when she didn't have a home. There was always somewhere she went back to. Always somewhere to tuck in at night and to write down on forms. That was supposed to be home. But she never knew what to say when someone asked her where she was from because she couldn't remember.

For as long as she knew, they were moving. Sometimes she knew it was coming. Her parents would tell her a few weeks ahead. She would have the chance to wonder where they were going and if there was anything she was going to miss. There rarely was. Unless it was the palm trees in the wind and the concrete burning her feet. Then she knew she would ache for it and hope there would be a time when they'd come back.

Other times she had no warning at all. In an instant, life simply changed, and she had no choice but to go along with it. She woke up in the morning in one place and went to bed in another. Sometimes only to wake in a third.

She had no idea where it started.

In a way, it didn't really matter. She couldn't really get to know people. There was always something she wasn't allowed to say or something she was supposed to know. On the way to the next stop, the next home, she'd find out the new details of her life. After a while, they all started to blend. That's when she stopped talking to people. She didn't want to say the wrong thing or give the wrong details. She didn't know who was asking or why. It was easier to be quiet.

The only thing that stayed consistent in her life was her martial arts training. No matter where they were, she didn't go more than a few days without training.

She was training that day. If she hadn't been, she would have been home. She was in the gym rather than there with her mother. It often crossed her mind that things could have turned out so differently. Just one choice, one move along a different path, and she could have been lying there right beside her mother, and it would have been her father to first walk through the blood.

That was the day moving turned to running. Danger defined her life. Even when she didn't know it. Even when she thought everything was exactly as it should be. She was always running. She kept running even after her mother's murder. That day everything in her changed. She didn't care about the art that she thought would pull her out of the chaotic world she knew and give her a life of her own. Her focus changed to only one thing. Understanding who killed her mother and why.

That was the day her feet found her father's footsteps. She didn't follow them exactly. Her feet wouldn't fit in them anyway, but she followed their shadows. She gave herself to learning everything she could about the danger that haunted her life and why she was always running.

She kept running until the day there were no more steps to follow.

That's when the question changed. It was no longer *where are you from...*

It was *where did you go?*

CHAPTER FIFTEEN

NOW

At some point, I fell asleep on the couch. I only know that because I wake up with my head buried in Jake's chest and cold air making me shiver. If it wasn't for the lamp still glowing in the corner, I might think the power went out again. As it is, it's just the ancient heater. Climbing off the still-sleeping Jake, I grab the quilt I left draped over the chair and wrap it around myself. He wakes up as I'm standing over the old furnace, glaring down into the grates with absolutely no idea what to do. The Bureau has trained me for many things, but the 'F' most certainly does not stand for 'furnace'. I don't even know what's under the grates.

"Everything okay?" Jake asks.

I glance over my shoulder and see him leaned over the back of the couch, looking at me. Sleepy eyes and tousled hair make him look younger than he is. The anger and hurt are gone from his face, but it won't be long until they're back. As long as there are questions left about his father, those feelings aren't going to go away. And even after those questions are answered, the pain will linger. The anger will never really go away. Jake might be able to tuck it away. He could compartmentalize it, so he's only forced to experience it when the walls break down. But it's part of him.

"Well, it seems like getting me through that last Arctic blast was the heater's swan song. It's not working," I tell him.

"Do you want me to take a look at it?" he asks.

"No, you don't have to do that. I can get in touch with the owner. I'm sure he'll send somebody over here to take care of it."

Or she. Not really knowing who I'm renting this cabin from might make getting the furnace fixed a bit of a challenge. But I don't want to let on.

"Are you sure?"

"Absolutely. I don't think you need me treating you like my handyman," I nod.

The icy air might make me rethink that. I pull the quilt closer around me and glare down into the furnace again. This would be the perfect moment for me to develop some sort of psychokinetic power. I only cling to that possibility for a few seconds before I turn back to Jake.

"Not your handyman," he says. "Just your man who happens to be handy."

It's cheesy to the point of being cringe-worthy, but damn if it isn't effective. He climbs over the back of the couch and slips his hands under the sides of the quilt so he can wrap his arms around my waist. His mouth finds mine, and the pressure of his body guides me back toward the wall. His kiss is deep and intense for a few seconds before he steps back. He brushes his lips over mine one more gentle time, and he brushes my hair away from my cheek. Something about the gesture makes me feel off balance like I haven't caught up from the first kiss.

"I'll let you know if he doesn't send somebody," I say.

Jake smiles. "Good. As much as I would rather stay here and keep you warm, I should probably go and make sure the bar is still standing, and Burke hasn't decided to take over permanently. Thank you again for being so amazing today. I don't know how I would have gotten through it without you."

"Of course," I tell him.

"Make sure they get this heater fixed fast. I don't like the idea of you being out here all alone in the cold for too long. If it's not up and working soon, you should come stay at my place."

He pulls the quilt closer around me, his hands running along the fabric.

"I'll let you know as soon as I'm back in the warmth."

I want to ask him to call me if he hears any more from the police, but don't want to fracture the calm that has come over him. It's temporary, but he deserves to have it for as long as it will stay.

I wait a few minutes after Jake leaves to grab my phone. The cold makes my fingers ache as I try to dial, but I finally get the number in. It rings a few times before I even wonder what time it is. It might be too late to catch anyone at the office.

"Hello?"

That was a ridiculous thought. It's never too late to catch anyone at the office. They live and breathe work, especially when they have major cases to juggle.

"Eric, it's me."

"Emma? Is everything okay? What's wrong?"

"Well, that's just encouraging as all hell. Have you been talking to Bellamy?" I ask.

"Sorry. I'm sure everything is absolutely perfect," he quips.

"I wouldn't quite jump that far. But I'll start with the fact that my eyes are going to freeze over because the furnace in my cabin decided now was the perfect time to lay down its life. Unfortunately, I don't know who Creagan got this place from, so I can't call and get it fixed."

"So, why aren't you calling Creagan?" he asks.

"Because I'd rather talk to you," I offer.

"I'd be flattered by that if it wasn't just a flagrant use of our friendship to avoid you having to talk to him because you know he's going to grill you about the case," Eric points out.

"That's not true," I argue. "It's a flagrant use of our friendship to avoid me having to talk to him because I'm afraid he'll call me Brittany again, and I just frankly don't have it in me to deal with his shit right now. I'll pretend to think he's funny some other time. Right now, I have bigger things to think about than the potential of my ass splintering into little ice chips if I sit down too hard."

"We can't have that," he says. "Hold on. Let me see if I can find anything."

"Thanks."

The phone clicks onto hold, and I shuffle my way back into the living room, sweeping the end of the quilt away from my feet with one hand while holding my phone with the other. Sitting on the edge of the couch cushion, I reach down into the alcove beneath the coffee table and pull out the stack of research I shoved there. It's jumbled up from my hasty clearing of the table, so I get to work trying to organize it again. I'm halfway through reconstructing them as I had them when the line clicks again.

"So, it turns out the house isn't really owned by anybody," Eric says.

"What?" I ask. "What do you mean it's not owned by anybody? Creagan had to have rented it from somebody. Besides, it has electricity, and water, and it's furnished. Obviously, no one has lived here consistently for a while, but it's not like it's been sitting abandoned for decades. "

"The town owns it. It was abandoned a while back, but you can imagine there's not a whole lot of real estate opportunity there. When someone is interested in visiting, especially when there are bodies piling up and the reputation of the town isn't exactly thriving, they offer up what they can."

"And of the options they gave him, this is what he went with. I wonder what that says about his image of me. Wait, so what does that mean for my furnace? If I have to keep staying here, I'm not going to make it without heat," I say.

"He said to find a repairman and charge it to your expenses."

"Perfect," I sigh.

"How is everything going?" he asks.

"Do you mean, have I figured out why all the people are disappearing and getting killed around here? No." I let out a sigh and rake my fingers back through my hair. I find the picture of the woman by the train tracks again and stare down at it. My skin tingles. "But I might be getting close. Eric, can you do something for me?"

"Do I have to talk to Creagan again? Because I think I might have used up all my leverage with that conversation."

"No. He's not necessary, but I do need you to do something for me," I say.

"What's that?"

"Do trains have cameras on them? Like cargo trains. Do they have cameras on the front to see what's happening on the tracks?" I ask.

"Most of them do. By now I'd say probably all of them do unless a company is using really outdated machinery. Why? What do you need?" Eric asks.

"If I send you a map of train tracks and a range of dates, can you figure out what trains were running during that time and get me the feeds off the cameras?"

"I'm sure I could. Does this have to do with the bodies?"

"It might."

"I thought the train company already examined all the trains and couldn't find one that might have hit either of them," he says.

"They did. That's not what I want to know. Can you get me the video?"

"I'll see what I can do."

"Thanks. I'll email you the information," I tell him. "Oh... Eric? Keep this between us. I don't know what it might mean yet, and I don't want to get anybody sniffing around if it doesn't pan out."

———

Two hours later, I'm sitting, listening to what sounds like the furnace repairman arbitrarily bashing whatever is inside a furnace when an email finally appears from Eric. Curling defensively into the corner of the couch so the repairman can't catch a glimpse of what's on my screen, I nestle my earbuds in my ears and open the first attached video.

There's no audio, and the image is choppy and slightly grainy. It's the type of video that comes from a surveillance video most people never intend on watching. A few second's time-lapse makes it look more like a series of pictures flashing by in rapid succession than a smooth video. The video covers several hours, three days before the body of the woman was found by the train tracks. I watch it carefully for markers to identify the specific area of the tracks I'm interested in seeing. Taking notes of what I see during that part of the tracks, I stop the video and move on to the next one.

By the fourth video, I'm able to skip ahead through much of the feed just to the small portion that shows what I need to see. This video is slightly different than the others. Recording the journey of a different train than the others, this one shows a camera position just off from where it should be. As if it's been knocked off center or was mounted incorrectly. The camera doesn't give a full view of the tracks. The screen shows a portion of the train itself and half the tracks along with the gravel bank on the side opposite the woods.

Something catches my eye in the corner of the screen, and I stop the video. I go back several seconds and watch again. Four times through later, I'm convinced I know what I'm seeing. I watch one more time for good measure, my stomach sinking.

"Son of a bitch."

"I'm working as fast as I can."

My eyes snap up to the repairman, and I shake my head, popping the buds I forgot I was wearing out of my ears.

"Not you. I'm sorry. You're doing fine. Um. Do you by chance, know how much longer it's going to be?" I ask.

He peers down at the furnace he appears to have gutted. "Give me another hour. Maybe an hour and a half."

I don't want to sit around waiting for him, but I'm also not going to leave him alone in my cabin. Wrapping the quilt around me again, I pull my computer onto my lap to settle in for the wait. My attention goes back to the man who died on my porch and the note clutched in his hand. Without giving him details why, I already asked Eric to run a check on the name Ron Murdock and see if anything came up, even though I was pretty sure it wouldn't. He wasn't swinging by for a friendly visit. I doubt he gave his real name at the hotel. In tiny places like the towns dotted around here, it isn't unusual for a hotel to not bother to check identification if someone pays cash. Even if they do, I've tossed enough faked credentials into the shredder to know it isn't hard to convince someone of anything if you pay attention to the details.

It's the details I want to know now. No one outside of the team knew I was coming here. The thing is, he didn't just find out I was here. To arrive so soon after me, he had to anticipate me coming. Just for fun, I ran a check on the name along with my own, but nothing came up. Another search with my father's name and a third with my mother's had equally dead ends. I wasn't going to get anywhere with searches like this. I needed more. But for now, there was nothing I could do but sit and wait.

In the dark.

"What just happened?" I call out.

"Sorry about that. Nothing to worry about. Just tripped the circuit a bit. I'll fix it." The repairman's footsteps disappear into the back of the cabin, and a few moments later, the lights pop back on. He comes back and crouches down near the furnace. "That box is a finicky thing. I've been tinkering on this house since way back, and it has always given me trouble. Tucked way the hell back there and all."

"Who lived here?" I ask.

"What's that?"

"You said you've been working on this house for a long time. When I rented it, they told me it was abandoned," I explain.

"Well, abandoned is a bit of a harsh word. The lady who lived here died, and no one claimed the property," he tells me.

"She didn't have any family?" I ask.

He runs his hand over his face and looks into the distance for a second.

"Seems to me she had a daughter. Never met her, but Wendy sometimes talked about her girl and a granddaughter who lived somewhere. She didn't get to see them."

"And they never came for the house or any of her things? Did the police get in touch with her after Wendy died?" I ask.

"Not my business. All I know is the house got taken over by the town, most of it cleaned out, and now it's rented out to folks wanting to visit Feathered Nest. Not that there are too many of those. Last gentleman came to stay didn't even stay for the full time he had booked. Just took his stuff and left. Door unlocked, lights on. Some people have no manners."

"Someone else stayed here recently?" I ask, surprised.

"Yep. Round about six months ago, I'd say," he muses.

"No one mentioned it to me."

"Now, why would they?" There's a touch of suspicion in his voice, and I try to come up with something to cover it, but the sound of the furnace roaring to life brings a smile to his face. "Would you listen to that? She still has some life in her, after all. It might take a little bit of time to get this place warmed up again but should be nice and toasty before you tuck in for the night."

"Thank you so much. Let me know what I owe you, and I'll write you a check."

CHAPTER SIXTEEN

I've never seen someone pack tools so slowly. The repairman meticulously wipes down each implement with a threadbare red rag before settling them into his bag. I get the distinct feeling he's stalling, trying to take up as much time as he can. I'm not sure if that's because he's trying to spend more time with me, or if he thinks something else in the cabin is about to go wrong. Either way, I'm not interested in the company. I hurry him along his way, and as soon as he heads outside with my check peeking out of his pocket, I rush to change into another layer of warm clothes and put on my boots.

I'm walking back toward the living room when the sound of the door opening makes my heart jump in my throat. The furnace muffles the sound slightly, but I can still hear the footsteps enter the house and stop. Very aware that my phone is in there on the table and even if I had it, the police likely wouldn't be much help anyway, I brace myself and walk out into the living room.

"Jake!" His name bursts out of me when I see him standing in the middle of the living room, holding his phone like he's getting ready to dial. "What are you doing?"

"I was getting ready to call you," he says.

"I mean, what are you doing *here*?" I ask.

He stuffs his phone into his pocket and points behind him. "You drove my car from Cole's house. You don't have your car. I thought I'd come bring it to you."

I let out a breath. "Oh. Thank you. Yeah, I didn't even think about that. I was actually just getting ready to leave."

"Leave? Where are you going?" he asks.

My plan was to go back into the woods to test my new theory, but I can't tell him that. I'll have to shuffle my plans.

"I need to go up to the police station," I tell him.

"The police station?"

"It's about the man," I say quickly. "I forgot to ask LaRoche something the last time they brought me in."

"I'll give you a ride up to your car. Ready to go?"

"Sure." I grab the satchel I filled before getting dressed and sling it over my shoulder. "Let's go."

We get into his car, and I peer back at the cabin as he pulls away from it.

"Something wrong?" Jake asks.

"Did you meet the guy who rented the cabin a few months ago?" I ask.

He glances over at me with a confused expression.

"What guy?"

"The man who came to repair the furnace said there was a guy who rented the place about six months ago but didn't stay the whole time."

Jake presses his lips together in thought, then shakes his head.

"No. I didn't even realize anyone else had stayed here in years. He must not have been very social while he was here."

"I wonder what he needed repaired," I muse.

"Don't know, but old Clancy must not have done a very good job if the guy left early."

"Maybe."

We get to the main street of town, and Jake pulls up behind my car. He walks me to the driver's side and leans into the door as I settle into the seat.

"Let me know if you find out anything," he says. "I don't like not knowing you're there when nobody knows what happened to that guy."

"I will."

He gives me a peck on the cheek and closes the door. Almost immediately, my phone rings. I put it on speaker and pull away from the curb.

"Why is Eric getting all the updates from you? Why don't I get to know anything?" Bellamy demands.

"Because he works for the FBI and can find things out for me," I tell her.

"I know stuff. I'm a consultant! I can consult for you," she argues.

"Can you help me access security camera footage and do a background check?" I ask.

"...No."

"And there we go."

"But I still want to know what's going on with you. I can help you... think," she says.

"You're right. Maybe I'm too deep in this and am missing something you might see."

"Lay it on me."

I drive to the police station as I fill her in on Jake's father, the train footage, and the path through the woods, then what I'd learned so far about the man from the porch. I'm still talking as I sit at the front of the station, watching the doors to see if any of the officers leave.

"Holy shit," she says once I finish.

"Yeah, that's pretty much the place I'm in right now, too."

"Is Eric going to tell the rest of the team about any of this?" she asks.

"No. I don't want to get Creagan involved. Not yet, anyway. It might not be anything, and I don't want to blow the entire investigation by acting too soon. There's not enough to go on yet."

"Just be careful."

"I will. Look, I've got to go," I tell her, starting to climb out of the car.

"Okay. Call me later."

"I will. Bye."

I feel a twinge of guilt at not being totally honest with her about the man on the porch, but I push it away. She's already worried enough. Besides, without knowing who he is or how he ended up on the porch, I don't know what kind of danger I could put Bellamy in by telling her. I learned a long time ago that information could be deadly. I can't put her at risk.

The receptionist looks up at me as I entered the lobby and let the door swing closed behind me.

"Can I help you, Ms. Monroe?" she asks.

"I just need to talk with Chief LaRoche," I tell her.

My eyes automatically swing over to the door, waiting for his usual appearance right after I summon him. But this time, the door stays closed.

"He isn't in the office right now. Is there something I can do for you?"

"No. Is Nicolas available?"

"Officer Greene is in the back. I'll see if he can take a minute to speak with you."

"I'm sure he can. Thank you," I say.

I slip past her and through the door into the back before she has a chance to stop me. Nicolas comes through a door as I'm heading down the hallway at a fast enough clip to avoid Esther. I do not put it past her to snatch me by the back of the coat if she can catch up.

"Ms. Monroe? What are you doing here?" he asks.

"I'm sorry, Officer Greene. I didn't think she would just come back," Esther says.

"I have a few questions I need to ask you," I say.

"I believe asking questions is my job," he frowns.

"Actually, it's Chief LaRoche's job, but he's not here, so I'm going to have to settle for you. Besides, I'm not trying to do your job. I just want to settle my own curiosity," I say.

And do my job.

He stares at me for a few seconds like he's trying to decide what to do, then nods.

"What is it you want to know?" he asks, gesturing into the room he just left.

I follow him into what turns out to be a small conference room and sit in one of the gray chairs at a round table.

"The woman whose body was found by the train tracks. What can you tell me about her?" I ask.

Nicolas's eyes narrow.

"Why do you want to know that?" he asks.

"Like I said, curiosity. You have to know the disappearances and murders are big news. And since I got wrapped up in it all the night I got here, I'm interested in finding out more," I tell him.

"We already told you that man's shooting was a random event. It didn't have anything to do with the other case," he says.

"Are you absolutely certain about that?" I try to needle him, to get him to reveal any bit of information I can use. Shooting? That's new. "It seems to me you don't even know who that man really is, much less why he was here. So how can you totally discount his being the responsibility of the same killer?"

"The other victims all have ties to the area. Cristela Jordan came from the next town over and was well-known in town. She was up at Jake's bar most weekends. Ron Murdock is a stranger. They have nothing to do with each other." He leans across the table toward me. "Look, Ms. Monroe. I can understand your interest. But I assure you, there's nothing for you to worry about. The shooting was an unfortunate accident. It doesn't have anything to do with the other cases. As for those, the investigation is ongoing, and we can't discuss it. Just know we are zeroing in on the truth."

His voice sounds slimy and insincere. It's the way officers talk when they don't want to admit to someone who has already confronted them that they haven't gotten any further. But something he said stands out to me.

"An unfortunate accident?" I ask.

"What else could it be?" he asks, but not before a flicker of undecipherable emotion crosses his eyes. "Cold weather means easy shots around here. But hunters don't want to admit they're out when the deer aren't in season."

"So, you think a hunter accidentally shot him?" I ask.

"It's the only explanation that makes sense." He nods and stands, starting toward the door. "Now that you've gotten your answer, I need to be getting back to work."

I don't point out that he didn't actually answer my question.

"Sure. Um. Where is the chief?" I ask casually.

"He got called away from the office."

I nod and smile. "I guess that's part of the job."

As I follow him out of the conference room, I notice a large board on the wall. It's covered with pictures of the missing people and the crime scenes. I have most of them, but I pause to look at it. A few images look like they were taken in the days after the official crime scene photos. My eyes scan over the pictures and the notes scribbled on them. A timeline in black marker at the bottom of the board stands out to me. I glance up and see that Nicolas is leaned out of the door, talking to someone down the hall. Snapping a picture of the timeline as fast as I can, I shove my phone back into my pocket. The next second, he looks in at me.

"That's part of the investigation, Ms. Monroe. I'm going to have to ask you to move along now," he says.

I flash him a smile. "No problem. Thanks for your help."

Esther peers at me over her glasses as I scurry past her out of the station.

My next stop is the hotel a few towns over, where Murdock checked in. The woman behind the desk could be a younger version of Esther and is looking at me with about as much trust.

"The footage was turned over to police," she tells me.

"I know. But it was saved on the cloud, wasn't it? You could just access it from the computer."

"Are you with the police?"

"I am definitely not with the police," I tell her.

"Then what's your fascination with the camera footage?"

"Ma'am, he died on my porch. I'd like to know what he looked like before that."

I probably could have used more tact, but this is the place I'm in. It seems to work. The woman's face goes pale, and her eyes widen. She scurries into the office, and I'm fairly certain she's going to come back with the manager to chase me out. At least if they call the police, I have a good chance of just being brought right back to the station. I can even see if LaRoche is back. I hear voices across the lobby and look up, ducking out of the way behind the wall beside the desk just in time.

No need to get myself arrested to see LaRoche again. He's right here at the hotel with a very blonde, very young woman teetering on ill-fitting heels and hanging on his every word. I stay out of sight while I watch them cross from the elevator to a side door tucked in an alcove. He looks different, not in his uniform, but it is definitely the chief. Pulling her up against him, he leans down for a long kiss. It ends suddenly, and LaRoche reaches into his pocket, pulling out his phone and putting it to his ear. His face darkens, and he mutters something I can't hear, but I also can't imagine is pleasant.

"Ma'am?"

I peek around the wall to see the woman has come back to the desk. Glancing over at LaRoche, I see him say something to the girl and slam through the door out into the parking lot. The woman behind the desk gives me a curious look as I slide back into place in front of her. There's no manager at her side, but she is holding a tiny white computer.

"I thought I saw someone I know," I offer with a smile. "But I'm not sure. Do you have any guests from Feathered Nest here today?"

She shakes her head. "Not in the last few weeks. Most recent check-in is a lady says she's from New Jersey."

"Says?" I ask. "You don't check identification?"

The woman shakes her head. "Not usually. No need when people pay cash. It's not like I'm running a five-star resort here. Just a place for people to lay their heads."

Or something.

I glance back toward the door. The blonde I'm guessing at least pretends to hail from New Jersey is gone. Turning back to the clerk, I gesture at the computer.

"Is that it?"

"Yes. I'm still not sure if I should show it to you."

"Did the police tell you not to?" I ask.

"Well… no," she frowns.

"Then, what's the harm? I just want a quick look."

She turns the screen toward me and clicks the mouse pad to start the video clip. I lean against the counter and watch the same woman moving around behind the desk. The angle of the camera shows her back and the top of her head, giving the perfect vantage point for the front door. After a few seconds of her dusting, sifting papers around, and watering a plant that has since been moved to the other side of the desk, the door opens. The man walks in, and my breath catches in my throat. He's wearing the same clothes he was in when he landed on my porch. Glancing at the bottom of the screen, I note the time stamp.

He walks up to the desk and says something to the woman. She nods and reaches into a drawer, sliding a form across the desk to him.

"What's that?" I ask.

"A registration card. I've always used them. I put the information into the computer now, but I still have the guests fill them out. Force of habit."

He fills out the card and hands it back to the clerk. I see him look around the lobby and notice something that strikes me as odd.

"He doesn't have any bags," I say. "Did he bring any in later?"

"No," the clerk says. "The police asked the same thing. Wanted to look through his personal effects. But he didn't have any. There wasn't anything in his room, and there was no car parked in the lot."

I watch the video for another few seconds while the man accepts his key card and heads to the elevator. Scanning through the recording, I see him come back out of the elevator and leave less than five minutes after going upstairs. I know by the timestamp, he never came back.

"Do you still have his registration card?" I ask.

She nods and pulls a binder out of the drawer. Flipping through it, she pulls out the card and shows it to me.

"Ron Murdock. Such a nice name."

I nod. "Do you mind if I snap a picture of it? I want to send a condolence letter to his family."

She shrugs. "Go ahead. I don't think privacy laws extend to the dearly departed."

"Thanks." I snap the picture and put my phone away. "I really appreciate your help." I start to walk away, then turn back to her. "Actually. There's one more thing you can do for me. I'm really thirsty. Do you have a bottle of water or something I could have?"

She looks at me strangely but nods. "Sure. I'll be right back."

As soon as she walks into the office with the computer, I turn the binder toward me and snap a picture of the entire page of registration cards tucked in their clear plastic sleeves. Flipping through the book to the end, I take another picture of the last page, then close the book. She comes out of the office just as I'm lowering the cover, and I slide the binder toward her. Accepting the miniature bottle of water she offers out to me, I smile.

"I appreciate it. Thank you, again."

I wave and head out of the hotel. I'm halfway across the lot to my car when the shot rings out.

CHAPTER SEVENTEEN

I hit the ground before I fully process the sound. It's the second shot that really sinks in and gets my mind spinning. My stomach scraping on the tiny bits of gravel scattered across the parking lot, I army crawl over to my car, so I have some cover. Reaching into my pocket, I wrench out my phone. The last picture I took is still up on the screen, and I swipe it away to dial.

Flickering bars taunt me from the top of the screen. The call won't connect, and I end it to dial again. It's still struggling when the front door to the hotel opens. The clerk rushes out, clutching a cordless phone.

"Go back inside!" I shout.

There haven't been any more shots, but that doesn't mean there won't be. She doesn't need to be running around out in the open making herself the perfect target. Though I don't think she's who the bullets are meant for.

"Are you alright?" she asks, rushing toward me and reaching for my hand.

"You shouldn't be out here," I tell her.

Seconds later, tires crunch across the gravel and her head snaps toward them, her face relaxing.

"Oh, thank goodness," she says.

I stand up cautiously, expecting to see a police car. Instead, a dark blue truck sits at a diagonal across three parking spots just inside the lot. I know that truck and the face that's going to come out of the driver's side any second. Watery eyes meet mine, and scuffed boots hit the ground.

"Chief, thank you for getting here so fast," the clerk says, rushing across the lot toward the truck.

"It's alright, Mirna. Just calm down and tell me what's going on," Chief LaRoche says.

It's the first time I've heard her name, and somehow it fits her perfectly. It's the casual familiarity between the two of them that makes me pause. He came here to get the recording from the surveillance video, so she knew he was involved. I know I just saw him inside, yet Mirna said no one from Feathered Nest had come to the hotel recently. Why would she lie?

Or maybe she didn't. The pictures I took might tell me more, but I don't have time to look at them right now.

"Someone shot at the hotel. They almost hit a lady," Mirna says.

I cringe. This is going to be a fun conversation.

"What lady?" he asks.

"Me."

I stand and walk out from around my car. LaRoche's eyes narrow as he takes a step toward me.

"What are you doing here, Ms. Monroe?" he demands.

"I could ask you the same question. You got here mighty fast coming in from three towns over, Chief. Come to think of it; it's a little strange that an emergency call from here would go all the way to Feathered Nest," I say.

"I have a police scanner in my truck," he explains. "Not that I need to justify anything to you. What are you doing here?"

"Is there a reason I need to justify anything to you?" I ask.

"When you're standing in a parking lot that just got shot up, not to mention interfering with an active investigation, yes, you do," he says.

"I'm not interfering with anything. I have every right to be here.

And what do you mean active investigation? I thought you said Ron Murdock was killed by the wayward bullet of a hunter. An accident."

"That is what happened."

"Then why would you need to investigate it? If you already know, and you are sure it's an accident, wouldn't it be closed?" I ask.

His eyes narrow, but before he can say anything else, Mirna takes an imploring step toward him.

"Am I safe?" she pleads. "Is someone after me?"

"Mirna, no one has any reason to be after you."

The way he said *you* hangs heavily in the air as the wail of sirens cuts through the tension, and blue and red lights sweep across his face. LaRoche's head snaps to the side to watch the police cars speed into the parking lot. The police Mirna actually called have arrived, and Mirna rushes up to them.

"Thank you for coming. I don't know what happened," she says.

I listen to her launch into the story of the shooting but can still feel LaRoche's eyes on me. He's staring through eyes rimmed with red over a jaw set so hard the muscles strain against his skin.

"You have no reason to be here, Ms. Monroe," he says, his voice low, his words slow. "You need to go on back to your cabin now."

"I'm sure the police will want to talk to me. I am the one who was outside when someone started shooting at the hotel," I point out.

"Likely, but when you're done, go home."

"Do you have me under surveillance for something, Chief?" I ask.

"No. Just don't want anyone else in danger," he says.

The threat slithers down the back of my neck and along my spine. I feel someone step up behind me, and I force myself to turn away from the chief. The officer behind me looks concerned as he grips a pad of paper and a pen as tightly as he can.

"Can I ask you a few questions about what happened?" he asks.

I nod, ignoring the feeling of LaRoche still glaring at me.

"Go ahead," I nod.

"Mirna says you were out in the parking lot when the shooting happened. Is that accurate?" he asks.

I'm not sure how there may be a lot of ambiguity in that concept, but I nod anyway.

"Yes. I was on my way to my car when I heard the shots," I tell him.

"How long did you stay at the hotel?"

"I wasn't actually staying here. I just stopped by for a few minutes."

His eyes lift up to me, and he looks at me questioningly.

"What were you doing here?" he asks.

"I would like to know the same thing," LaRoche calls from behind me.

The officer looks over my shoulder at him.

"Chief LaRoche, I'm surprised to see you here," he says.

"Just trying to help. I'll be on my way. Ms. Monroe… " he pauses like he's going over what he might say, then changes his mind. "Have a nice day."

The officer turns back to me and asks a few routine questions. I answer them as quickly as I can, not wanting to hover around here any longer than I have to. I head directly back to my cabin. Not because the chief told me to, but because I want to look through the pictures I got and see if they can tell me anything. Something makes me hesitate as I climb the steps onto the front porch. It's a tugging feeling in my gut, like it's trying to stop me, but I don't know why. I hesitate and stare down at the darkened place on the porch before turning to look out over the lake.

Something is bothering me, pricking at the back of my mind. It doesn't add up, but I can't put my finger on it. Forcing past the discomfort crawling along the back of my neck, I go into the cabin and take my pictures and notes out from their hiding place. Attaching my phone to my photo dock, I start the process of printing off the pictures I took at the hotel. My stomach rumbles, and I try to think back to the last time I had a truly substantial meal. By the time I come back from the kitchen with a bowl full of mixed nuts and a cup of coffee, the pictures are waiting for me. I scoop them up and scan them.

The registration card filled out by the mysterious man offers the exact information the police chief gave me. He said his name was Ron

Murdock. The rest of the card is scantily filled out, with many of the questions left blank. I get the impression Mirna isn't exactly a stickler for having all the pertinent details about the guests at her hotel. From the look of the blonde woman stuffed in the alcove with LaRoche, I wouldn't be surprised to find out a good portion of her clientele drifts in and out on a fairly regular basis and doesn't always stay the whole night.

One piece of information the card does list is an address. I open my laptop and put the address into the search engine. It's an Iowa address, which instantly strikes me as odd. Feathered Nest is out in the middle of nowhere for someone who lives in Virginia to get to. Iowa seems obscenely far away for someone to just happen on a porch on the first night the cabin it's attached to has been occupied in months.

When the results come up, it's no longer the distance that seems strange. Instead, it's that I'm not looking at a neighborhood or a city street. There's a house, but the old-fashioned white farmhouse is barely visible at the edge of the photo that came up. Most of the image is a baseball field carved into a cornfield.

"That is the fucking Field of Dreams," I mutter.

I'm not a Hollywood expert or anything, but I'm fairly certain no one's putting their head down on the pitching mound to sleep at night.

"What the hell is going on?"

I add the name 'Ron Murdock' to the search engine but find no connection between the name and the movie. Or the state of Iowa. Or anything else that makes any sense.

Tucking that information in the back of my mind to simmer, I move on to the last page of registration cards. I'm fairly certain the blonde woman wasn't Joseph or Abernathy. The petty part of me wants her name to be something like Bambi or Sugar, but that isn't showing up. The only card left belongs to Andrea Layne. Assuming she isn't also lying, the address listed has her living just one town over from the hotel. I put it into the search engine just to make sure it doesn't come up as another movie icon or an empty field. Instead, it shows a modest house that reminds me of the ones built in the fifties for the soldiers growing their families after the war. Not exactly what some might immediately think when they looked at the woman cozied up to the police chief, but I have been on the job long enough to know people are rarely as predictable as we want them to be.

No one is listed on the registration card with Miss Layne, much less Chief LaRoche. That's not a surprise. The way Mirna spoke to him when he showed up after the shooting tells me she had no idea he was making himself comfortable in one of her rooms last night. Or at least today. She only checked in yesterday. My eyes scan over the card a few more times, taking in as much of the information as I can and hoping something more will pop out at me. It's obvious LaRoche is very friendly with this woman, but there's a clenching feeling in my gut that tells me it's more than that.

CHAPTER EIGHTEEN

The sun is all the way down now, and the air feels thin and cold enough to shatter if I breathe too hard. But that doesn't stop me from adding another layer, tying my scarf around my mouth, and heading outside. Like every night in Feathered Nest, everything is eerily quiet. It isn't late. It's barely after when I'd usually eat dinner, but it feels like everything around me has totally shut down. The memory of the gunshots ring through my head as I step down off the porch and let the beam of my flashlight sweep over the ground in front of me.

It's not enough to chase me back into the cabin. That wasn't the first time I've been shot at, and I can't help but believe it's not the last, either. I just hope the next time isn't going to be tonight while I'm out in the woods. My phone rings as I make my way around the back of the cabin. It's a video call from Bellamy, and the wide smile she has when I first answer almost instantly melts to a concerned expression.

"Did your furnace go out again? I thought you just got that fixed."

"Talking to Eric?" I ask. "I didn't realize the two of you have gotten so close."

"It's just because you aren't here to be between us, so we ended up just kind of sliding into the space you left. Like when you put too much jelly on a peanut butter and jelly sandwich," she offers.

"Exactly how much jelly-ing has been happening?" I raise an eyebrow.

"Not that much," she assures me. "We just happen to know you have the bad habit of only giving each one of us pieces of what's going on. So, we started comparing notes."

"Well, my furnace did not go out again. It's lovely and warm inside the cabin right now," I tell her.

"Are you telling me you are not inside the cabin right now?" she asks.

She's curled up in her favorite plush white bathrobe on her white sofa. Bellamy likes things in very specific ways, and that's one of them.

"That would be what I'm telling you. I'm going into the woods behind the cabin," I say.

"Don't you think it's a little cold for a nice after-dinner stroll? Not to mention it's darker than the inside of a witch's hoo-ha at a pumpkin festival?"

That is also one of them.

"I don't know what that means, B."

"It's so dark, all I see is you. It's very fake documentary," she says.

"Well, you're a step ahead of me. I can't even see myself. Let's hope my flashlight sticks it out."

"What are you doing out there?" she asks.

"I'm checking on a theory," I explain.

"What theory?"

"The last time I came out here, I found a path that leads straight to the train tracks where the two bodies were found. I didn't even notice it the first time I went out there to see the scene. I'm sure you know I asked Eric to look into some things for me."

"He said something about trains," she says.

"Right. I wanted to see the feed from the cameras on the trains that went down the tracks in the days before the girl was found. The police officially linked her murder to the others, but they haven't figured out exactly what happened, and from what I see, aren't really making a ton of progress, either. One of the biggest questions is why the killer would go to so much effort to hide all the others so they wouldn't be found, then just dump one right out in the open. It doesn't make sense," I tell her.

Talking to her carries me the first several steps into the woods. Darkness closes around me.

"But they found another body, too, right? Close to there."

"Yes. A man. His body was further up the tracks, but it wasn't nearly as mangled as hers."

"Maybe he was trying to get attention," Bellamy points out. "The killer wanted to show off a little, so he left the bodies where they would be found."

"He was already getting plenty of attention. If he wanted more, he would have left one of the identified missing people out to be found. Maybe it's the opposite. Maybe he thought he was getting too much attention, and so he left the other body out for the specific reason of making them look connected. And to stop investigators from digging too deep into the first one. My point is, maybe this isn't what it seems," I say.

"What do you mean?"

"Nobody really knows what happened to either of the bodies. They were too damaged to give any real conclusive evidence. But the running theory has been the girl was put on the train tracks so a train would hit her."

"But that's not what you think happened."

"No, I don't. The last time I came out here, I found a dog collar attached to a tree. It was deep in the ground, like it had been there for a while, and someone had tried to cover it with leaves. The crime scene pictures of what was left of the girl showed damage to her neck, like something was wrapped around it. There is absolutely no record of her for days before she was found. The police interviewed people from her hometown and from the bar here, and no one could remember seeing or speaking to her. There's a gap of time that isn't accounted for."

"And you think she spent that time on the other end of a dog leash," Bellamy muses.

"I think it's possible. The train videos don't show a lot. The cameras are positioned badly, and it's hard to really see much of anything. But I watched them closely, and after seeing the same thing a few times, I noticed something different. There's a flicker of movement. It's not much. But it's enough to make me believe Cristela Jordan wasn't killed and then dumped there, or even put on the tracks to die. I believe she was in the woods and managed to escape. She ran out of the trees in a panic and didn't realize the train was coming until it was too late. The train killed her when the corner of it hit her on the edge of the tracks. It dragged her for a while; then she tumbled to the side. That's where they found her."

"But the injuries on her body," Bellamy points out. "Wouldn't they have realized they were from a train and not a person?"

"I believe she was tortured. There were injuries on her body consistent with knife wounds and blunt force that happened prior to death. That tells me the police noticed those injuries and just went with their first assumption. It happens more often than people would like to think," I tell her. "If I'm right, that means she might have survived and gotten to help. Her getting hit by that train might be the only reason the killer's still out there."

"Why do you say that like you know more than what you're telling me?" she asks.

"Someone might have shot at me today," I tell her.

"What?" she snaps.

I pull the phone away from my face, cringing at the high pitch of her voice, then tell her about the shooting at the hotel.

"It seems like someone feels like I'm getting too close. And I'm pretty sure I know exactly who that is," I say.

"Then you need to call the police," Bellamy insists.

My hurried steps have brought me onto the path that weaves through the train tracks, and I'm only a few feet from the tree with the dog collar.

"I can't," I tell her.

"What do you mean you can't?" she asks. "If you know who killed those people, you have to tell them. That's the whole reason you were put on this job."

I get to the tree and touch my fingertips to the dig in the bark where the chain used to be. My heart sinks. Crouching down, I dig through the cold, wet leaves hoping the metal just gave way, and the collar would still be there. But it's not. I let out a sigh.

"I can't tell the police because the man responsible for the murders is the police chief," I say.

"Shit."

"And he knows I'm on to him. He was at the hotel right before the shooting and showed up seconds after it happened, acting like he didn't know anything. And he came back for the dog collar in the woods. He knows and doesn't want me to be able to piece it together."

"You don't have to piece it together. You already have enough. Call Creagan and get them there," Bellamy insists.

I shake my head, pushing the leaves back into place, so it looks like they weren't disturbed. I don't want LaRoche coming back through here and notice I've come this way and realized the collar is missing.

"I can't call them yet."

"Emma, look where you are. It is pitch black, and you're tromping through the frozen woods on the heels of a murderer. I know you want to prove yourself and make up for the last time, but this isn't the way to do it. Putting your life on the line to make a point isn't worth it. The FBI can come in with a team that will end this, and you'll get to walk out of it alive."

"That's just the thing," I reply. "My life is on the line, right now, already. I don't have enough to call Creagan. A hunch and some evidence won't get them very far. I need something far more concrete to convince them to come all the way out here and further the investigation. If they raise up a fuss now, it will tip LaRoche off, and if they can't nail him, more people will die. Possibly including me. I can't risk that. I have to have a solid case to hand them, and then I'll let them take it."

"You will?" she begs.

"Yes. As soon as I can give them all the evidence they need to arrest LaRoche and investigate the disappearance and murders, I'll happily pass it along and step back to watch Eric and Company tie it up in a nice little bow," I promise.

"I don't know if I'm convinced."

A twig snaps in the distance. That's one of those sounds you think you know enough that it won't startle you. It seems familiar and mundane, a simple cracking sound that could mean something as simple as an animal passing through or a coating of ice breaking through a weak twig. It's not until you hear it in the silent black distance, and the awareness of a presence settles onto your skin like a fine mist that you know how chilling that sound can really be.

"Bellamy," I lower my voice, "I need you to not talk."

"That's just because you know I'm right. You don't want to listen to me, and you don't want to hear it, but you know I'm right," she says.

I shake my head and put my finger across my lips to quiet her.

"Someone else is here," I whisper. "Stay with me. Don't say a word. I'm going to turn off my screen."

Pressing the button on the side of my phone, I make the screen go black. Turning my flashlight off sends me into total darkness, but that's what I need. If LaRoche is out there, I don't want to make it any easier for him to find me. There's no need to send up tracking beams through the dark woods. Keeping Bellamy on the line is my security. She can't see me anymore, but she can hear everything that's happening. I trust her to listen to the sound of my breath and the speed of my footsteps. I can't say anything to her. I can't tell her where I am or what's happening. But I can hold the phone close so she can hear me breathe. I can make sure if something goes wrong, I won't be one of the missing. Not for long. She will know where I was and all my suspicions.

I can't move too quickly. Running will make me lose control of the sound my feet make on the dry leaves and sticks that litter the ground. I can't afford that. I need to stay aware of what's around me. I need to be able to hear what might be coming toward me and sense movement in the dark skeletons of the trees. Through the phone, I can hear Bellamy trying to keep her breath steady.

The next stick snaps closer to me, and something rustles in the leaves. I don't let myself look. Every second is another second I could be closer to the safety of the cabin, and that has to be my focus. With nothing but the glow of the moon and the meager starlight filtering through the tree branches, I follow the memory of my steps to make my way back through the woods, hoping I don't accidentally run into the lake. The cold is intense now, biting at my exposed skin and sinking through my skin and into my bones.

I feel eyes on my back. It's an unmistakable feeling I thought I knew before going into the Bureau but learned so much more acutely in the field. It's a feeling I can only believe is a throwback to our ancestors when being watched meant a predator was nearby. It's what I feel now. I'm being hunted.

In the distance, I see a faint glow. It's like one of the stars overhead but shimmering through the trees. As I move closer, it gets bigger, and the air rushes out of my lungs when I realize it's the light on the side of the cabin. Now I can run.

Turning the screen back on my phone, I use the light to guide me through the thick undergrowth until I reach the porch.

"Bellamy?" I say loudly when I get to the front of the cabin. "I'm back."

As I unlock the front door to the cabin, something moves out of the corner of my eye. I look to the side just in time to see a shadow sink back toward the darkness of the woods.

CHAPTER NINETEEN

"Are you okay? Emma, tell me you're okay."

I have to give it to her; at least Bellamy made it until I was inside the cabin, and the door was locked behind me to panic.

"I'm fine. I'm back inside my cabin now," I tell her.

"Was it him? Was he following you?" she asks.

"I don't know for sure. I didn't see him. But it definitely sounded like somebody was out there with me."

"You need to stay inside at night until this is all over with," she says. "You're all alone out there."

"I wasn't alone. I had you," I reply.

She scoffs.

"I'm several hundred miles away from you. What is it you expect me to do? All the good I would be for is pinpointing the moment you were killed. That's not helpful."

"It depends on how you look at it," I say.

"Well, how I look at it is I'd much rather my best friend get back here alive. That means proving this LaRoche guy kidnapped and killed those people, siccing the FBI on him, and getting the hell out of there before you end up another notch on his belt."

"I don't think he actually adds notches to his belt for every person he kills," I muse. "That wouldn't make for a very subtle approach."

I'm trying to calm her down, to make her feel better. It doesn't work.

"I'm serious, Emma. You agreed to go undercover to investigate and do what the local police force weren't doing. Not to hunt this guy down yourself. You need to get your job done and come home."

"As soon as I know I have enough, I'll call the team in. Until then, I promise I'll be as careful as I can."

"I guess that's the best I'm going to get," she sighs. "Just make sure you really are careful."

I get off the phone and head to the bathroom to take a shower. The feeling of the scrutinizing eyes watching me hasn't completely left my skin, and I make sure the shade is pulled down tightly over the window above before undressing. I'm not used to feeling vulnerable in a space that is supposed to belong to me, even temporarily. I'm the type to shower with the door open because it means one less obstacle between getting out and getting on with my day. But I've also never been in quite this position. I've always had the comfort of knowing the rest of my team is close by. Even when I'm the only one in the building, or it seems to others watching that I'm alone, I know I'm not. There are always agents close enough to get to me within a matter of seconds. Not tonight. After six months out of the field, I'm truly by myself, and for the first time in my adult life, I lock the bathroom door before taking my shower.

The thought of being watched in the woods and the locked door makes me angry as I stand under the stream of water so hot it stings my skin. I hate the thought of anyone having that power over me. He shouldn't have the power to make me afraid.

I step out of the shower and unlock the door. When I'm done, I get into my pajamas. Not wanting to leave the warm steam of the bathroom and enter the cold cabin with wet hair, I blast it with my hairdryer. Finally, as close to warm as I think I'm going to get until I'm totally dry, I head into the living room and curl up on the couch.

I stay there for most of the night, going through the pictures and all the notes I've taken. I need to piece this together. I take out the picture of Cristela Jordan, thinking again about just how similar she looks to the blonde woman draped over Chief LaRoche at the hotel. It could be a coincidence. Or it could be a pattern.

When I can't keep my eyes open anymore, I bury myself in a pile of blankets on the bed and fall into an almost instant sleep. My father always used to tell me that dreams are our brain's way of entertaining ourselves during the long hours of sleep. While our bodies go about the work of repairing themselves and preparing for the next day, all our thoughts and impulses come together to create little stories to tell us.

That's not what these dreams are. This isn't entertainment or even a sequential story. I dream in flashes of thought, memory, and sensation. It's real enough to taste the damp earth of the woods on the back of my tongue when I take a deep breath and feel the cold claw with stinging precision along my skin.

The same things repeat in my mind over and over again. I see Cristela's face in the slightly blurry image published in newspapers. An instant later, it melts away into the battered, mangled remnants left at the side of the train track. From there, my mind wanders over to Andrea Layne. They look so similar. Not in any way that's unique or special. In fact, their similarity is in their normalcy. Both tall and thin. Both well-endowed beneath tight clothing. Both old enough to have started the experience of life. Both young enough for it to hurt a little more to think about their deaths.

I snap awake as the image of red-tipped fingers stroking along LaRoche's skin turn to droplets of blood. I know what I have to do.

I get dressed as quickly as I can and grab a bagel to bring with me on the way. The morning air is crisp and chilly, but I don't mind. I get into my car and drive off.

Three cars parked at different strategic points in the lot make the hotel look almost busy in comparison to the way it was when I visited yesterday. There are no signs of the shooting. Not that there would be. There were only two shots, and they didn't hit anything. That's something I never quite get over. After my years in the Bureau and knowing what my father experienced during his own service, crime is rarely a truly shocking thing to me. It's just a part of my everyday life. I have learned over time to live alongside it.

Some agents are able to completely push thoughts of the horrific people they encounter out of their minds. It's like they have strong metal safes inside their head and when it's time to go home after work, they're able to just stuff everything inside and close the door. That's not me. Every case I've worked, every person I've encountered has affected me in some way. Not that it's broken me down or made me question that I chose the right career path. More so, it just makes me look at people and things a little differently. That's why I am always a little surprised when I visit a crime scene again and realize it has gone right back to what it was before that moment in time.

It's the opposite of crime scenes left bloody or strewn with lingering remnants of police investigations. Instead of the shock of seeing the pieces of the horror left behind, there is the eerie feeling of seeing no reminder at all. There should be something. Crime makes an impact. It leaves a scar on the atmosphere of the place where it happened. People should be able to feel it. When there's nothing, it's like life has layered on top of that scar, glossing it over.

But there's only one reason I'm back at this hotel, and it has nothing to do with the two bullets that came flying at me. Cristela is still on my mind, and I need to answer a question burning in my thoughts.

Rather than going right through the doors into the lobby, I walk past and glance to the side through the glass. If Mirna is in her place behind the counter, I don't want to just walk inside. She's not there, but I quickly remember the security camera directed at the door. If I just walk inside, it will record me, and I don't want that to happen. Continuing around the side of the hotel, I walk past the door that must be connected to the alcove where I saw Andrea and LaRoche. I go around the corner to the back and through an empty parking lot. This many spaces seems extremely optimistic for a hotel this far away from everything.

A middle-aged man in a housekeeping uniform leans against the brick back wall smoking a cigarette and staring out into the distance. He's wearing short sleeves, but the temperature doesn't seem to bother him. I go back around the corner to prevent him from seeing me and listen. A few moments later, I hear a chastising voice, and when I peek back around the corner, the man is gone. Making my way quickly along the back wall, I look for the door I hope is at the end of the long hallway to the side of the counter. It's there, but it's locked, a card reader positioned at the side to allow guests to let themselves in.

I could go back around to the front of the hotel, but I can't risk Mirna seeing me and wondering why I'm here. Instead, I take my chances. If anyone is nearby, my knock will probably startle the hell out of them. With any luck, the man guilted back inside from his smoke break is still nearby.

I tap lightly on the glass. The door opens, and he peers out at me. I force a smile that I hope looks apologetic and believable.

"Hi, I'm so sorry, I must have left my key in my room, and my sister isn't answering her phone," I say.

He looks at me for a few scrutinizing seconds, and I rub my hands together. As if he's first noticing the cold, he nods and steps back, holding the door for me.

"Come into the heat," he instructs.

"Thank you so much."

I scoot past him and take the few steps to dip into the stairwell. Peering out of the pane of glass set into the center of the door, I wait for him to go back into the room standing open, then slip out. I don't hesitate but rush past the room toward the lobby. Just before going around the corner, I drop down to my knees so I can crawl behind the counter out of sight of the camera.

"This is fucking ridiculous," I mutter to myself.

Mirna still isn't behind the counter, but I doubt I have much time. She won't leave the lobby unattended all day. Pulling up onto the balls of my feet in front of the drawers, I tug on the one where I saw Mirna get the registration book. Unlike the door, the drawer isn't secured. The metal screeches slightly as it grinds together. I cringe and open the drawer the rest of the way so I can reach inside. My fingers touch the edge of the book just as I hear Mirna's voice in the office.

I grab out the book, close the drawer, and scramble my way back into the hallway. Holding the book under my arm, I run to the end of the hall and into the stairwell. Once behind the door, I start flipping the pages, scanning the registration cards to find the right range of dates. Before I get a chance to find exactly what I need, a door opens above me, and footsteps head down the stairs.

Of course, now is the time for one of Mirna's handful of guests to decide to be health-conscious and use the stairs rather than hopping in the elevator.

I meant to come here and snap a few pictures the way I did yesterday, leaving the book behind so no one would be the wiser. Instead, I find myself tucking the entire thing under my arm and running for the door at the end of the hall. Maybe Creagan was right. Maybe I have lost my touch. Maybe everything going on with my father and with Greg took something out of me.

I make it out unseen. Tossing the book onto the passenger seat, I drive out of the parking lot and head back down the road.

My curiosity lures me into the parking lot of a tiny hamburger stand at the side of the road, and I yank the book over into my lap. Flipping through the pages again as my eyes scan over the registration cards, my hand suddenly stops, and a smile comes to my lips.

Creagan was wrong. I haven't lost anything.

CHAPTER TWENTY

A shadow falls through my window over the registration card I pulled from the plastic sleeve in the book. My breath catches in my throat, and I snap my eyes toward the figure looming close to the car. My hand instinctively moves to the lock, though I know it's engaged. Even when I drove around in the first lumbering hunk of metal that amounted to my first car, engaging the manual locks was the first thing I did after closing the door. The locks in my car drop into place automatically, but I'm not so lucky with the car Creagan chose for this job. I've had to get back into the habit of locking the doors myself.

I look up, and the face staring in at me looks more startled than I am. Wide brown eyes in a face that seems far too young for the pink and white striped waitress uniform blink.

"Can I get you something?"

Her voice is muffled by the glass of the window, but I can make out the uncertainty in the offer. I roll the window down and lean slightly out of it.

"What?" I ask.

"Can I get you something?" she repeats, her head tilting slightly toward the hamburger stand.

"Oh," I say, looking through the windshield at the old-fashioned walk-up restaurant. The menu made up of a whiteboard with individually placed black letters looks like it might have been totally untouched for the last several decades. Which means the food is bound to be incredible. "Sure. What's good?"

"Burgers and fries are the most popular," she answers.

I notice the narrow white name tag pinned to her chest says 'Evergreen', and my heart gives a nostalgic flutter for the hippie mentality still flowing strongly through the veins of rural Southern towns. The ideals may have shifted, but the energy is the same.

"It's not even ten-thirty in the morning," I point out.

"We have an egg biscuit special," she offers.

I contemplate the options and shrug.

"Burger and fries sound great." The young waitress nods and starts back toward the restaurant. I lean from the window. "And a milkshake."

She waves over her head at me to acknowledge the request, and I go back to the registration card.

Cristela Jordan. Most of the rest of the information filled out on the card are details I already know, thanks to the investigation records made available to me. But it's the information that wasn't in those records that stands out to me. No one mentioned she checked into Mirna's hotel four days before she was found dead. And apparently never checked out. The line on the card with the guest's signature and a date and timestamp is blank. I look at the other cards in the pages and the ones in front of and behind it. All have the signature line filled in. The only other card I've seen without this line complete is the one belonging to the supposed Ron Murdock.

An idea strikes me just as Evergreen appears at the window again. She smiles and holds up the tray holding my food and milkshake. My thoughts immediately go to my mother as I roll down the window and take the massive Styrofoam cup. During her younger years in the ballet, she never would have been allowed to enjoy treats like this. Her ballerina body depended on a strict diet that left her longing for some semblance of a realistic relationship with food. That came when she left Russia and came to the United States. Here she learned to indulge.

Milkshakes were always a favorite. Though my father made sure she had one whenever the thought even crossed her mind, she would still pretend to sneak them and act like it was a secret for the two of us to share.

The waitress knits her eyebrows together as she scans the papers spread out around me.

"Are you some sort of reporter or something?" she asks.

I take the cardboard container of fries and paper-wrapped burger from her.

"Something like that," I tell her.

She smiles. "That's amazing. I want to be a newscaster one day."

"You do?" I ask.

I breathe in the hot, oily smell of the fries and can't resist plucking one from the box and biting down on it.

"Always have," she says, then looks around wistfully. "But it's not like there are a lot of news stations around here."

"So, go somewhere where there is one," I tell her.

"Easier said than done," she muses.

"I did it," I tell her.

"Really?"

"Absolutely. When you really want something, don't let something like where you came from stop you. This is all just a steppingstone. Make it happen."

She smiles and makes her way back across the parking lot toward the cook barking at her through the open window. It might not have been the complete transparent truth, but my story doesn't veer too far from that path. At least it seemed to inspire her, so the shaky details are worth it.

Following the thought that came to me, I go back through each page of the registration cards, reading over them as I go. It doesn't take long to find another card with Cristela's name, then a few pages before that another, and then another. With the four cards spread in front of me, I note the differences in the information provided on them. Everything is the same except for the check-out line. On the other three cards, the line is properly filled out and signed. It's only the most recent that's left blank.

There's only one reason why Cristela Jordan would be staying at the hotel. There might be more, but none of the others seem applicable when stacked up with everything else. Nicolas told me Cristela came from the town over on the other side of Feathered Nest but was a regular in the area. She frequented Jake's bar and was known by just about everybody in town. Yet she ended up on the opposite side of town, three towns over, in a tiny hotel. It doesn't make sense. Until you look at it through the lens of Andrea Layne.

Andrea has two registration cards in the book. The one from this stay and one other. Going back through the cards, I can't find a single other card with her name on it. Even going back to the very beginning of the book with dates years ago, she doesn't show up anywhere else. It is only those two, both after Cristela's death. Like she got slipped into a position recently vacated.

The date on the first card with her name on it is particularly interesting to me. It's from just two days before Ron Murdock showed up. Which makes me wonder about LaRoche's story about looking into his identity. It never sat right with me that the chief said he discovered the surveillance footage of Murdock checking into the hotel after canvassing the area. The hotel is hardly in his area, and there's little reason he would go out of his way to go to that particular hotel to ask about a stranger and just happen to get security footage. Unless he already knew he was there. If LaRoche went to the hotel to meet with Andrea Layne, he might have seen Murdock coming into the hotel or even walking to his room.

I think back to the first time I spoke to the chief after finding the man dead on my porch. There was something in his eyes I didn't trust even then. It was hiding something.

There's little more to find out about Cristela that I think will help. It makes more sense to concentrate on Andrea. Learning more about her might be just the key I need. Wiping the salt and grease off my fingers, I pick up my phone and open it to the web browser. I type in her name and the name of the town she put on the registration card. There's always the chance she put down a fake one, too, but it's a place to start. Almost immediately, I find listings for her social media. The smiling face tilted into the profile picture is unmistakably her, and when I click on the link, I find several dozen more.

Not surprisingly, Andrea has a fondness of taking pictures of herself and sharing them with the thousands of supposed friends she has never met, spoken to, or interacted with on any truly meaningful level. She's far too young to be cozied up with Chief LaRoche, and that general theme pervades her platforms. There isn't a single picture or mention of him as I scroll back through her posts and shares. I go back to the day she checked into the hotel and find a vague reference to 'hitting the road for an adventure'. It could mean literally anything from an epic cross-country road trip to spontaneously going in search of the best Indian food in town. That phrase is the common cold of obsessive social media posts. People are so wrapped up in their virtual existence and their perception that so many people care about what they are doing every moment that they can't bear to skip updating. When they come to something that can't be shared outright, they slap the 'adventure' label on it and consider it enticing.

The effect is lost on me. Partially because I have no patience for people who forego living in the actual world and experiencing life through their real senses rather than through a screen and the filter of social approval. Partially because I know exactly what adventure she's referencing. And I really don't want to think about.

The vast majority of her pages cover the minutia of her life, from what she ate to the color sunglasses she was wearing that day. But tucked among all the worthless swathes of over-information, I manage to find something valuable. Several pictures show Andrea in a black t-shirt standing behind a bar. In one, she's mixing a cocktail. In another, she's drinking a shot directly from the bottle. In another, she appears to be dancing. The caption of one simply reads 'work'.

Evergreen comes to the window and holds out a small foam cup with steam trailing up from it. I smell the rich sweetness before even taking a sip.

"I thought you could use some hot chocolate," she says. "Since you've been sitting out here in the cold and all."

It's the first moment I realize I never rolled the window back up after she gave me my food. I've been sitting here with the thin, sharp wind blowing in but have been so wrapped up in my thoughts and ideas I haven't even noticed the cold. But now that she's mentioned it, my brain magnifies the effect, and suddenly, I feel like I'm filled with ice. I accept the hot chocolate gratefully and take a deep sip. Expecting reliable Swiss-Miss, the thick, intense flavor takes me by surprise. I swallow and give her an approving look.

"That's delicious," I tell her.

"My grandmother taught me to make it," she nods. "It's one of my favorite things in the winter."

"Well, thank you very much."

"Absolutely. Is there anything else I can get for you?"

She takes the trash I hand out to her, then I show her the pictures from Andrea's social media.

"Do you happen to know where this picture was taken?" I ask.

She only looks at the picture for a brief second before nodding.

"That's Lacy's. It's not too far from here," she tells me, then gives me brief directions on how to get there.

"Have you been there?" I ask.

She shakes her head. "No. Too young. But my brother has gone a few times, and I've heard him talking about it. Apparently, they have good potato skins, and the bartenders are all really cute."

I laugh. "I don't think the potato skin angle is going to be very helpful. But the bartenders might."

Fishing money out of my wallet, I hand her more than she needs and give her a smile that says I hope for the best for her.

"I hope your story turns out well," the young waitress says.

"And I hope to see you on TV soon," I tell her, and I mean it.

She beams as I pull away from the hamburger stand and head in the direction she pointed me. I'm suddenly in the mood for some potato skins.

CHAPTER TWENTY-ONE

Lacy's has a completely different feeling than Teddy's. Jake's tavern has a warm, broken-in feeling, like sitting in the same spot on a soft leather couch every day for years. It's comfortable and familiar, if somewhat awkward for someone new. This place is taut, vibrant, and alive. Even with only a few people at the tables, there's an energy about the place that makes it feel like walking into the set of a movie. At any point, I expect attractive young men to start tossing bottles of liquor in the air and suggestively clad girls to climb up on the bar like they just spontaneously know the same dance.

There are two young women behind the bar. Without patrons looking to start getting tipsy before lunchtime, they don't have much to do, so they're leaned back against the rail talking. It's not hard to tell which I'm here to see. Andrea's blonde hair is a stark contrast to the thick dark curls piled on top of the other girl's head. I cross the room and slide up onto one of the stools along the edge of the bar. Almost instantly, Andrea turns a bright smile to me. I wait to see if there is any flicker of recognition, even a question or touch of confusion when she sees my face. I don't see either. She must not have noticed me at the hotel.

"Hi, there," she says cheerfully. "What can I get for you?"

My burger and fries are still taking up the vast majority of my stomach real estate, and most of my milkshake is keeping chilled in the car. But I don't want to look suspicious by wandering into a bar in the early afternoon and not ordering anything.

"I've heard you have really good potato skins," I tell her.

She nods. "Best in the area. Do you want bacon?"

"Sure."

"I'll get that right up for you," she says and turns to disappear into the kitchen.

The other bartender glances in my direction.

"Are you new around here?" she asks.

"Just got here, as a matter of fact," I confirm.

"I thought so. Don't think I've seen you around here before."

"You get a lot of regulars?" I ask.

She nods. "We tend to know people's faces."

"I bet you get a lot of people coming in to see the two of you behind the bar," I chuckle.

It does the trick. Her icy demeanor thaws with a smile as she tries to look away humbly. But it's obvious her high opinion of herself is well-supported.

"I guess," she says. "More for Andrea."

She reaches for a cup and fills it with water from the soda fountain.

"Oh?" I ask, accepting the cup as she slides it across the bar to me.

"People just can't seem to get enough of her. She gets all the tips, and guys swarm in here just to sit around and talk to her. Sometimes I feel like the only reason I get any attention at all is because of runoff from her."

To her credit, the dark-haired woman laughs.

"Anyone in particular?" I ask. "I know you said there are a lot of regulars who come around here, but is there any one specific guy who seems to be around more than others?"

The question could go either way. Either she's going to think I'm just getting in some gossipy girl talk in my new town and indulge me, or she's going to think I'm prying and get suspicious. I'm going to hope for the former.

"Well," the bartender starts, leaning toward me in a way that says she's going that direction, "there is this one guy. He's come in a few times and seems really fixated on her. Doesn't say much and only ever orders bourbon. Just one, nothing to eat. He sits in the corner and just watches her."

My interest perks up.

"That sounds intriguing," I say, trying not to give away my curiosity. "Do you know who he is?"

She shakes her head.

"He doesn't talk. I don't even know his name. But I saw Andrea meet up with him after work in the alley behind the bar. She didn't know I was looking, and I saw her get into his car and ride off."

The kitchen door opens, and the other bartender straightens up sharply. Andrea eyes us suspiciously.

"What are the two of you talking about?" she asks.

The dark-haired girl smiles. "Just your admirer who likes to sit at the bar and watch you work."

Andrea shakes her head at the teasing. "He's not my admirer. He just likes to come drink a bourbon at the end of the day sometimes. Besides, I've told you, I think he comes to watch you, not me."

Flashing me a knowing look, the other bartender swishes off to talk to a couple who have just come in and perched themselves on the opposite side of the bar. Andrea sets a huge plate of potato skins in front of me, and the smell of bacon, sour cream, and cheese almost counteracts my fullness.

"Don't listen to her," Andrea says. "Kenley just likes to come up with dramatic, romantic stories to keep herself entertained."

"So, this mystery guy really isn't anybody?" I ask.

"Just a guy like any other customer who comes in. He shows up a little more often than some of the others, but I think that's just because he's lonely, maybe. Doesn't have anybody to go home to, you know? Even though he doesn't say much or interact with anybody, he can come here and feel like he's part of something. At least he's not sitting home and drinking his bourbon alone."

"You have a point," I tell her. I glance around, taking in the rest of the bar. "So, tell me about this place."

"What do you want to know?" she asks.

"Anything you can tell me," I say with a laugh. "Just trying to get a feel for the area."

"Well, there isn't much going on around here. Not that I'm complaining. I love it around here," she tells me.

"Did you grow up here?" I ask.

"Born and raised," she smiles.

"What about the surrounding areas? I saw a sign for somewhere called Feathered Nest. What's that all about?"

She looks slightly taken aback by the question, but quickly brushes off the reaction and shakes her head.

"I don't really know anything about it. I don't spend time out there or really know anyone from there. Well, I should leave you to your potato skins. The lunch rush will be starting soon. I don't like when it takes me by surprise."

Andrea gives me another warm smile and walks away. I watch her go up to Kenley and place her hand on her back as she leans around to talk to the couple. Taking out my phone, I pretend to be invested in something on it while I continue watching what's going on around me. Andrea is obviously hiding something. She doesn't want to talk about Feathered Nest or about getting in the car with LaRoche after he visits. That in and of itself isn't all that unusual. By the way they were acting in the hotel, I wouldn't jump right to calling their relationship out in the open. She wants to keep it to herself, but it seems like more than that. Not revealing her actual connection to the mystery man showing up at the bar is one thing. Pretending she doesn't know anyone from a nearby town when I know for a fact she's seeing someone there is suspicious.

After almost an hour at the bar, I manage to make progress on two of the potato skins. Andrea comes back over and looks at the plate through narrowed eyes.

"You didn't like them?" she asks.

"They're delicious," I protest. "I guess I just wasn't as hungry as I thought I was."

She picks up the plate. "Do you want me to put them in a box for you?"

"That would be great. Thanks."

As she carries the food back into the kitchen, I take out money and toss it on the bar. I accept the box from her, and she slides the money into the pocket of the small apron tied low around her hips.

"I hope you'll stop in again sometime soon," she smiles.

"Maybe I will," I tell her. "Have a good day."

Kenley turns around, and we wave at each other before I step back out into the cold afternoon. I reach behind me to put the box on the back seat and feel a sharp pain in the heel of my hand. My breath hisses through my teeth as I snap my hand back and hold it in my other palm to examine where the pain was. Something's glittering in my skin, and a trickle of blood bubbles up around it. Using my fingernail, I gently pry the glittering piece away to find a small shard of glass. Pulling it out causes more blood to slip down my hand and onto my wrist. Muttering a few profanities, I lean across the car to open the glove compartment in search of a tissue.

Once I have my hand wrapped, I turn around to look in the back seat. I haven't put anything glass back there since getting in the car. Is it possible one of the windows is broken, and I just didn't notice when coming out of the bar? Shards of glass in various sizes scattered across the seat look like they could have come from something shattering, but it's not vehicle window glass. All the windows are intact. I climb out of the car and test both back doors. They're locked. I know I unlocked the driver's side door before getting in, and the passenger door is secured as well. All that's left is the trunk. I try to open it, but it doesn't budge.

Getting back in the car, I lock my door and head for Feathered Nest. In any other circumstances, I'd go right to the police to show them the strange event. But that's not an option now. Someone's leaving me a message, and I'm on my own to find out what it means.

When I get back to the cabin, I snap several pictures of the glass but don't touch it. The remaining potato skins go right in the trash can sitting to the side of the porch. I'm fairly certain the Styrofoam is sturdy enough to withstand sitting on the glass without it getting through, but I'm not risking it. The lid to the trash can slams closed, and I'm turning around to head onto the porch when the light attached to the side of the cabin catches my eye. I take a few steps back and look up at it.

It's shattered.

The light that led me back here out of the woods last night is destroyed. Only the metal rim and one jagged piece of glass are left where the dome around the bulb used to be. A chill runs down my spine, joined by a shock of searing hot anger. They twist together, making my palms sweat and my head throb.

I didn't imagine it. He was following me last night, and he followed me today. It isn't just the glass strewn in my car that's the message. It's the destruction of what brought me to safety. He's getting closer, and at some point, one of us has to strike.

CHAPTER TWENTY-TWO

I am wrapping the cut on my hand in the cabin bathroom when my phone rings. Not bothering to look at the screen, I hit the speakerphone button and answer.

"Do you want to come up and have dinner tonight?"

I don't even want to think about food right now, but hearing Jake's voice brings a slight, much-needed smile to my lips. I realize I haven't even checked in with him since he dropped me off at my car, and he doesn't know about anything that's happened since then. I don't want to give him too much information. He has enough to think about right now without having to worry about me getting shot at and chased through the woods. Especially considering the person doing those things is the same one he's relying on to resolve the situation with his father's grave desecration.

"Absolutely," I tell him. "What time?"

"Meet me up here around 7?"

"Sounds perfect to me. I'll see you then," I tell him and disconnect.

It will do me good to get out of the cabin and clear my mind. I need time to think about everything and find the threads to tie it all together. Being at the bar with Jake will help me think about something else while the deeper parts of my mind tumble through the clues and evidence I have found so I can finally fit all the pieces together.

As soon as the thought goes through my mind, sadness tugs on my heart. Part of me has lost myself in this persona in so many ways I've gotten used to being here and living this life. I've gotten used to Jake. But soon it'll be time to leave all that behind and go back to my real world. Until now, I haven't even thought about that or considered what I'm going to do when this is over. I'll have to find a way to explain myself, and I dread how he may react.

I walk into the tavern exactly on time and feel the rush of warmth. It's not that everyone here is friendly or even welcoming. In the time I've spent in Feathered Nest, I've learned well enough that's not true. This town is all secrets and dark corners. The people here hide more than they show. But despite all that, there's still an overriding sense of camaraderie and a rhythm of life stitched into the fiber of each person who lives here.

Jake sees me when I'm only a few steps inside the door and gives me a broad smile. It's good to see his eyes sparkle again. I know he hasn't completely gotten over what happened, but he seems to be moving past it. He gestures at me, pointing to a spot at the bar he has reserved with an empty pint glass and a menu.

"Hi," he says happily when I take my place and accept a quick kiss to my forehead.

"How are you?" I ask.

He nods, letting out a sigh and looking around like he's surveying the surroundings and making sure nothing has gone wrong before he answers.

"Going well. Good to be here and have plenty to distract me."

He laughs. "How about you?" His eyes drop to my hands folded on the bar. I try to move them out of the way before he sees the bandage, but I'm not fast enough. "What happened?"

"Nothing. It's fine," I protest.

Jake reaches out and puts his hand over mine, gently easing it across the bar toward him. He turns it over in his palm and runs his fingertips over the bandage.

"This doesn't look like nothing."

"There was some broken glass," I explain. "I just wasn't paying attention and got cut on it. It's really not a big deal."

He searches my eyes like he's trying to see if I'm being honest with him. He must be satisfied with what he sees because he tenderly lifts my hand and touches his lips to the bandage. My heart aches even more. I never thought I would be the type of woman to get confused by emotions or things like this. The closest I've ever gotten to being wrapped up in my feelings and struggling with them is when Greg broke up with me. Our relationship felt like it was going so well, and things were moving forward. Then it was suddenly over, and just as abruptly, he was gone.

Now I'm tangled in a way I couldn't imagine. Struggling with my feelings for both men and what either of them really are is confusing. It feels close to betrayal, but it's hard to tell which of the men I think I am betraying more. Greg for developing any feelings for Jake at all, or Jake for letting him fall for me when he only knows a fabricated version.

"What were you up to today when you weren't cutting yourself on glass?" he asks.

"I did a little driving around."

"Anywhere in particular?"

"Not really. Just exploring. How about you?" I ask.

"Just work stuff. I did go up to the police station and talk to the chief about what's going on with my father," he explains.

"You did? Any new developments?" I ask.

"You could say that," he mutters.

Before he can continue, the door behind him opens, and a man with a round belly and cheeks so red they are almost glowing comes out from the kitchen. I recognize him as the cook who brought us the basket of French fries when we stood in Jake's office talking to Nicolas the day they found his father's bones. He hands two plates to Jake, who gestures for me to follow him with a nod of his head. I hop down from the stool as he comes around the bar and leads me to a booth. We sit across from each other, and he slides one of the plates toward me. Meatloaf, mashed potatoes and gravy, and vegetables. It smells amazing.

"What's the new development?" I ask.

The tines of my fork gather a scoop of the potatoes and gravy, and I slide it off onto my tongue. The flavor is rich, savory, and nostalgic. Jake eats a few bites, staring down at his plate. A bartender brings each of us a beer, and he washes his bite down before looking at me.

"They let him go," he says.

"What?"

"Cole Barnes. The cops let him go. Just opened up the door and let him wander on home," he vents angrily.

"They must have had a reason," I say.

"They're terrible at their job. That's the reason. How could they just let him go like that? They had him. He couldn't do anything else. Finally, he was going to be the one to answer for what he did. But they couldn't even manage to keep hold of him."

"Jake, it's not like he escaped. They released him," I point out.

He takes another deep swallow of his beer.

"Why? What good reason could they possibly have for not holding onto him? They have everything stacked up against him. Everybody in this town knows the blood went bad between Barnes and my father well before he died, and that the way my father met his end is up for debate. Then his grave gets destroyed, and his body stolen, only to be found in Barnes's shed. How can any of that be open for interpretation?" he asks. "He did it, and they know he did it."

"They might know he did it, but they can't just throw him into a cell and toss away the key. It doesn't work that way. They have to charge him and have him indicted. He has to face trial. It's a process and one they really only get one good shot at. I've seen a lot of cases where the evidence is completely clear-cut, but they don't hold the suspect because they believe there's even more evidence they can find. Especially these days, with the way lawyers can talk circles through just about anything, the more evidence, the better. Usually, police can only hold a person for about twenty-four hours before they have to either file formal charges or let them go," I explain.

It's not until I notice him staring back at me that I realize the spiel I just went on.

"What do you mean you've seen cases?" he asks.

I shrug. "I like to watch a lot of true crime TV. It's kind of my guilty pleasure. But anyway, that's probably what's happening here. They got up to that time limit and didn't want to file charges yet. They believe a defense attorney could talk his way out of the charges, or at least minimize them. So, they let him go until they find more to go on and can be absolutely positive the charges have the best chances of sticking."

Jake nods and reaches for my hand. He holds it carefully, avoiding the bandage over my cut. The injury has started throbbing, and as delicious as the food is, I don't want to eat any more of it. I lean back and draw in a breath. Jake tilts his head to look into my face.

"Are you alright?" he asks.

"I'm just feeling a little lightheaded. It's been kind of a long day, and I didn't get much sleep last night. I'm really sorry, but do you mind giving me a rain check for dinner?"

"Of course. Let me bring you back to the cabin," he offers.

I shake my head. "No. You don't need to do that."

"It's not a problem," Jake insists.

"I don't want the hassle of coming to pick my car up again and everything, either," I reply. "It still feels a little isolating being out there so close to the woods, and I like knowing my car is available."

"That makes sense. Well, I'm still going to drive behind you to make sure you get back safe. There are enough staff here to keep an eye on the bar while I'm gone."

There's no point arguing with him. I'm not going to be able to convince him I don't need him to come home with me. It will be easier just to ease his mind by letting him follow me. He guides me into the office so he can get his keys and pauses by the desk to flip through a small notebook I didn't notice the first time I was in here. Taking his phone out of his pocket, he glances at the screen, then leans over the notebook and makes a notation on the last page.

"What's that?" I ask when he puts his hand on my lower back and steers me out of the bar.

"The log of people who get escorted home from here. I like to keep track of them. It helps me know who to really keep an eye on and maybe offer a ride to the next time they come in. It also means if one of them ends up wandering back out of their house and gets into trouble, they can't possibly blame me. A buddy of mine owned a bar a few towns over and ended up having to shut down because a man got drunk at the bar, he escorted him home, and that guy then left and got hit by a car."

"Oh, my lord," I whisper.

"He survived, but the car that hit him swerved and got mashed up on a tree and hurt the driver. They blamed my buddy, and the insurance totally knocked him down. He couldn't face the charges and ended up closing down his bar. It devastated him. I'm not looking to have anything like that happen to me. I started escorting people home because I want them to be safe if they drink too much. And when people started disappearing and getting killed, I did it even more to make sure people weren't hurt heading home from my place. I care about them, but I also need to cover my own ass," he explains.

"I definitely understand that," I nod.

Jake pulls into the driveway right behind me, and when I climb out of the car, I see him standing beside his, staring at the broken light.

"That wasn't like that the last time I was here," he says.

"I know. It just broke today," I tell him.

"You need to call Clancy and have that fixed. It's too dark out here for you to not have that light," he insists.

I nod. "I will. First thing in the morning, I'll call him."

He walks with me into the cabin. I'm about to offer him a hot drink to thaw him out before he heads back to the bar when I notice him staring to the side. I follow his eyes and see them locked on the coffee table. And the pictures strewn across it.

CHAPTER TWENTY-THREE

Jake walks over to the table and stares down at the pictures. The one on top is a particularly gruesome close-up of Cristela Jordan's body. The blood makes her hair dark red, the tumble from the train tracks leaving the skin along the side of her face torn and discolored.

"What is all this?" he asks. "Why would you have all this?"

His hands gesture over the pictures, falling back down to his sides like he can't believe what he's seeing and is at a loss for words.

"I've been researching the disappearances and murders around here," I explain.

"Why? What's going on here, Emma?"

I can understand his suspicion and scramble to come up with a way to answer him.

"When I first came here and you told me all about what's been happening, it intrigued me. Like I told you, I'm fascinated by true crime. If I'm thinking about moving out here, I should probably know everything that's going on, don't you agree?" I try, already cursing myself. I could have come up with something way better than that.

He looks at me with a distant, almost pained expression in his eyes. There's something in that look that hangs heavy, dragging down the usually vibrant, alive blue. It's close to betrayal.

"Everyone around here is doing everything they can to ignore this. It's horrible, and none of us want anything to do with it. We want nothing to do with our town going from barely showing up on maps to being splashed around on the news because of all this horror. But you want to do everything you can to experience it?" he asks.

"That's not it. I'm not trying to experience it. It's not like that, Jake."

"Then what is it? Because it seems to me you came here telling everybody you wanted to move somewhere peaceful and quiet, to start a new life for yourself somewhere without the burden of your past. But what you really wanted to do is come gawk at the town of the damned and make a spectacle of us."

He sounds angry, and I find myself wanting to calm him down and reassure him.

"No, Jake. That's not it at all. That's not what's going on here. I came here because I want a new start and am thinking about moving into the area. I thought this would be a calm, easy-going place to take some time to myself and decide what I'm going to do next. But then I found out about everything, and I just needed to know more. So, I started studying it and found more and more... I just got swept up in it," I say.

I reach out for his hand, and our fingers intertwine. As they do, his knuckle nudges the ring Greg gave me, and the edge of the gold knot presses into the side of my finger. This isn't the way this is supposed to be. I'm fighting to keep Jake from thinking badly of me, not to maintain the secrecy of my mission. I don't want him to be upset or hurt, or to change his opinion of me. I shouldn't have let myself make this connection with him in the first place. It's unfair to both of us, and it's unfair to everything I have in my real life. The ring is a reminder of that. Maybe not of what I will one day have, but of what I did have and what I know is the way it should be. Greg wouldn't have just walked away from his life. Something happened to him, and I feel obligated to find out what.

Yet, I'm still looking to Jake for approval. Like he's my anchor here away from everything I know. Soon I'm going to have to be honest with him about why I'm really here, but until then, I need him to stay consistent.

"Alright," he finally says, accepting my explanation. "I'm sorry. I guess it's just been forced down my throat so much over the last two years I don't understand why anyone would want to have it around even more. But people probably didn't get my grandmother's obsession with thimbles, either. Everyone has their own thing."

"What's your thing?"

I ask the question despite the pain. I shouldn't be doing this to myself. I shouldn't be letting myself get deeper. The less I know about him, the better. It's easier to destroy the trust of someone you don't know well. Easier to walk away from the potential of something you haven't explored far. If I keep him at a distance, it won't be as difficult when the time comes for me to leave Feathered Nest. But I've already gotten too far, and I can't help myself to want to keep inching farther.

"Archery," he smiles.

I tilt my head back in surprise, looking at him under slightly furrowed brows.

"Really?" I ask.

"Really. Why does that surprise you so much?" he asks.

"I don't know. It just... does," I shrug.

"I learned when I was a lot younger. We used to have big targets set up in the backyard, and I'd go out there and practice for so long my parents would have to come out and force me back inside. I never wanted to stop. Not until I got it perfect. My dream was always to achieve the Robin Hood trick of splitting an arrow."

Jake laughs, and I feel the compulsion to wrap my arms around his waist and give him a squeeze.

"Did you?" I ask.

"Yes. Finally. Maybe that's why I haven't touched a bow in years. It's my thing, but I think I hit my peak. Don't want to go down from there."

I laugh. "Such a sacrifice."

He kisses me and then sighs, stepping back from me.

"As much as I would rather stay here with you, I should probably get back to the bar. Will I see you tomorrow?"

I nod. "Yes. And since I'm the one who ruined dinner tonight, let me take care of the plans. Do you think you could get away for lunch? I just found this place I think you would really like."

"Absolutely." We start toward the door, and he glances back over his shoulder at me. "What flavor milkshake did you have, by the way?"

I stop in my tracks, my throat tightening, and my blood running cold. "What?" I ask.

Jake turns around to look at me, his head tilting as he gives me a strange expression, then gestures back toward the coffee table.

"Milkshake. What flavor did you have?"

I notice the cup sitting there, the spot where the waitress wrote 'shake' across it in black marker turned toward us. The breath streams from my lungs, and I shake my head to get rid of the disquieting thoughts.

"Strawberry," I tell him.

"I'm a chocolate kind of guy," he smiles.

I nod. "I can see that."

I'm looking forward to another strawberry milkshake the next day as I walk up the long driveway to Cole Barnes's house. Without all the chaos of the police cars and listening to Jake scream, I can really look at the house and its surroundings. Like most of the other houses around Feathered Nest, it's modest and relatively well kept. There are bits and pieces of it that look like they could use a little bit of attention. Windowsills need a touch of paint, a crack along the sidewalk spreads dried, brown weeds across stones. One section of the gutter appears to be sagging slightly. But Cole doesn't look like the kind of man who could quite handle the physical work of this type of upkeep anymore. He has the body of a man who was in good shape when he was younger but let time and bad habits take control and fade away all the signs of youth. Climbing up to the top of a ladder to fix a gutter probably isn't in his future.

Which makes me wonder how he could manage to dig up a grave and get an entire skeleton of bones back to his shed without anyone noticing. The door at the front of the house opens when I'm still making my way up the driveway, and a version of Cole that looks even more run down than the one I saw shackled in the backyard stares out at me. His firmly set jaw covered in white and gray bristles, his eyes deeply set into his face and nearly concealed by heavy bags beneath them, he looks like he's on the edge of destruction.

"What do you want?" he snaps.

"Mr. Barnes? My name is Emma. I just came by to talk to you for a few minutes if you have the time," I say.

I don't stop walking toward the house. It's harder for people to push you away when you're close to them. When you are confident and insistent, taking the space you need and putting yourself in a position to get what you want, people are much less likely to try to get in your way.

"Are you a reporter?" he asks. "I don't want to talk to any reporters. I don't want to be on the news. I don't want to get in the newspaper. I just want everybody to stay out of my business."

"I'm not a reporter," I tell him honestly. "But I do want to know more about what happened."

"Why?" he asks, but as I get closer to him, recognition seems to settle over his face. "You were here. You were here the day they locked me up. With Jake."

I nod. "Yes. I'm a friend of his."

Cole shakes his head adamantly and steps back into the house, moving his hand to push the door shut. I hurry up onto the porch and position myself so he can still see me.

"I don't want anything to do with this. I've already talked to the police and told them my side. There's nothing else I have to say."

"I just want to know what really happened," I say.

"Did Jake put you up to this? Did he tell you to come talk to me and try to get me to slip up and say something?" he asks.

"No." I shake my head. "Jake doesn't even know I'm here. This is for me. He told me a little bit about his father, and I know the two of you used to be best friends."

"That was a long time ago. Things changed," he says.

"I know. But I don't know why, and Jake wouldn't tell me enough to make me understand why you would want to do something like this."

"I couldn't do something like this," Cole insists. "I don't know what happened or how those bones ended up in my shed. It certainly wasn't me. That day I was out in some of my old fields I'm thinking about selling, and when I came home, my place was crawling with cops. They slapped the cuffs on me before they even told me what was happening."

"But you knew about the desecration of Jake's father's grave," I point out.

"No," Cole protests. "I had no idea. They just showed up telling me I dug him up and put him in my shed."

"What happened between the two of you?" I ask.

He shakes his head again. "I'm not going to get into all that. That was years ago, and I put it behind me. When John died, he took all that with him. I'm willing to let it stay buried."

"That's just the thing. It didn't stay buried. Neither did he. Someone wanted people thinking about the two of you again. Can you think of any reason why?"

"I told you, I don't want to talk about it. I just want all this to go away," he says.

"But it's not going to. They are either going to keep pushing with these charges and you're going to end up in jail soon, or it's just going to keep haunting you while they investigate and investigate trying to figure out what happened."

"Why does it matter to you? Jake thinks I did it. He's hated me since everything that happened."

"What happened? Why would Jake hate you?"

"I'm not going to talk about that. I told you, I don't want to talk about John, and I don't want to talk about Jake. I don't want to talk about any of this. Just leave."

He moves to close the door again, but I step forward and push my hand against it to stop it.

"Fine. We don't have to talk about it. What about the disappearances?"

Cole looks at me strangely.

"What about them?" he asks.

"If you didn't dig up Jake's father's grave and stash his bones behind your house, somebody else did. Do you think you could have anything to do with the people who have been murdered?" I ask.

"Now you're accusing me of murder, too? I already faced that enough with all the whispers after John died."

"No. But somebody's trying to get people to look at you again. What do you know about Police Chief LaRoche?"

As soon as the name is out of my mouth, Cole recoils. A look of fear crosses his face.

"That's enough. I'm done. You need to get on out of here now and don't come back. Just leave me be."

"What can you tell me?" I ask. "I know his father was Chief before him. What happened back then?"

"You need to leave. Now. I'm not answering any more questions. Just leave me in peace."

Cole slams the door shut, forcing me back. The encounter tingles on my skin. I struck a nerve. Seeing Cole again only confirmed my doubts, he couldn't have managed the desecration on his own. It would take a strong, young man hours to dig up a grave. Someone Cole's age, with his obvious ill health, would never be able to pull something like that off as quickly as it would need to be for no one to see what was happening.

Someone was finishing what they started... or what was started for them.

CHAPTER TWENTY-FOUR

I want to knock on the door again and try to pull more out of Cole, but I doubt he would open it. The look of terror on his face and what he did say will be enough for now. I move back down the driveway at a faster clip and hop into my car. Riding on the slight high of getting closer to the truth, I head out to the edge of town and the cemetery on the hill.

It's quiet now with the police cars gone and the ground strewn with scattered snow rather than officers. Parking in almost the same place as Jake did, I walk through the iron gate and follow the same path toward his father's grave. It wasn't until Cole said it that I realized I hadn't heard Jake's father's name yet. His tombstone lay in pieces around the gaping hole of his grave the last time I was here, so I didn't get a chance to read it. Now I know his name had been John. John Logan. That's the kind of name people called a solid name. The kind attached to the successful, honest businessman Jake told me about.

I stop at the edge of the grave and stare down at it. It's filled again, the dirt dark and damp where it's mounded slightly above the level of the frozen grass around it. I didn't think they would refill the grave until the bones were released to be re-interred. Something feels unsettling about the idea of them having to open up the grave yet again to put John's body back inside when all this is finally over. I hate the thought of Jake having to go through the trauma of choosing a casket for his father for a second time. The one originally buried with him was destroyed, and there was no way they could salvage it to bury him again. Part of me wonders if it's still down there. They could have just left the remnants sitting in the ground and put the dirt back over it.

The headstone hasn't been replaced, and the fractured base still sits in its original spot. It's a scar and a testament. If something this horrific happened to my mother's grave, I don't know what I would want to do. Part of me would want that jagged, broken piece of stone gone as soon as possible, so I wouldn't have to look at it or think about what happened. There's another part of me that believes I would keep it in place. Even after adding a new stone to mark the grave properly, leaving that piece behind would just be another way to honor the story and legacy that continues.

I look to the grave closest to one side and see it is one of the older ones of the cemetery, dating back several decades before John's death. The one to the other side is slightly more recent but still older, like his grave was wedged in a free space between two unrelated plots as space became limited. I walk behind the headstone and look at the next stone. It's from only a few years before John, but the name doesn't ring any bells. It's not until I reach another grave that something stands out to me.

"Melanie Logan," I whisper, slowly crouching down over the grave and reading the beautifully scrolled tombstone.

Jake's wife. I can still hear the tremor in his voice when he said her name the day he told me about her. The day he told me about how he fell in love with her and their short, loving marriage. The day he told me about her horrible, sudden death. I look beneath the etched image of an angel in the center of the stone to the birth and death dates. The date on the stone is just a year before John's death.

"Who do you think you are?"

The voice suddenly booming through the cemetery makes me

jump to my feet and whip around defensively. My muscles tighten, ready to lash out if I need to. Chief LaRoche's eyes burn into mine as he stalks through the tombstones toward me, and my muscles don't relax.

"Excuse me?" I ask.

"Who the *fuck* do you think you are?" he repeats with embellishment.

"What are you doing here?" I ask. "Did you just drive around looking for me?"

I want him to slip. If I can just get him to admit something, I can end this.

"You best fucking believe I came looking for you. I should have known you'd end up here. Can't keep your nose out of anything that has nothing to do with you," he growls.

My heartbeat quickens, but I keep my face calm and under control. I focus on the outline of my phone in my pocket. It might not have the best reception this far out, but it's enough that I can contact somebody if LaRoche gets violent.

"What are you talking about?" I ask. "I was here the day Jake found out someone dug up John's grave. With Jake. He brought me here."

"John? You're on a first name basis with him now?" LaRoche spits.

I refuse to give into him. I'm not going to rise to his bait and give him the satisfaction of riling me up or seeing me afraid.

"You need to tell me what you're doing here. The last time I checked, I'm not a suspect in any crime, and you don't have me under investigation for anything. Unless that's changed for some reason, you have no right to be on my ass like this. And if it has changed, now would be a fantastic time for you to tell me that," I state flatly.

"You know exactly why I'm here," he fires back angrily.

"Enlighten me."

"What were you doing going up to Lacy's?" he asks.

LaRoche's voice lowers until he's almost whispering, like he's trying to keep the words away from anyone who might be too quiet among the tombstones for us to know they're there.

"It's a nice spot, don't you think? I heard the potato skins were amazing, and I just needed to find out for myself," I offer.

"Don't give me that shit. You went in and started asking questions. I want to know why," he snaps.

I narrow my eyes and toss my head to the side, searching his face and keeping my expression as open and innocent as I can.

"I don't know what you're talking about," I say.

"Stop playing stupid. You went up there and started poking around, trying to find out more about Andrea," he hisses through his teeth.

"And how would you know that?" I ask. "Do you make it a habit of following women around?"

"I didn't follow you. She told me you were there."

"I didn't even tell her my name. How could she possibly tell you I was there?"

"She said some woman she never saw came up to the bar and was sniffing around asking questions about Feathered Nest and the people who go up there. Said she was tall and blonde. Didn't take a whole lot of stretch of the imagination to figure out it was you," LaRoche says.

"Tall and blonde. Interesting. Sounds very much like Andrea, doesn't it?" I point out. "And Cristela Jordan, for that matter."

"What are you getting at?"

"I saw you and Andrea at the hotel the day I went up there. The day someone shot at me," I say. "You looked awfully friendly for someone who says she doesn't know anyone in this town and has never been here. Of course, the hotel isn't *technically* in Feathered Nest, so I guess she might not have been lying. Did you just not tell her who you really are?"

"Where do you get off shoving your nose in my private business?" he sputters.

"When dead people wind up on my porch, bullets come flying at my head, someone follows me in the woods, and broken glass from my outside light ends up on the backseat of my car, everything becomes my business," I say.

"What are you talking about?" he asks.

"Now who's playing dumb? I know you were there when I was at Lacy's. The other bartender, Kenley, told me you go sit up there and watch Andrea all the time. I must have chosen just the perfect time. Even if you weren't following me, you showed up at the bar and saw my car. Thought you'd leave me a little message."

His eyes darken, and heightened awareness pricks at the back of my neck. I'm on a slippery slope now. This confrontation might have gone too far. But I want to push him. I want to get him to the very brink and shove him over, to force him to reveal all the cracks that will soon make him shatter. He takes a step toward me, but his eyes snap over my shoulder before he says anything.

"Emma?"

I turn to the sound of Jake's voice and see him walking toward us, holding flowers in one hand and a bottle in the other. He looks distinctly unhappy to see me there.

"Jake... " I start.

"What are you doing here?" he asks.

"I just came to look…"

"At my father's grave? You wanted to gawk at it again? See if anything else horrible happened to it?"

He sounds angry, and I take a step closer to him.

"Cole Barnes said…"

"You went to talk to Cole Barnes?" he demands.

"What the hell is with you and interfering with active investigations?" LaRoche growls from behind me. "Barnes was just released. He's still being investigated, and anything he says needs to be on record. Not babbled out to some nosy woman who doesn't know how to keep her distance."

"How dare you talk to me like that?" I say, turning back to look at LaRoche.

"He's right," Jake says.

I whip around to face him.

"Excuse me?"

"You said you've always been interested in true crime, and it fascinates you?"

"Yes."

"If you were so invested in it, you would have known about the disappearances and murders around here. It's been going on for two years. Two years, Emma. People have been losing their lives, and no one can stop it. News about it has been splashed all over every channel and newspaper across the damn country. If you had even the slightest interest in crime, you would have heard about it. But you said you found out about it and started getting interested after you got here, and I told you."

"It's just…"

"It's just you're nosy and unbelievably insensitive. I can almost understand you having some curiosity about it and wanting to know more, especially after you and I started getting closer. You want to know what's happening," he says.

"Exactly. I just want to know."

"That's not enough," he snaps, cutting me off. "Being curious is one thing. Being inappropriate and pushing yourself into situations where you don't belong is something entirely different. Do you have any idea how much all this has hurt me? How many wounds it's opened up? I trusted you. I leaned on you to help me get through it. Then I find you creeping around the cemetery prying into my father… into my *wife*."

"Jake, I'm sorry. I know I should have told you before I went to talk to Barnes, but there were some things I just needed to know."

"So, you went behind my back to talk to the man who is responsible for all this pain and torment. For what reason? What did you possibly think you could get out of that?" Jake asks.

"She gets off on it," LaRoche sneers. "It's the same reason she went up to the hotel."

"What hotel?" Jake asks.

"The one where Ron Murdock, the man shot dead on her porch, was staying. She went up there, asking questions."

"I was trying to find out more about him," I protest. "I don't think it's that strange to want to know more about a man I watched die."

"It is that strange when you didn't even know him, and you've already gotten an explanation about what happened to him," the chief says. "You're prodding around trying to make more out of things than you should. I'd think you would learn after someone shot at you."

Jake's hand grabs my wrist and pulls me around to face him.

"Someone shot at you?" he demands. "When did this happen? Why didn't you tell me?"

"I didn't want you to worry about me," I tell him. "The police don't even know who did it. It could have just been an accident, or some stupid kids joy riding and shooting without thinking about where the bullets might end up."

I can feel LaRoche staring at me, the same searing, threatening feeling from the woods. I want my words to throw him off, to keep him guessing about how much I know so he will trip himself up.

"You still think that after your light got broken?" Jake asks. He shakes his head and takes a step back from me. "I can't do this. I can't handle worrying about you on top of everything else."

He storms away, heading back toward the entrance to the cemetery.

"Jake, please. Just let me explain," I call after him.

He hesitates and looks back at me. "You need to watch yourself, Emma. If you aren't more careful, someone could get hurt."

CHAPTER TWENTY-FIVE

"Listen to him," LaRoche says. "Sounds like he knows what he's talking about."

"I don't need your advice," I snap. "You haven't even explained to me why you were up at the hotel that day."

"Like I said, I don't need to justify anything to you. But since it seems you're determined to play Miss Marple, I'll tell you. It's not like I need to deal with getting your obnoxious little ass killed. I was up at the hotel to see Andrea. But you already know that. You saw us together. We're having an affair. I'd appreciate it if you kept your mouth shut about that. You don't need to go around messing up people's lives over two adults wanting to spend some time together."

"But why meet her all the way out there?" I ask.

"Ever heard of discretion? I don't particularly want people around here knowing what's going on between the two of us," he says.

"Because it's happened before?" I ask. "I imagine you've made some people pretty unhappy with your dalliances."

"You don't know what you're talking about," he glowers.

"I know what Kenley told me. Why are you so willing to hang around stalking Andrea at work, but won't let her be seen around here?"

"Like I told you before, I don't know what you're talking about. All I know is ever since you got here, you've been causing trouble. You need to back off and leave people alone. I don't want to have to tell you again."

With those words hanging heavily in the air around us, the police chief walks around me and leaves the cemetery. I stand beside John Logan's grave for another few seconds before making my way back to my car and heading toward Teddy's.

When I walk into the bar, I see two of the usual bartenders pouring beer and a few of the regulars scattered at the tables, but don't see Jake. Walking up to the bar, I flatten my hands down on it and lean over toward one of the bartenders. I know I met him, but his name isn't popping to my mind.

"Hey, buddy," I call to him.

Fortunately, he turns my way.

"Hey, Emma. Good to see you."

"Good to see you, too. Is Jake around? Maybe he's in the office?"

The bartender shakes his head. "Haven't seen him. He called up here earlier to say he was heading to the cemetery to pay his respects. It's a hard day for him, you know."

"It is?" I ask.

He nods, looking at me strangely as if I should know what he's talking about.

"Yeah. It's the anniversary of his wife's death."

"Oh, shit," I mutter, hanging my head. "How did I not realize that?"

"It's been a long time, but he's still really broken up about it. You know, he's been happier since you came here than I've seen him in a long time."

"Really?"

"Absolutely. People see Jake and he seems so full of life and goofiness. He's always the one trying to lift people up and make them feel better. But it's all because he's still hurting so much. Not to say he isn't a great guy or is always all gloom and doom, or anything. But there's part of him that's been closed ever since Melanie died. He wasn't ever the happiest and most social person before he met her, but she changed everything. Then when all that happened, it's like something inside him broke, and he closed off. He shut down. Then his father died, and he took this place over. Life started again for him. He woke up and became the happy, jovial Jake people know. But that little bit of emptiness inside him was still there. I didn't think it would ever go away. Then you came along. Now maybe he'll have a chance."

My throat aches, and I have trouble drawing a breath all the way into my lungs, but I force it in and then out in a long stream.

"It sounds like you've known Jake a long time," I say.

"Ever since he was a kid. I didn't know him real well or anything. He wasn't the kind to come hang out with other kids or invite people over to his house. But we were friendly enough. I got to know him better after he met Melanie. He's a good guy. Despite everything, he's a good guy."

I nod and step back from the bar. "Thanks."

He gives me a little half wave, and I leave the bar to get back in my car. My next stop is Jake's house, and I'm relieved to see his car parked there. I know he leaves the door unlocked, so I don't bother knocking. He probably wouldn't answer the door, anyway, and I need to talk to him.

"Jake?" I call out when I step inside the house. "It's me."

He doesn't answer, and I continue past the first room and into the cozy den set at the center of the house. There I find Jake sitting on the couch, slumped down far enough, so his head rests on the back as he stares at the picture album open on his lap. There's no expression on his face. His eyes seem almost glazed over, like he's not even seeing what he's looking at. I step cautiously closer.

"I want to apologize," I start.

He flips a page of the photo album slowly but doesn't say anything to me. He hasn't directly told me to leave, so I get a little bit closer. Giving myself time to work up the words I'm going to say to him, I ease down onto the couch cushion beside him and look at the album across his thighs. It's not the same one I looked through the last time I was at his house, but it's put together in the same way. I have a feeling the same person put both of them together. Somebody wanted very much for the family memories to be kept close and safe. These pages hold moments of time that slipped by long ago. Without them, those moments might be totally forgotten. But each of these pictures crystallizes them so Jake can look back and relive the times that obviously mean so much to him.

"Today is…" he starts, but his voice cracks, and he stops.

"I know," I whisper. "I'm so sorry. I had no idea."

"I thought spending some time with you today would help me get through it. Every year I go to the cemetery and leave flowers for her. I bring a bottle of her favorite wine and make a toast to her. It makes it seem more of a celebration of her life than a marker of her death. I try to tell myself one day, it won't hurt anymore. It never works. Today I was going to do that early so I could see you for lunch. I hoped that would be all it would take to make the pain…less."

"I'm sorry, Jake. I wish there was something I could say to make it better for you. There's no way to imagine what that feels like. "

"When it happened, I didn't know what to do. I couldn't wrap my head around it. No matter how many times I heard it or the things I had to go through after it happened, there was a part of me that didn't really believe it. I went to identify her body. I saw her lying there, cold and discolored. The next day I went to the funeral home and arranged her funeral. I watched them bury her. Everything rolled past like it was barely even happening. My mind told me any minute she was going to come home, and it would have been someone else."

"I know how that feels," I tell him. "Not in the same way, but close."

"After that, all that was left in Feathered Nest was my father and me. My brother and sister came back home for the funeral, but when they left again, it felt even emptier here than it had before. My father was gone a year later. And it was just me. I never missed my grandmother more than I did in those first few weeks after he died." He lets out a mirthless laugh. "I missed her even more than I missed my father."

He touches the page of the album in front of him. The picture of his grandmother is similar to the one in the other album. She's wearing the same dress, but rather than standing on a step, she's sitting on a porch swing. The focus is tight around her, not letting me see much of her surroundings, but there's enough to reveal green leaves and bits of grass. I remember what Jake told me about celebrating Easter with his grandmother and siblings. I imagine her sitting there watching them search for the eggs she hid.

"I can understand that. Sometimes it's even harder to cope with the people you lost longer ago than it is the ones who have just passed. It's safer to miss them more because you've been doing it for longer. Besides, from what you've told me about your grandmother, I know she's the one you relied on the most to help you through hard times. She comforted you and made you feel better when things were difficult. Losing your wife and your father within a year of each other is something harder than most people will ever have to face. I can understand why you would start longing for her when you were going through that," I tell him.

"Then can you understand why it is so hard for me to think of you in any danger. I hate the idea of anything happening to you," he says, looking over at me.

"I thought you were mad at me," I say.

"I am. I can't pretend it doesn't make me angry to think about you going to talk to Cole Barnes or that it doesn't bother me to see all those pictures in your cabin. And I hate that you didn't even trust me enough to talk to me," he says. "But being worried about you is more important right now. I can get over being angry. But I can't get over the possibility of losing you."

"Jake, I…" I stop the words trying to come out of my mouth. I don't want to keep spiraling. I don't want to keep building lie upon lie, so I'm never able to pull myself out of it. This is all going to explode soon enough. At least maybe this way I won't have to try to survive it alone. "I'm sorry I worried you. That's exactly what I didn't want to do. But there are some things you don't understand."

"Then tell me. Help me understand," he begs. "Because right now I can't figure out why you would want to have anything to do with things the rest of the town is trying as hard as we can to escape."

"Chief LaRoche was in the cemetery with me today because I

found something out about him, and he wanted to confront me about it," I tell him.

"What did you find out?" Jake asks.

"I was telling the truth when I told you I went to that hotel to find out more about the man who was shot and died on my cabin porch. I needed to know more about him and didn't think the police were giving me enough information. They were brushing me off and acting like it wasn't a big deal, so I decided to go find out for myself. All I wanted to do was find out his real name and where he came from."

"His real name?" Jake asks.

I nod. "The name they found out for him just didn't sound right. I did some research on it but couldn't find him. So, I went to the hotel and asked the owner about him."

"Did you find out anything else?"

"Not really. His registration card had the name Ron Murdock on it, and the address wasn't a real house. That's all the information it had. But while I was there, I saw Chief LaRoche with a woman. They were very friendly with each other. When I asked the owner about who else was staying at the hotel, she said no one from Feathered Nest had checked in there in weeks. He was hiding that he was there. He left before I did. When I walked out into the parking lot, there were two shots. I didn't see any car or anything. Then just a minute later, LaRoche showed back up and acted like he just happened to be in the area and heard over the police scanner that there was a shooting. He even spoke with the owner of the hotel and acted like he hadn't been there at all."

"Are you saying you think LaRoche shot at you?" he asks. "Why would he do that?"

"Because he thinks I know something he doesn't want me to know, possibly. I ended up tracing the girl he was with, Andrea and found out she works in a bar in another town. I went to see her, but she acted like she didn't know anyone from Feathered Nest, even though the other bartender told me a man comes and watches her work all the time, and she's seen Andrea get in a car with him. Jake, she looks so much like Cristela Jordan," I say.

CHAPTER TWENTY-SIX

A s soon as I say it, it's obvious the name strikes a nerve. Jake pulls back slightly, his eyebrows lowering.

"Cristela, who used to come into my bar?" he asks.

I nod. "The one murdered and found by the train tracks."

I'm starting to say more, but Jake shakes his head and reaches to take my hand.

"Emma, you have to calm down. I think you've gotten in over your head with this. Just like he said, you are giving significance to things that don't have any," he says.

"He's having an affair with Andrea. He admitted it. And the first time she stayed in the hotel was after Cristela died."

"That could just be a coincidence."

"Cristela was staying at that hotel, too. She stayed there several times. You knew her, Jake. You knew she lived just on the other side of Feathered Nest. Why would she go stay in a hotel three towns over clear in the opposite direction of where she lived?"

"I don't know," he admits.

"Unless she was meeting someone, and she didn't want anyone to know. And, Jake, think about it. You know, as well as I do, Barnes couldn't have dug up that grave and moved your father's bones himself. He just doesn't have the strength. You told me yourself LaRoche's father got involved when things happened between your father and Barnes years ago. People thought finding your father's bones could have something to do with the murders and disappearances because Barnes did it. But what if it's because LaRoche wanted a distraction? He wanted to confuse people and get them thinking about all that again rather than what's going on now."

"Why would he do that?" Jake asks.

"I'm not sure, other than to screw with people. But I do know when I went out in the woods the other night; I felt someone watching me."

"This isn't safe for you, Emma. You need to tell someone what you know," he insists.

"Who should I tell? The police? I can't tell anyone anything until I have something more concrete to go on. And you have to promise me you aren't going to say anything, either. I'm trusting you with this."

"Emma... "

"Jake, I'm trusting you. I only told you because I don't want you worrying about something you don't know. And I want you to be on your guard. I know you're still going to be interacting with him as he pretends to investigate Barnes. You have to be aware."

"How am I supposed to just sit by and not say anything when I know what this man has done? To me, to you, to all of us? He's supposed to be the most trusted member of our community, and he's picking us off one right after the other. Now he's coming for you."

"I will be fine, Jake. You have to trust me," I say.

"I don't want you out at that cabin by yourself at night. It's too dangerous. Come stay here with me."

"No, Jake. I'm not going to let him chase me out of my cabin. I'm not going to give him that kind of power," I argue.

"It's not giving him power," he says. "It's being smart and safe. He was sending you a message with that glass, and you know just as well as I do, he's not going to back down now. If he has even the slightest clue of how much you know about him and what he's been up to, he's going to do anything he can to make sure you don't tell anybody. Keep in mind, you're tall and blonde, too."

I hesitate, hating the idea of giving LaRoche the satisfaction of forcing me out of my cabin. But at the same time, Jake's words ring and swell in my ears. I know I'm looking at this too closely. I'm too deep, too sharply focused to make the right decisions. I need to pull back and look at the situation like I would with the witnesses I've worked with on other cases. If a woman involved in an abduction and murder case experienced as many threats as I have, there's no way I would let her be alone for a single second, much less staying alone in an isolated location where I knew the suspects could easily find her and already had.

"Let me go get a few things, and I'll come back," I tell him.

He nods. "The guys at the bar are expecting me to show up for a while tonight, but I'll make it fast and then come right back here. You stay put."

I shake my head. "No, Jake. That's what I'm talking about. I'm already having to uproot my existence because of this. I'm not going to let you do it, too. You go to the bar just like you would have anyway. Do what you need to do. You need the routine and the consistency to help you through all of this. Besides, we don't want to look suspicious or like we're trying to hide from anything. I'll be fine."

"Do you want to come up there with me? We didn't get to have our lunch today. It's not the best replacement in the world, but we can have some beer and fries up at the Den, and when I'm done for the night, take a drive up to that hamburger stand for a late-night snack," he suggests.

"Please don't take this the wrong way, but I think I need a little break from the bar. I just don't want to deal with a lot of people right now. I'd rather spend some time in the quiet just relaxing, if that's alright with you," I say.

"Of course, it is. As long as you promise to keep the doors locked and your phone right beside you so if you need me you can call me. I'll be back to you in a second."

"I know you will. It won't take me long to get my things from the cabin. I'll be back soon."

"Do you need any help?" he asks.

Shaking my head, I lean forward to brush my lips across his.

"No. I'll be fine."

I stand up from the couch, and he gently tugs my hand to stop me from walking away. Pausing, I look down at him.

"Be careful."

I nod and leave, feeling like a weight has been lifted off my shoulders, knowing I don't have to carry all of this on my own. I'll still have to come clean to Jake about who I really am and why I came here, but for now, I don't have to think about that. I've been honest with him about part of what's happening. That's a start.

Caution makes me drive slowly up the long driveway to cabin number 13. I want to be aware of any movement around me or anything that might be amiss before something can go wrong. Everything seems exactly as it was when I left. I walk into the empty cabin and feel the heavy warmth pumping from the furnace. It's finally cozy and relaxing inside, and I'm leaving. Sighing, I walk back into the bedroom and drag my bag out from under the bed. I fill it with a few sets of clothes and my toiletries. Though I'm tempted to just go ahead and bring everything, that feels too extreme. I'm not giving in to him. I'm not abandoning the cabin and cowering. Going to Jake's house is a precaution and also a way to make him feel better, which will help ensure he doesn't bubble over and blow the progress I've made.

I'm gathering up my notes and pictures when my phone rings. I glance at the screen before answering.

"Hey, Eric," I say.

"Hey, yourself. Are you close to your computer? If not, you can see this on your phone, but it will be better on a bigger screen," he starts.

"Yeah. Just give me a second."

I sit down on the edge of the couch and open my computer. It takes a second for the screen to come up, and I open my email inbox.

"Alright. Go ahead. What's going on?" I ask.

"I did what you asked and looked into that guy. Turns out you were right. As far as I can tell, his name is not Ron Murdock," Eric continues.

"I can't believe I didn't tell you. I went to the hotel and looked at his registration card. The address he has listed comes up as ..."

"The Field of Dreams? I know. I found that, too."

"How did you find that? Never mind. Doesn't matter. What else?"

"Turns out, winding up around you was no coincidence. I'm pretty sure he wasn't intending on dying, but he was definitely trying to get to you. I'm sending you a message. Tell me what you see," he says.

"Alright. Go ahead."

An instant later, a new email pops up in my inbox, and I click on it. There are no words, only an image. It takes a second for the entire thing to appear, and when it does, my breath catches in my throat.

"Is that...?"

"That would be your Mr. Not Ron Murdock with your parents," Eric tells me.

It confirms exactly what I thought I was seeing, but part of my brain convinced me I had to be wrong. The picture is old, showing my parents years younger than they even were when my mother died. They're smiling, their eyes hidden behind dark sunglasses as they stand with their arms around a man standing in the middle of them. He's huge and hulking, but the smile on his face is genuine. His face is smooth, and he doesn't have the streaks of gray through his hair, but it's unmistakable. That's the man who fell dead on my front porch.

"What is this? Where did you find it?" I ask.

"I'll admit it took a little bit of doing. It doesn't seem our elusive friend wants to have much of a presence in the world. I'm not even sure what his real name is or where he comes from. For all intents and purposes, he doesn't exist. But I found this picture in a deep archive related to your father. This is Florida, April 1998," he says.

"1998? I remember being in Florida then. It was one of the few instances we stayed in place for long enough; I really remember it. I wonder where I was when they were taking this picture."

"I don't know. It seems you would be with them. It says they're at the opening of Disney World Animal Kingdom."

"The opening of Animal Kingdom? I don't remember going to that." What he said suddenly sinks in, and a strange feeling roils in my stomach. "Did you say 1998?"

"Yes. April twenty-second," Eric confirms.

"And that was the opening? Of the whole park? Not just a ride or attraction or something?" I ask.

I hear clicking and know he's looking the information up on his computer just to make sure.

"Yep. That's the day the entire park opened. Why?"

"Did you find out anything else about him? How my parents know him? Why he was following me?"

"No, not yet. I'm working on it, though," he says.

"Keep me updated. I'll talk to you soon."

"Is there something wrong, Emma?" he asks.

"Just let me know if you find out anything else. And since I know you'll be talking to her, save me the third degree from Bellamy and let her know I'm fine," I add. "Thanks for doing all this for me. Call you later."

I hang up before Eric says anything else and immediately dial Jake.

"Did you change your mind about needing help?" he asks by way of greeting.

"Can you explain to me how you went to a theme park five years before it opened?"

CHAPTER TWENTY-SEVEN

"What?" Jake asks.

"You told me you remember going on vacation with your family to Florida when you were seven years old. You went to Animal Kingdom and loved watching the elephants because you didn't realize how big they actually were," I say.

"Yeah, it was an amazing trip. Some of my favorite childhood memories with the entire family. I don't understand why you sound so upset," he says.

"Because none of those memories can be real," I explain.

"What are you talking about? I can show you the pictures."

"The park wasn't open, Jake. The park didn't open until 1998. You were twelve years old. You couldn't have gone there when you were seven. Why did you lie to me?"

There's a long pause.

"What happened between the last time we spoke and now?" he asks.

"I found out you lied to me about these precious childhood memories you supposedly have with your family. If you lied to me about those, what else are you lying to me about?" I ask.

"I'm not lying to you, Emma. Those memories are real."

"They can't be. I thought I could trust you."

I hang up the phone, shaking and fighting the feeling of tears stinging in the back of my eyes. I don't want to think about why those tears are there. There are too many emotions that could create them, and I don't want to deal with any of them. Grabbing my bag, I carry it back to my bedroom and angrily start unpacking and shoving everything back in the drawers and onto shelves. I'm still fuming when my phone rings, and I don't even bother to look down on it. I don't need to. It's Jake calling me, and I don't want to hear his voice.

When everything is back in place, I go into the living room to bury myself back into the case. I can't focus, and after more than half an hour passes, I realize it's because the spare key Jake gave me is still sitting in the bottom of my pocket. Usually, he doesn't lock his door, but he insisted on me bringing the key with me and to lock the door behind me when I left to come to the cabin. I don't want it anywhere near me. I impulsively grab my coat and head out to my car. He's probably at the bar by now. I can go up there, leave his key, and be back in less than 20 minutes. Then I'll have nothing left to distract me from getting this done and moving on.

It seems most of Feathered Nest has the same idea. All the spots in front of the bar are full when I arrive. I have to drive around to the back of the tavern. I'm only partway down the alley when I notice two figures behind the building. Stopping, I look more closely and realize it's Jake and LaRoche. They're close together, speaking animatedly, but not loudly enough for me to hear them. Their gestures get bigger and angrier. It looks like Jake is doing exactly what I asked him not to and confronting the police chief about what I know. An instant later, LaRoche grabs Jake by the front of his shirt and slams him up against the brick wall of the bar. He brings his face close to Jake's and says something, then turns and stomps away.

Jake steps forward and combs his fingers angrily back through his hair, then turns and stalks back into the bar, slamming the door behind him. I put my car in reverse and back out of the alley. Now isn't the time for me to confront him anymore. I don't know what just happened between the two men, and I don't want rumors spreading among the regulars in the bar. The fewer people who know about my suspicions, the better. I'll wait until the bar closes and then talk to him.

Back at the cabin, I find myself unable to focus. I can't get my brain to settle down and concentrate. Finally, I curl up on the couch and put an old favorite movie on my computer. It's one I've seen probably a hundred times in my life, and I can repeat every line by heart. There's something soothing in that. The predictability takes away all anticipation and lets me just completely relax. My brain wanders, and I don't have to feel like I'm missing anything if I realize I've drifted into thoughts for any stretch of time. This is a technique I learned a long time ago when I couldn't get my thoughts to straighten out. Just having something familiar to rely on was often all it took to get myself back into a place where I could think.

That's not how it works this time. The next thing I know, I am waking up, and the cabin is dark. The only light I had left on before sitting on the couch was the kitchen, and it gives just enough light for me to see around the room. My computer screen has long-since gone into standby mode, and all around me, the cabin had fallen asleep with me. It's disorienting waking up and having no idea what time it is or how long I've been asleep. Rubbing the mouse pad on my computer, I wake up the screen and see it's already the middle of the night. My lack of sleep over the last several days must have finally caught up with me. I've been out for several hours.

Climbing off the couch, I stretch muscles and joints made tight and tense with staying in the same awkward position for too long. My throat is dry, and my lips feel sticky from the open-mouth position I tend to assume when I fall into a deep sleep. I can thank Bellamy for my knowledge about that. A particularly unflattering picture posted on the refrigerator in our tiny shared apartment was restitution for crashing in the middle of an all-nighter back in college. That image will never leave my memories or her rotation of embarrassing stories.

I make my way into the kitchen and squint as my eyes become accustomed to the light. Pouring myself a glass of water, I feel in my pocket for my phone. It's not there. I head back into the living room and see it sitting on the side table. I realize I left it there in my rush to return the key to Jake. It's blinking with a notification, and I see I have a text message sent to me hours ago. It's from Jake. I open it, half expecting a long, rambling explanation and plea for a second chance. Instead, there's only one sentence.

"It was Busch Gardens Tampa," I whisper.

Pulling up a search engine, I type in the name of the amusement park. It opened decades earlier than Animal Kingdom, well enough time for Jake to have visited with his family when he was 7. The African theme of the park means his memories of the elephants are accurate. It was just the park that wasn't. I instantly feel guilty for snapping at him the way I did without even giving him the benefit of the doubt. Going back into the bedroom, I repack my bag and make my way to his house. He should be there by now, and I look forward to surprising him.

But when I drive up to the house, it's completely dark. His car isn't in the driveway. It's possible the bar is still going at this hour, but he should be wrapping things up soon. I'll just wait inside for him. Using the key from my pocket, I let myself into the house and drop my bag at the door to the living room. I turn on several of the lights to chase away the shadows and flip on the TV to bring some sound to the still-ness. I haven't been in here enough to feel totally comfortable yet, but it will feel better when Jake's here.

Two reruns of a baking competition show later, Jake still isn't home. The patrons must have been harder to chase out into the cold tonight. Either that or he had several people he needed to escort home. I can only imagine after what I told him; he's going to be more on edge and want to keep track of as many of his customers as possi-ble. Depending on how many he can stuff into his truck and if he can convince one of the bartenders to help him, it may take some time to get them all home safely. He's going to be exhausted when he gets here, and likely starving. I go into the kitchen and explore the refrig-erator and cabinets trying to find something to make for him.

By the time the bowl of apples withering up in the corner of the counter has turned into pie, and a simple pasta sauce is simmering on the stove, it's late enough that I can't deny the worry creeping up the back of my neck. I wipe my hands on a towel I tucked into my belt loop and pick up my phone to call Jake. He doesn't answer. I call again, but there's still no answer. Telling myself he's probably just driving and doesn't want to be distracted by the call, I set my phone within easy reach and sit back down for more of the baking marathon. Ten minutes later, my phone rings.

Relief washes over me as I answer.

"Jake?"

"Sorry I missed your call. I was bringing some people home," he says.

His voice is cautious, unsure of what to expect from me.

"That's what I figured you were doing. Will you be home soon?" I ask.

There's a slight pause.

"Are you at my house?" he asks.

"Yes. Along with an apple pie and a pot of pasta. Which you should absolutely eat in that order," I tell him.

"I'm so glad you're there," he sighs.

"Me, too. I'm sorry about earlier. I just… "

"It's forgotten. The magic of apple pie has done its work."

"You haven't even tasted it," I laugh.

"I don't have to. I know it's perfect because you made it. And apple pie is my favorite, so you've already got a lot going for you," he tells me.

"Have any vanilla ice cream in the freezer at the bar?" I ask.

"I'll check. There's one more person waiting for a ride, and then I'll be there."

"See you soon."

I feel better as I hang up the phone. But as the minutes tick by and the headlights of his truck don't sweep over the wall, the good feeling starts fading. I try to push the returning worry away by getting up to boil the pasta, so it's hot and ready for him when he walks into the house. By the time it splashes into the colander, and I snag a wayward piece out of the drain, it has fully returned. Three unanswered calls turn the worry to fear.

The confrontation I witnessed between Jake and LaRoche comes back into my mind. My stomach twists into knots. Grabbing the key and my phone, I run out to my car and drive as fast as I can to Teddy's. I want to see cars and lights. People trying to convince Jake to let them in for one last drink to end the night. Jake standing outside, trying to help a drunken customer make his way to his truck so he can finally get him home.

Instead, there's nothing. The street is dark and empty; only the moonlight illuminating the sidewalk in front of the door. I park haphazardly and run to the door. It should be locked. Jake may be willing to leave his home unlocked, but even he secures his business before he goes home at night. But the door gives easily under my hand. I open it slowly. It's dark inside, only a glow from the exit sign at the very back, providing any break from the blackness.

I take a second to orient myself and envision the layout of the bar, remembering the position of each table and the plate of switches behind the bar. If I can navigate to the side of the bar, I can reach over and turn on the lights. I use the flashlight on my phone to provide enough light for my feet to follow and make it to the bar. My hand hits the switch and slips across it.

Lights burst on overhead. I press my other hand across my mouth to muffle my scream.

CHAPTER TWENTY-EIGHT

The blood shimmering like oil on my hand is still liquid enough to prove whoever turned off the light left the smears not too long ago. To my side, more splatters the bar and pools on the floor behind it. A handprint grasping the side of the kitchen door makes my heart tighten and my stomach turn. I shouldn't get near it. I know I shouldn't. Every bit of training and experience I've had tells me to step back and call for help, but I can't. I run to the door and push it open with my shoulder to avoid leaving any fingerprints. The light switch is by the side of the door, but I don't touch it. Instead, I take my phone out again and send the beam around the kitchen.

"Oh, god."

Smatters of blood create a path across the tile floor and toward the back door. Another handprint mars the brushed metal prep counter, and silverware scattered across the floor shows where Jake tried to grab at something to get control of himself and pulled down a rack of clean dishes. From where I'm standing, I can see the back door standing partially open and a sliver of the gravel parking area behind. I walk toward it gingerly, avoiding the blood and not touching anything. Leaning toward the crack in the door, I try to see anything beyond it. There's a small pool of blood just outside the door and a few drops leading a couple of feet away, but then nothing. He must have been dragged into a car, waiting just outside the door.

Running back through the bar and outside, I lock myself in my car and drive to the police station. Esther looks up at me when I storm through the door, but I don't even pause to acknowledge her. Keeping the hand coated with Jake's blood to my side, I wrench the door to the back open and stalk down the hallway. The aging receptionist is close behind me, but there's nothing she can do to stop me. I'm already at LaRoche's door.

"He's not here," Esther gasps when she catches up to me. "The chief isn't here."

I jiggle the handle of his office door, but it's locked. My jaw aches with tension as I stare her down.

"Where is he?"

"I don't know. He got a call a few hours ago and hasn't come back."

The words are no sooner out of her mouth than the front door opens, and LaRoche walks into the hallway. He's wearing a crisp, clean shirt and adjusts the buttons at one cuff as he comes toward us. I push past Esther and rush him, the intensity of my approach, forcing him back a step.

"Ms. Monroe, what… "

"What did you do to him?" I growl through gritted teeth. "What the fuck did you do to him?"

His face darkens.

"What are you talking about? What did I do to who?"

"Don't play that game with me. Not again. Not now. You know exactly who I'm talking about." He continues to stare at me in confusion, and I lift my bloodied hand to press it into his face. "Does this help refresh your memory?"

LaRoche takes hold of my wrist and looks at Esther.

"Thank you. I can take it from here. You go on back to your desk," he says.

She seems hesitant but does what he asks. As soon as she's back through the door, the chief pulls me over to his office. He unlocks the door and yanks me inside. I wrench my wrist from him and stand in the middle of the room. My muscles ache from wanting to tear him to pieces, but I have to leave him with the ability to speak if I want to find out what he did with Jake and possibly find him. There's a chance he's still alive. I have to do anything I can to keep him that way.

"Where is Jake?" I ask.

"Emma, you need to tell me what's going on," LaRoche says.

"I found the blood in Jake's bar. He's gone, and you know where he is," I tell him forcefully.

"Blood?" he asks. "There's blood at Teddy's? How long has it been since you've heard from Jake?"

"Three hours," I say. "Esther said you've been gone from the station for a few hours. I would think you would come up with a better story than you got a call."

LaRoche ignores me and opens the door to his office.

"Every available officer here, now!" he shouts. As if he leads a force of more than four. Nicolas and another officer appear in the hallway, and I meet eyes with the young officer before he turns back to the chief. "Get to Teddy's immediately. Call forensics from Hinkley. Now. Jake's missing, and Ms. Monroe says she found blood. Now! Go!"

They scramble away from him, and he turns back to me.

"Hinkley?" I ask.

"It's the nearest town with a forensic department. You need to tell me everything. What did you find?"

He looks genuinely concerned, but I don't buy it.

"I was supposed to meet him at his house tonight, but he didn't show up. I called him, and he said he had one more person looking for a ride home from the bar, then he'd be home. But more and more time passed, and he didn't get there, so I went looking for him," I explain.

"And you didn't find him?" LaRoche asks.

"No, but I found the bar unlocked and a hell of a lot of blood."

"Come on," he says, heading out of the office.

"I'm not going anywhere with you," I tell him.

"Yes, you are. We're going back to Teddy's. You are officially a part of an abduction and potential murder investigation."

I follow him out to the car and try to keep my breath calm as I sit beside him. My hand moves down to my phone in my pocket, readying myself to call my own number and record a voice message of whatever happens in the car if I need to.

"How long are you going to pretend?" I ask. "You're just going to put on this show and try to convince everyone you have no idea what's happening?"

He doesn't answer me.

When we get to the bar, he gets out and heads inside in a few long strides. I rush to follow him inside to see Nicolas and the other officer starting to record the scene. The forensic team hasn't arrived, but they've turned on more of the lights, and the extra illumination, along with separation from the immediate shock of the scene, makes me aware of even more blood throughout the space. It's soaked into the carpet and smeared across the bar. Fine blood spatter covers the mirror behind the liquor, and large drops are starting to dry on the glasses.

"Fuck," LaRoche mutters under his breath. "That's too much blood. No one could survive that."

"There are handprints," I point out. "One on the door leading into the kitchen and one on the counter. He was alive when he got into the kitchen."

"But not much longer," the chief says. "No one can bleed this much and keep going. Not without immediate medical intervention, a trans-fusion, and a miracle. I doubt he got any of those wherever he is."

"What do you want us to do after we photograph everything?" Nicolas asks.

An idea comes into my head, and I rush across the room toward Jake's office. LaRoche follows close behind me.

"What do you think you're doing? This is a crime scene. You already tromped through it enough. You can't just go wherever you want to," he grumbles as I push my way into the office. "What are you doing?"

"When I was on the phone with Jake, he told me he had one more person to give a ride home. The last time I was in here with him, he told me he takes meticulous notes of the people he brings home. He doesn't want to be held responsible for anything happening to them. So, he writes them all down," I search the top of his desk and find the notebook, "in this. I'm sure most, if any, of the people he brings home know about his notes. Probably a good thing. Some might not be so quick to accept his help if they knew it was going to be recorded."

I stop and stare down at the page of notations from tonight. LaRoche steps up beside me and looks down at the book.

"It's torn," he notes. "Half the page is gone."

"I guess you didn't want anyone seeing your name on his list," I snap, slamming the book closed and tossing it down onto the desk.

"You need to stop talking in riddles," he frowns.

"I'm not talking in riddles. I'm saying it straight out. You did this. You hurt Jake, and you took him somewhere, just like you did the others. Tell me, was this always your plan? Do you have some sort of checklist, and his name came up or was it spontaneous because of what he knows about you?" I ask.

My heart pounds so hard in my chest it might crack my ribs. Sweat beads on the back of my neck and stings in my palms. Being this close in the same space as LaRoche makes me sick, but I doubt he'll try anything with the other officers right outside. I just need him to say something, anything.

"Do you seriously fucking believe I have something to do with all this?" he demands.

"I saw the two of you arguing in the alley earlier! I know he told you."

"Told me what?" he asks.

"That I know what's going on."

"I'm not going to stand here and listen to this insanity. In case you missed it, there's been another probable murder."

He starts out of the office, but I can't let him go. Not yet.

"When will the hero complex kick in?" I rant. "When are you going to decide you've killed enough, and it's time to start solving all the mysteries so you can be the most impressive chief this town has ever seen? You'll get all the glory, all the recognition. All throughout the country, people are going to know your name. That's pretty appealing. When does that happen? Is Jake the last one?"

LaRoche slams the office door shut again and steps up so close to me I can feel his breath on my face.

"I didn't do this," he growls. "I don't have anything to do with whatever happened to Jake."

"Just like you didn't have anything to do with any of the others? With Cristela?" My mind churns, and I square off against him. "What about the baby? Is that what made you do it, or was it just a casualty of the circumstances?"

"How did you know about the baby?" he shouts.

A smile curls my lips. Got him.

"You just told me."

CHAPTER TWENTY-NINE

The door opens, and Nicolas looks in at us.

"Chief? I think you need to see this," he says.

LaRoche doesn't take his eyes from me.

"On my way. Have Daniel bring Ms. Monroe back to her cabin and get her statement."

I shake my head. "Absolutely not. I'm not going anywhere."

"Have him get all the details of everything she saw when she got here tonight and set up surveillance at her cabin. She needs her rest, and I want to make sure there is no movement in or out."

He's trapping me. He's locking me down.

"No," I insist. "I'll give my statement here. I don't need anyone to come back to the cabin with me."

"That's not your choice."

LaRoche walks out of the office, and seconds later, the other officer appears at the door. He gestures for me to step out in front of him, and my stomach sinks as I do it. In the time LaRoche and I were in the office, the forensic team from the other town had arrived, and now they are moving around the bar like bugs crawling around the scene. People in masks take pictures and swab blood spatters. A woman in a suit near the door mutters into a recorder in her hand. I feel like I'm looking through a window into a moment of my life. I've been on that side. I've watched forensic teams scramble through a new crime scene and gather evidence.

Now, I'm on the other side. Every bit of blood they gather is a piece of Jake. Every picture they take is capturing a space he moved through in some of his last moments. It's invasive and impersonal at the same time. I want to step through the looking glass and be on the other side. I can protect him from there. Maybe I could see more and know what happened if I just turned everything around and was standing beside that woman rather than walking out of the bar led by the officer assigned to control me.

I'm not thinking any more clearly when I get back to the cabin. Daniel insists on going inside before me and sweeping the cabin. It's useless. I know it is, and I can't help but feel he does, too. The one responsible for this isn't hunkering in a corner in the bedroom or hiding in one of the closets, waiting for me to be alone. Not that Daniel really knows that. Not the way I do.

When he finally lets me inside, I head straight for the kitchen to make a pot of tea. My body shakes from the inside, like my bones aren't strong enough to hold me up. Minutes later, I'm sitting in the living room as the young officer stares at me, taking careful notes of everything I say.

I describe getting to Teddy's and discovering the bloody scene. He has me go over the story three times. He's checking for consistency, making sure I give the same details and show the same emotion each time. He's not at all subtle about it. While some more mature and tenured officers might ask the same general question several times, slightly changing the wording or manipulating the connotation to see if I give a different answer, Daniel just asks me to say it all again.

As soon as I'm done, he stands up.

"I'll be outside if you need anything," he announces.

"You really don't have to do that," I say. "I'll be fine."

Daniel shakes his head. "Chief LaRoche assigned me to you. He wants me to watch over you and the cabin tonight, and that's what I'm going to do. Tonight has been very difficult for you, and you should get some rest."

He sounds like he's reading out of a brochure, but I can't really blame him. There's little to prepare someone for a situation like this.

"I don't think I'm going to be able to," I tell him.

"Try. If you need anything or are worried at any point, I'm right outside. Lock the door behind me."

He leaves, and I follow his instructions. As my hand pulls away from the lock, I see the streaks of Jake's blood. I tremble as I walk into the bathroom, shoving my hand beneath the faucet to wash it away. The water reconstitutes the dried stains, creating bright red swirls as it spins down the drain. My mind feels the same way. I can't stop thinking about LaRoche's revelation. Cristela Jordan was pregnant when she died. Or at least, he thought she was.

But that wasn't in the autopsy. Pulling out the papers, I look over them again. The notes from the medical examiner admit the body was so badly mangled he couldn't glean total information from them. The lower half of her body was largely intact when they found her, but her torso was crushed and nearly sliced through, destroying her organs. There was no way they would be able to determine a pregnancy unless she was already far enough along for the fetus to be visible.

LaRoche was convinced, though. And the way he asked me how I knew about it tells me he wasn't too pleased at the idea of co-parenting with a woman he didn't even want people to know he was seeing. Far too many women are killed because of an unexpected, unwanted pregnancy. It wouldn't be a leap to think that would lead LaRoche to kill her, even if there was the slim possibility he cared for her at one time.

For the next few hours, I pace through the cabin, occasionally glancing out the window at Daniel's car. Each time I do, he looks right back at me through the windshield. He doesn't leave. He doesn't sleep. And neither do I.

My phone rings just after the sun comes up. It's the last person I want to talk to, but I can't avoid him.

"Hello?"

"What the hell is going on, Griffin?" Creagan demands. "I turn on the news this morning to find out I've sent an agent undercover to find a serial killer and someone else died."

"He's missing," I point out quickly, feeling the strange compulsion to put that out into the world. "There's no body."

"But you know there's a lot of blood because you're the one who found the scene," he says. "What was going on between the two of you?"

"What do you mean?" I ask.

"Everyone's saying the two of you were an item. I didn't send you on this job so you could fill the void in your life. You're not being paid to date the townsfolk."

"I don't have a void in my life, Creagan. Jake and I have gotten close since I got here, I'll admit that. But if it wasn't for him, I wouldn't know a fraction of what I do about this town and the people in it. He's made it possible for me to be accepted around here so I can do my job," I tell him.

"And now he's another victim. You didn't do your job. I knew you weren't ready to go back out into the field. You got there and were too distracted to do what you needed to do, and it's cost the town another life. I'm shutting this whole thing down. Pack up. As soon as the police there say you're free to go, you're coming back."

Panic jumps into my throat.

"No," I say defiantly.

"Excuse me? What did you just say?"

"I said no. I'm not coming back there now, and you're not shutting this down. I'm close to getting you exactly what you need," I say.

"It doesn't matter. You had your time," he tells me.

"And you're going to give me more," I push back. "This isn't just about the original victims. This is personal now. I've been in touch with Eric, and as soon as I know we can put together a strong enough case, I'll call you in."

"I'm not just going to leave you on your own anymore," Creagan says. "Look where it's gotten you. The police department wasn't doing its job investigating, but at least the bodies stopped piling up."

"Two more days," I demand through gritted teeth, trying to stop myself from lashing out at him for the way he is dismissing the victims. "Give me two more days. If I haven't done what I came here to do, I'll go back, and you can handle the case however you see fit. But this is mine. I've been putting in the work, and now someone close to me has been victimized. I'm not walking away from this."

Creagan hesitates but finally relents.

"Two days, Griffin. But know if you come back here, and I have to fix the mess you left behind; your badge is mine."

The call ends, and cold, steely resolution flows over me. I take a fast shower in a blast of stinging water to wake myself up and clear my mind, then get dressed and walk out of the cabin. Daniel opens the door and stands up, pulling a blanket close around him.

"The night's over. You don't have to watch me anymore," I tell him.

"The chief hasn't given me instructions," he says.

"I am. You can go home now. I'm sure your shift was over a long time ago."

He watches me walk over to my car and takes a few steps closer.

"You aren't supposed to leave," he says. "LaRoche says no one was supposed to go in or out."

"You can take it up with him. I'm sure he'll be where I'm going," I reply.

Unlocking my door, I get into my car and drive toward Teddy's. Daniel is close behind, and I can see him talking into his radio, undoubtedly telling LaRoche I've left the cabin and am on the move. It doesn't matter. He's not holding me anymore. I've gotten answers to some of my questions, and then those answers just created more questions. I'm working on borrowed time now, and I'm not willing to give up my badge for someone like this man.

Police tape draped across the front of the bar isn't a deterrent. I duck under it and walk past the officer coming to stop me and into the bar. LaRoche stands close with a man in a suit beside the bar, and he looks up when I walk in. Excusing himself, he comes toward me with an expression that says he's losing patience with me.

"You are supposed to be at your cabin," he growls. "Daniel was supposed to ensure that."

"He did. He kept me there all night. But it's morning now, and I'm not staying there anymore. I want to know more about Cristela Jordan."

LaRoche looks around almost frantically and leans closer.

"Someone is going to hear you," he hisses.

"Is that what you were worried about?" I ask. "You didn't want anyone to know about the two of you?"

"Come with me," he says, guiding me toward Jake's office again. He shuts the door and turns his glare directly at me. "I don't know what is wrong with you, but you need to let go of this notion that I have anything to do with Jake's disappearance, Cristela's death, or any of the others."

"Her autopsy doesn't say she was pregnant," I point out. "Did you do that on purpose? When you had her tied up, did you make sure you destroyed any evidence of the baby so no one would find out and possibly do testing? You knew if they did, it would show you were the father of her baby."

"Tied her up?" he asks. "What are you talking about? They found Cristela's body by the train tracks. She wasn't bound."

"She had marks on her and a bruise around her neck consistent with something tied around it. Like a dog collar. Convenient, one was tied to a tree not far from where they found her and then disappeared. I heard you have a dog you like to walk around out in those woods."

"I have a dog I like to walk out there. Not one I like to tie up out there. I would never put my dog on a collar attached to a tree. I don't know what you think you know, but it's far off base. Cristela thought she was pregnant. She told me just a few days before she died. We hadn't even really had the chance to talk about it. Neither one of us were expecting that, but it's not like we're teenagers. I'm not afraid of my responsibilities."

"But you're afraid of people knowing who you're sleeping with," I point out.

"There's a difference between being afraid and not wanting my personal life broadcasted out to the entire town. I don't want to settle down. At least not now. So, I keep a girl or two on the side. That might not make me the most upstanding man in the world, but it also doesn't make me a murderer. I would never hurt Cristela. And I had nothing to do with Jake's disappearance."

"And how am I supposed to believe that?" I ask.

"Because I was with Andrea last night. You can call her if you want to. She's still at the hotel."

CHAPTER THIRTY

I feel like all words, thoughts, and sense have been pulled out of me for an instant. I blink and shake my head, trying to bring myself back into the moment.

"What?" I ask.

"Yeah. Go ahead, call her. I'm sure you know the number to the hotel by now. If not, it's in my phone. I'd be happy to give it to you. We were in room two-twelve. She checked in yesterday and is planning on checking out this morning. But that might change because of all this."

"You were with her?"

"Yes."

"All evening?" I ask.

"Since the afternoon. I came back to the station long enough to fill out some paperwork. Esther must have thought I was here longer, but if you look at my computer, you'll see the times I signed on and off."

"I saw you here," I point out.

"Yes. After I left the station, I came by here before going back to the hotel. I needed to talk to Jake about what he told you."

"What he told me?" I ask, confused.

LaRoche narrows his eyes, his head tilting slightly.

"You mean, he didn't tell you about Andrea and Cristela?"

"Jake knew?" I ask, startled by the revelation.

"Of course, he knew. He helped me. When Cristela came into town, Jake brought her to the hotel. He made sure it seemed like he was giving her a ride home to keep her safe. They would leave the bar and go around the back way to the hotel. If you check his records, I'm sure you'll see her name."

"She checked into the hotel days before she died, and there's no signature when she checked out," I tell him.

"That's because I checked us out. I was waiting for her at the hotel. She was supposed to do just as she always did. Go to Teddy's, spend a couple hours there, then have Jake bring her to me. But she never showed up."

"At the hotel?" I ask.

"At Teddy's. She left the hotel to go back to her house because she thought she left something. Jake called me hours later to tell me she never made it to the bar. I dropped the hotel key in the deposit box beside the desk, took her stuff with me, and left. I figured her boyfriend caught wind of what was going on or something, and I'd hear from her within a day or two. That happened before. But then I didn't hear from her. Then…"

"They found her body," I finish his sentence. He nods. "And when they did, you didn't point out you were with her? That you had her belongings or were supposed to see her that night?"

"I didn't make the best choices. I know that. But I didn't know how else to handle it," he says.

"I guess making too big of a deal out of the whole thing would make it harder for you to keep up your thing with Andrea," I muse. "Wouldn't want her knowing your last fling ended up dead."

"My attraction to Andrea wasn't planned. But I shouldn't have to justify it. I told you already my relationship with Cristela wasn't committed. It was consensual fun for both of us. That doesn't mean I didn't care about her well-being, but I wasn't obligated to her."

My skin crawls, listening to him. He disgusts me even more now than he did before.

"A small town is plagued by disappearances and murders, and the police department can't seem to figure it out or make it stop. Then it turns out one of the victims was screwing the police chief. You don't think that should have warranted more discretion than just going to a hotel a few towns over with your new friend with benefits?" I ask.

"Look, I know this looks bad. That's why I didn't say anything. It could have put my entire career in jeopardy."

"I don't know if you really should have been so worried. It's not like your corrupt father had any problems."

"Excuse me?" he asks, his voice lowering angrily. "What did you say about my father?"

"Jake told me about the problems his father had with Cole Barnes and with the rest of the town. He said he was an honest businessman, and that rubbed some people, including your father, the wrong way."

"John Logan was a lot of things, but an honest businessman wasn't one of them. Now, I don't know what happened between him and Barnes, but it had nothing to do with Barnes swindling anybody or my father covering anything up," he says.

"I don't understand," I frown.

LaRoche seems to let go of some of the tight, angry tension built up through his shoulders and along his spine.

"Sometimes, we tell stories to make things seem better than they really are. It's easier for Jake to think of the rest of the town having a grudge against his father because he was the honest and upstanding one among the riffraff. But I'll be the one to tell you when there were questions about how his father died, it wasn't necessarily who might have been willing to help him along to the other side, but who wouldn't have. Now Jake's gone, too, and I have to be the one to figure out if they have anything to do with each other."

"Why would you think that?" I ask.

"You're the one who pointed out to Cole Barnes he wouldn't have been strong enough to haul those bones up to his property by himself.

I find it hard to believe someone would do that just for show," LaRoche explains.

"Who else knew Jake's father helped Barnes build that shed?" I ask.

"What shed?" he asks.

"The one where the bones were found."

"How did you know about that? That wasn't released to the public."

This takes me slightly aback.

"We must have heard it at the crime scene when Jake ran up."

"Probably. Those investigators aren't exactly known for being discreet. I would appreciate if you didn't share that with anyone. We're purposely keeping that bit of information out of the media. Now, you need to leave."

"I'll tell you now there's no point in putting another officer outside the cabin. They aren't going to stop me," I say.

"No, Emma. I didn't mean leave here. I meant leave Feathered Nest."

"Excuse me?"

So much has just come at me I think I must have misheard him.

"The danger we all hoped had moved on is obviously back. Until we find out who is responsible for these disappearances and killings, everyone in this town is at risk. I'm under enough pressure trying to protect the people of the town who have been here through all of this. I can't be responsible for you, too. Especially when you consider how close you and Jake were getting. You're too unpredictable and emotional about this. You're just going to get in the way," he says.

"I don't care how *emotional* you think I am. I'm not going anywhere, and there's nothing you can do to force me. If you had done your job in the first place, this wouldn't be happening. I'm not leaving until Jake is found."

I pull open the door to the office, but LaRoche steps up close to the opening, so I can't go through.

"Stay out of our way, Emma. You don't know what you're getting yourself into," he warns.

"You have no idea who you're talking to," I tell him, and push past him and outside.

For the next three hours, I drive slowly around Feathered Nest. I have no idea exactly what I'm looking for, but I'm waiting for something, anything to stand out at me. LaRoche did his best to pretty-talk his way out of my suspicion, but I still don't trust him. Call me crazy, but I don't often find myself taking the word of an unethical, devious, lying, manipulative womanizer as gold. He's unreliable, to give him the very best, and I can't bring myself to wholly believe anything he says.

But some of what he said has started gears turning in my brain. No matter how deep I've explored in to Feathered Nest, there always seems to be another layer just beneath. My car stopped in front of the cemetery almost automatically. I can't even remember driving here. My mind was somewhere else, and my hands brought me along in autopilot. I climb out and walk back through the huge gate to the tombstones I've come to know. My eyes anticipate the names and carvings before I even get to the graves, and I know when I'm steps away from the edge of John Logan's empty resting place.

Just behind him and slightly to the side is Melanie. Briefly, Jake's wife, but his devotion for a lifetime. I look around at the surrounding graves. I haven't paid much attention to them in the other times I've visited the cemetery, and now I'm noticing something strange about them. None of the rest of them carry the Logan name. I walk several paces away from Melanie's grave and across the yard to either side, but find no other stones suggesting they belong to a member of Jake's family. I suddenly remember he mentioned a family cemetery, which is where they buried his grandmother. I assume that means the rest of his family is there. But if that's the case, why are John and Melanie out here?

Above me, rain clouds I hadn't even noticed forming crack open, and the first droplets of a chilling winter storm fall down on me. The sensation of them soaking through my clothes and slipping across my skin reminds me of the first time I came here with Jake. Standing there shivering beneath the umbrella as the rain mixed with the tears falling down his face and into the remnants of his father's destroyed grave.

The rain starts coming faster, so I hurry back toward my car. I can't remember what I did with the umbrella after that day. I probably tossed it back into Jake's car. He didn't have his truck that day. I found the umbrella tucked under the passenger seat. I look around inside my car but find nothing to block the rain, so I abandon any further exploration of the cemetery and head back to the cabin. There's little hope the call ringing through my phone as I will my cold, stiff hands to unlock the door is a conversation I actually want to have, so I delay answering it as long as I can. It doesn't stop ringing, and finally, I'm inside standing over the furnace when I answer.

"Hello, Eric," I say.

"I heard what happened. Are you alright?" he asks.

"No," I answer. "Is anyone ever really alright when someone asks that?"

"Probably not," he admits.

"What did Creagan tell you?"

"That the guy you've been seeing was murdered, and you have two days before we have to take back over for you."

"Shit," I grumble, putting my face down in my hand and rubbing away the exhaustion grinding like sand on my eyes.

"What are you going to do?" he asks.

"I'm going to spend the next two days finishing what I started. I can't just let him win."

"Creagan?"

"Creagan. LaRoche. Any of them," I mutter.

"You sound tired," Eric points out.

"I didn't sleep last night."

"You need to get some rest."

"I can't. I don't have the time."

"Time isn't going to mean shit if you're not even going to be functional enough to know what you've figured out. You need to get some sleep. Go wrap up in one of those amazing quilts you kept emailing me about when you first got there and get a few hours of rest," he instructs.

Just as I open my mouth to answer him, the lights around me shut off. The furnace lets out a mournful groan and goes silent. I let out an involuntary gasp and press my hand to my chest to calm my heartbeat.

"Damn it," I sigh.

"What's wrong?" Eric asks.

"The power just went out. Fun little habit of this place when it rains or the wind picks up. Just hang tight, I'm taking you with me to fix it."

I walk through the house into the back hallway. Since Eric is on the phone, I can't use the flashlight feature and have to rely on what little glow is coming from the screen to help me through. I get through the laundry room and down the two steps into the bathroom, open the closet, and feel around for the breaker box. When I finally find it, I throw the switches, and the lights come back on.

"Did you get it?" Eric asks in response to my sigh.

"Yeah. That is such a pain in the ass. Someone must have gotten a good laugh planning where to put that thing when they built this house."

I stop at the dryer and open it to pull out the fresh load of laundry. The first is the quilt. I don't bother to fold it, knowing I'm probably going to be using it soon. Next is a ball of t-shirts and pajamas. Finally, I get to my pants.

"Did someone at least show you around when you got there so you would know where stuff was?" Eric asks.

I turn my pants over to adjust the cuffs, and as I fold them, I notice loose strings. I follow them to a snag in the fabric at the back of one leg.

"No," I say. "I just had to figure it out."

"Sounds like fun," Eric says sarcastically.

I nod, even though he can't see me. My head buzzes, and my lips tingle. I reach over into the basket and pull out the unfolded quilt. My hand runs over the fabric, each of its uneven pieces unique, pattern against pattern, color against color.

"Eric?"

"Yeah?"

"I don't need the two days. Start getting the team ready to roll in."

"Why? What's going on?"

I stuff my feet back into my boots and slip into my coat.

"You're just going to have to trust me."

CHAPTER THIRTY-ONE

*S*ometimes *we tell stories to make things seem better than they really are.*

    I step out onto the porch and walk over to the side. Holding onto one of the supports with one hand, I climb up onto the railing so I can reach the roof. My fingertips run over the brown paint and feel the rough patches where someone covered up deep holes. Holes big enough for the hooks to suspend a porch swing.

We'd spend all afternoon hunting for eggs she hid in the yard.

I go back into the cabin and make my way to the back door. Like the ceiling of the porch, the door has seen many coats of paint in an effort to liven it back up and take away some of the signs of wear and tear. But the olive green has done little to conceal deep gashes along the side of the door under the doorknob. They're long and even, uniformly spaced.

That's Mocha. She was obsessed with that dog. My father found him as a puppy in the woods. He never was too interested in being domesticated.

I pull open the door and step out into the backyard. The rain has slowed down, but I still pull up the hood of my coat to stay warm. I walk out to the edge of the yard and push the branches of bushes away to see the round, browned spot of matted down weeds where a birdbath once stood. I look back at the house. In my mind, I can see a woman standing on the steps wearing a floral dress.

That dress was her favorite.

Over the years, the dress would have faded and started to look worn, the floral pattern becoming more muted and the fibers loosening and becoming weaker with every wash and wear. But that made it perfect for the day when she cut it up and added it to her bag to stitch it into a quilt.

My mind goes to the quilt in the laundry basket, and the pair of pants discarded beside it. The tips of my fingers can still feel the sharp point of metal under the seat that snagged my pants. That piece of metal could cause a serious injury to the back of the leg of someone dragged out of the passenger seat.

Better to have your good memories than someone around who doesn't want to make any more of them.

I take off into the woods, heading directly for the path that leads to the railroad tracks.

How much of it was real? How much was his fantasy?

It wasn't coincidences. The cabin didn't just seem familiar or sound like the stories Jake told. It was his grandmother's cabin. It was the place where he hid and found comfort when he was a child. The woods where he played with his siblings.

But was it? There are no graves, no history. No one has mentioned his family except for his father. What is real, and what did he create?

My head spins as I make it to the path. I know what it's like to not be able to trust my own mind. I know I can't rely on what I think are my memories. For every story of what happened to my mother or where my father might have gone, there was another one to contradict the first, and a third to retell the second. Sometimes, I never know what's really real. Could that be what's happening with Jake? Does he know what he's crafted in his mind? He convinced himself so much of the life he told me about, enough to go after Cole Barnes, threatening to tear him to pieces with his bare hands. All based on the kind of man he told himself his father was.

But could that have fed him into the hands of a killer? What did he retell, what did he change or uncover that made it necessary to silence him? What story would end that way? If I can figure that out, maybe I can find him and the others. Maybe no one else has to die.

Rather than heading down the path toward the train tracks, I start in the direction I've never gone. It weaves deep into the woods, quickly becoming narrower and more neglected the further I walk. The path seems to go on for miles but isn't leading anywhere. It twists and dips, occasionally turning back on itself for a few paces before bending around again. I want to give up, but I can't. I've come this far, and I need to see what's on the other end. Finally, ahead of me, the thick trees start to thin out. I can see what looks like a clearing. When I get to the end of the path, I immediately feel like I've stepped back in time.

The house in front of me is nothing like anything I've ever seen in real life. It's sagging and dilapidated, but through the rot and neglect, I can see what a strong and beautifully built home it was once. I don't know how long it's been standing here, but it looks like it's seen centuries. The area surrounding it holds similar remnants of another time. An unusable, rusted pump sits at the edge of a well. A trough once filled with food for animals of some kind is now filled with grime and fallen leaves.

I take out my phone and call LaRoche.

"Have you found him?" I ask.

"Have you left Feathered Nest?" he asks.

"Have you found Jake?"

"I told you to stay out of our way, Emma."

"There's a house in the woods behind the cabin."

"It's been searched," he tells me.

"What is this place?" I ask.

"It used to be a house. It was there long before the town even was. I can't ever remember someone living there. It was abandoned a long time ago and then condemned. No one lives there. No one goes there," he explains.

"Where did Jake grow up?" I ask.

"What?"

"Where did Jake grow up? One of the bartenders at Teddy's told me he knew him when he was much younger, but he never went to visit his house or anything. He didn't mention his siblings."

"I didn't know Jake had any siblings. All I knew of him was he was John's son. I always knew of them living in the apartment up over the tavern."

"How about his grandmother? Did you know her?"

"What grandmother?" LaRoche asks.

"He never told you about his grandmother?"

"No. Like I said, all I knew of him was he was John's son. It was just the two of them. He didn't talk much when he was young, but sometimes when he did, he would mention his mother. It was always in passing and sometimes sounded like he was talking about the past. We all just assumed his mother died when he was really little, and he hadn't quite gotten over it."

"Thanks. Tell me if you find out anything," I say.

My phone starts to crackle. The connection is becoming weaker, the closer I get to the house. It's like the years looming around the place are sucking me in, closing out everything from the outside world.

"You are not a part of this investigation. You still need to leave Feathered Nest," LaRoche says.

I hang up and look around. Jake told me so much about playing in the woods when he was younger. There's no way he could have been so active if he really did spend all his time in the apartment over the tavern. I notice details about the house that remind me of stories he told me and the memories he shared. They don't sit well with me. Some of his memories are concrete, like the stories of the cabin and the details of this house. But others are fleeting, not seeming to have any anchor in reality.

I think back on everything Jake told me, trying to pinpoint anything that might help. I let the stories of his childhood home draw me into the house. This is where he lived, hidden away from the rest of a world that barely even knew he existed. I know when I get through the front door, there will be an entryway and then a sitting room to one side.

The door gives way after only a firm push. I step into the damp, musty interior of the house. It's obvious no one has lived in this home for many years. Old furniture and belongings scatter rooms caked in dust and dirt. In some places, the forest has started reclaiming the house. Vines grow along the walls, and trees sprout up in between the cushions of a couch. Somewhere in the distance, a skittering sound tells me animals are more than happy to claim this as their space.

There are a few signs of a cursory search by the local police. It's not a surprise that it wasn't very thorough. They know this place from one perspective, and that perspective keeps them from considering anything any different. They are exceptional to work with when it comes to local places and people because they know well enough to notice when things are amiss. But they can also rely too heavily on this knowledge and stop, not thinking to go any further.

But I won't stop. This is where I'm supposed to be. Jake's stories brought me here. Now they'll tell me why.

As I make my way through the rooms, I try to find details or places that spark memories of comments he made or stories he told me. So many of these stories were told about the woods outside. There's not much to go on inside.

But I eventually find a door leading down into the basement. The heavy, dank smell is oppressive. An uncomfortable chill rolls through me. I hold my breath and tense myself, trying to keep my wits about me. My phone provides enough light to get me through the dirty space. Cobweb-encrusted shelves sag under the weight of ancient cans and bottles of food. Crates and boxes hunker in the corners, their contents unknown.

Whenever it felt like it was all too much, and I just wanted to be alone with my thoughts, I used to hide in my secret room. It was like a fort, only so much better.

This basement can't possibly be it. There's nothing comforting or fort-like about it, and it's certainly not secret. There has to be another place, a secret compartment or hidden room. This is a very old house, and it's not unheard of for places like this to have secret rooms, tunnels, and compartments. They were used for all kinds of purposes but were often forgotten when those purposes were no longer important. That left only the family and those very familiar with the house to know the hidden places were even there.

I keep walking through, my ears straining for any sound more than the occasional scuttle of rodent feet and the drip of water from where raindrops have worn the structure down over the years and finally broken through. Toward the back of the basement, I find a large wardrobe pushed up against the wall. It seems so out of place I can't resist walking up to it. The streaked mirror shows the reflection of my flashlight and my scrutinizing eyes. There has to be something more to this piece of furniture than just a wardrobe.

I run my hands along the edge of the base, then up over the curved top. My fingertips hit something uneven, and I move it until it shifts and depresses down into the wood. With a slight creak, the wardrobe moves out of place just a few inches. I grab onto the edge and pull it away from the wall.

Right in front of me is a narrow door built into the wall. It opens to a set of steps leading down into a sub-basement, possibly a storm cellar designed to be out of the way. At the bottom of the steps is another door. But I immediately recognize that this door is not original to the rest of the house. It's newer, added to the end of the steps to create a separation between the entry and what lies beyond.

My hand hesitates on the doorknob for only a few breaths before I push it open. The smell knocks me back onto the steps, and I sag against them, trying to catch my breath, trying to wrap my head around what I saw in the brief instant I stood in the sub-basement.

In that instant, I know what happened to all the missing people.

CHAPTER THIRTY-TWO

My hands grip the step on either side of me, squeezing hard enough to make my knuckles ache. I'm shaking as I draw in a breath, trying to ignore the thick smell that comes along with the air. It forces itself heavily into my lungs and stings at the back of my throat. My stomach turns, rolling until I think I'll be sick, but I force it down. I have to stay in control. This is why I'm here. It's why I was sent. I have to know the truth.

Holding my phone tightly, I stand and open the door again. I take measured, cautious steps into the room. I need to be careful, aware of my surroundings, so I don't possibly damage or contaminate anything. Almost as soon as I'm all the way in the room, the door behind me automatically swings shut. The sound of it clicking into place hits me in the center of the chest, and I throw myself against it, desperately grasping the knob on this side. It doesn't move. Unlocked on the outside, this door is designed to lock anyone who steps past it inside the room.

I wonder if that's what happened to any of the missing people who are no longer missing.

In a structure this old, I don't think I can hope for a simple light switch beside the door to give me any light. Instead, I shine the flashlight of my phone up above my head and sweep it back and forth. The light catches a variety of strange objects before it finally finds what I was looking for. The beaded metal strand hangs just low enough for me to catch it with the tips of my fingers if I stand as high on my toes as I can possibly reach. Even at my height, it was designed to be turned on by someone taller.

Pulling the chain doesn't just turn on the single bulb overhead. It also activates several strands of Christmas lights, a lamp, and a vintage Lite Brite game set up on a table several paces away from me. The room is larger than I would have anticipated, and the light creates a brighter pool in the middle before melting out to shadows at the edges and corners.

And all around me, the light illuminates the bodies.

I've walked into scenes of corpses many times. I've reported to mass burials, bodies hidden away in walls, and those long dead strewn across fields, streets, and floors. But I've never experienced anything like this. The bodies aren't just lying on the floor or on tables. They haven't been stored here. They've been posed.

All around the room, more than a dozen bodies have been taxidermized and manipulated into poses creating vignettes of everyday life.

In one corner, four sit and stand around a Christmas tree. A middle-aged man has his hand rested against the branches of the tree as if setting an ornament into place, while a woman sits on a chair at his side, poised as if ready to hand him the next decoration. A young man and woman are on a shaggy rug wrapping a gift.

Several feet away, another version of the family sits around a dining room table, frozen around a meal. Fighting to control my revulsion, I walk up to the table and touch the loaf of bread sitting among platters of food. The food is hard and cold beneath my touch.

I'm suddenly aware of the weight of my phone still in my hand. I turn off the flashlight and try to dial for help. There's nothing. I put in Eric's number, but it still won't connect. I have no service down here. Fear starts to sink into my mind, taking over my thoughts. I'm locked down in this hidden basement room with corpses crafted into some mind-boggling playland. Without phone service. Without anything to save me.

I have to stay calm. I turn on the camera on my phone and start taking pictures of everything I see, starting with the vision of Christmas. Forcing my emotions down and pulling the trained agent up to the surface, I block out the grisly reality of what is around me and break it down into its elements, turning it into evidence and exhibits. This lets me step up close to each of the bodies and take pictures of their faces, their hands, the wire contraptions supporting them in their chosen positions. Some of the bodies are far older than others and are starting to degrade despite the efforts at preserving them. Their features are warped, and their hair replaced by wigs.

But I can still recognize them. As I move from the Christmas scene to the dinner, the images of the missing people I've stared at for weeks flash through my head. I see them smiling in life, living moments that belonged to them, and superimpose those images onto the cold, taut faces forced into these false realities.

From the dinner scene, I move to an older man and young man playing a board game. From there, an older woman and younger woman holding teacups as they lean toward each other as if in conversation. I take picture after picture, needing to record every inch of this place. It's the last of the scenes, the smallest and simplest, that is the most horrifying to me. In this vignette, a young woman who looks very different from the others sits in a rocking chair, cradling a wrapped baby in her arms. My hand shakes as I reach for the edge of the blanket. I don't want to see what's beneath it. It's horrific enough to see what he was capable of with the adults strewn around this room. To think he could kill an innocent baby just for the sake of using it as a prop creates a visceral reaction inside me.

But I have to be able to photograph it. I need to record the proof and get it to someone else, so no matter what happens to me or to this room, someone else will know.

In one movement, I pull the corner of the blanket away from the baby's head. A shock of bright blonde hair tied with a pink bow sits above wide, vibrant blue eyes. The breath I didn't even realize I was holding gushes out of me. It's a doll. The woman is cradling a doll.

As the initial shock and horror of the discovery fades, and my mind clears, I start noticing odd features of some of the bodies. They don't look exactly right, as if parts of them are not proportioned correctly or are positioned oddly.

When I've gotten all the way around the room and taken pictures of every one of the bodies, I attach them to an email to send to Eric.

Without service, it doesn't send. I let out an exasperated sound.

The smell of the room and the feeling of the cold air on my skin is getting into my mind again. It twists my thoughts and steals my control. Time keeps slipping by. I try the door again. Tugging and twisting at the doorknob is useless. It's securely locked. I try several hard kicks to the area around the lock. I try slamming my shoulder into the center of the door. None of it works. It's solid and thick. It doesn't yield to me after several attempts, and finally, I step back, rubbing my throbbing shoulder as I look around the room for another option.

There has to be a way to get out of here. This can't just be a sealed cube of stone.

There are no windows. I'm far underground, beneath even the basement of the house. I look for another door, a vent, anything that might offer a way to either get out of the room or alert someone I'm here.

An hour passes and then another. Every few seconds, I look down at my phone, hoping somehow my service will return, but no matter where I'm standing, there's nothing. No connection to the outside world.

Another hour passes, and then a fourth. The day is slipping past. I wonder if anyone has noticed I'm gone. LaRoche told me to leave. Maybe not hearing from me or seeing me will tell him I did what he asked rather than raise any alarm.

The fifth hour is coming to a close when I hear a sound above me. My heart jumps. The sound of footsteps on the stairs right outside the door is loud in my ears. The doorknob turns impossibly, torturously slow. I duck into the dark corner behind the Christmas tree. Out of sight. A scented ornament tucked deep into the branches is old and nearly dry, but gives off the very faint scent of pine, and I find refuge in it. From this vantage point, I can watch the door.

The door opens, and Jake's tall silhouette appears in the doorway. His expression is frozen and unreadable as he turns his head slowly, sweeping his eyes across the entire room. I stay perfectly still, holding my breath and keeping my hands away from the tree, so I don't accidentally shake it. One hand keeps the door propped open as he looks around. It's only a few steps away. If I can distract him and move fast enough, I can get past him through the door and out of the basement.

Moving as carefully as I possibly can, I slip one of the ornaments off the nearest tree branch. When his head turns in the opposite direction, I throw the ornament to the other side of the basement. It smashes against the wall in an impossibly loud shatter, and Jake's head snaps toward it. He takes a step in the direction of the sound but hesitates. His gaze scours the room again, searching each of his displays with the familiar, scrutinizing eye of an artist and the exacting precision of a butcher.

I inch around to the side of the tree to put myself in a better position to run for the door. Fear creates droplets that slide down my face like ice and pool in my palms as I ready my shaking body for the sprint. My phone tucked away in my pocket to free both of my hands; I release the old metal hook on the top of another ornament. This time I aim for the corner of the room diagonal from him. I throw it, but it doesn't sail directly into the wall the way I intended. Instead, it hits the game board set up on the table and sends pieces skittering down onto the floor.

Jake draws in a sharp breath and takes a protective step toward the scene. That movement is my cue. I dart out from behind the tree, heading for the door.

But Jake has already stepped away and released it, allowing it to swing shut.

I throw my body toward it. I just need to get out. It doesn't matter how. I hit the ground and scramble toward the opening in the door. A second later, the door crushes down on my hips, sending a sharp pain through me.

His rough hands grab my ankles. I cry out, thrashing against Jake's grip. I take hold of the doorknob and use it for leverage to pull myself up, but his hand moves to my thigh, keeping me from moving the rest of the way out of the door. I snap my elbow back, striking him as hard as I can. In the brief second his hold on me loosens, I try to shove myself the rest of the way through the door. I know he has a key, but all I need is a chance.

I don't get it. The door falls on my fingers, crushing them. I scream and pull my hand back, making the door shut and lock. Pressing my hands flat to the door, I drop my forehead against it and let out a sob.

Jake's hand runs up my thigh and onto my hip, then traces its way over my waist until it brushes my hair away from my neck so he can touch a kiss to my sweaty skin.

CHAPTER THIRTY-THREE

"Don't touch me," I say, my voice calm and even. I don't want him to mistake for a second what I'm saying to him.

"But, Emma, I'm so happy you're here," he croons.

I almost don't recognize his voice. It sounds different than it ever has, but I can't put my finger on exactly why.

"Let me out, Jake."

"I can't. I've been waiting too long to have you here with me," he says.

The door remains firmly closed, but he at least relents and steps back from me so I can turn around. A large bandage wrapped around his arm has tinges of red at the edges. Despite everything, a surge of worry rushes up in my chest. I'm sickened by my own reaction.

"The blood in the bar," I say, gesturing with my eyes toward the bandage.

Jake nods and runs his hand along it.

"I've been slowly collecting it for a while now, but I knew I needed as much fresh as I could spare when it was time. But don't worry, the cut will heal. I've gotten very skilled at stitching up wounds."

The comment makes bile roll into my throat.

"There was too much blood," I tell him. "Everyone thinks you're dead."

He smiles. "They do? That's perfect. It's exactly what I want."

"I don't understand. Why fake your own death? Eventually, you're going to be found," I say.

"That's just what I intend to happen. But I won't need to be found. I'm going to make it easy on everybody and show back up in Feathered Nest in a few days."

"Why? Why would you go through all this if you were just going to give yourself up?" I ask.

I shift to the side, and my crushed hand hits the door. Hissing at the pain, I pull it against my chest and cover it protectively with the other. Jake rushes up to me; concern etched on his face.

"Oh, sweetheart. Does it hurt? I'm so sorry. That wasn't supposed to happen. Nothing was supposed to happen to you. I would never want to hurt you," he says. "That was never what I wanted."

"You shot at me," I spit. "You tried to kill me."

"No," he frowns, shaking his head. "No, I never would have let you get hit. Those bullets were nowhere near you."

"Then why?" I ask.

"To keep you guessing. So you felt like you were on the right track. From the very beginning, I knew you were suspicious of LaRoche. It was perfect. I couldn't have even planned it that well. That's what all this," he gestures at the bandage on his arm, "was for. You weren't supposed to come after me. You were supposed to be in Feathered Nest with the others, searching for me, and be the one I dragged myself to when I escaped."

"Escaped?" I ask.

"Yes. You see, when you showed up, it was like I was being given a new chance. I could have a life again. Have everything I've wanted. But that meant ending the mystery for good. When you started digging around into it, the ideal solution just showed itself. If you already thought LaRoche was responsible, I would make sure everyone agreed with you. The dots were already there. I just had to help connect them."

"You didn't write Cristela in your notebook the last night she was at the bar," I say. "But you drove her."

Jake laughs. "No one else knows that. How do you?"

"The piece of metal under your passenger seat. It snagged my pants the day we went to the cemetery. When I was looking at a picture of Cristela's body, I noticed a cut on the back of her leg in the same spot. She caught her leg on that piece of metal when you dragged her out of the car and tied her up in the woods."

"It would have been so much easier for her if she had just cooperated. She would have been perfect," he says. "But it turns out she still was. Just for a different purpose than I could have imagined."

"Did you know she was pregnant?" I ask.

He shakes his head. "No, she wasn't. At least, not that night. She decided to do away with her baby. It was too much of a hassle for her, and she didn't want to have to deal with raising a child she didn't want alongside someone like LaRoche. She confided in me when she first found out. Of course, I told her I thought she should keep it. That she would enjoy being a mother, no matter what. But she didn't listen. That made it easier for me to choose her. If she hadn't made that choice, she would still be alive."

I want to steer the conversation away from the terrifying, damaging rhetoric. I don't need to hear it, and it changes nothing.

"You said she was perfect."

He nods. "She was. When I first considered her, I wanted her for one of the scenes. But when it didn't go as I planned, and everyone realized the disappearances were connected, suspicion started ramping up. You connecting her to LaRoche has actually created the ideal foundation. So, this new plan was born. I'm sure by now, the police have called in a forensic team to investigate the bar."

"Yes."

"They'll examine the blood and do swabs to test it, hoping they find traces of DNA other than mine they might be able to use to link to my killer. And they're going to find other DNA. A lot of it. They'll also find that much of the blood around there isn't exactly... fresh."

"It's been frozen," I say.

Jake smiles and nods. "You're catching on. See, people like predictability. They like formulas. So, when someone disappears, the first thing anyone does is find the last place they were and start trying to find the path from there. But if they don't really know where that last place was, they can't find the path. Blood splattered around in conspicuous places is always good for starting an investigation in the wrong direction. I've kept extra blood frozen, not knowing what to do with it until now. When they realize the DNA isn't all mine and the scene has been staged, they're going to look to the person who has the most experience with crime scenes and what investigators look for."

"LaRoche," I murmur.

"It will seem like he contaminated the scene purposely to throw off the search and confuse people. It won't take much for people to start making connections and finding the same threads you did. I'm sure Andrea will be more than happy to come forward when she thinks one of the men she trusted is dead, and the other one killed him."

"You're the one who sat at the bar watching her. Not LaRoche."

"A couple times a week. He wanted to make sure she wasn't cozying up with anyone else. Of course, she didn't want anyone around to know who I was or that I was bringing her to see him so often. I don't know what this hold he has over women is, but he's able to convince them it's for the best that they keep any connection to him totally hidden," Jake explains.

"I don't understand. Why would you do that for him? Why would you go out of your way to help him have these relationships and keep the women a secret? I thought it disgusted you."

Jake shrugs. "Keep your friends close."

And your enemies closer.

"What happens when Andrea does come forward and people start to suspect him?" I ask.

"That's where you were supposed to come in. I knew you would keep searching. You wouldn't just take what you saw for face value. Already convinced it was LaRoche, you would keep digging and tying up those threads. After a few days, I would emerge from the woods, battered, starved, and tormented, but alive. Safe again in your arms. I would tell the harrowing story of LaRoche blackmailing me because of a secret he knows about my past. He used it for leverage to get me to cooperate with his affairs, but when I found out about the killings, he put me on his list. He abducted me, dragged me out into the woods, and kept me hostage there. But I managed to escape. It's a convincing story, especially with someone like you standing beside me, telling them everything you already suspected about him."

"And the town would be desperate to put the case to rest. It wouldn't take much to convince them."

"As confused as your version of the events is, it makes enough sense to warrant an arrest and keeping him in jail during a long, drawn-out murder investigation. And you probably know what happens to lawmen in jail," he says.

"They'd kill him," I confirm.

"Most likely. But if he did happen to survive, he would likely be convicted. Even if he wasn't, he'd never be able to show his face around here again. I'd have everything I ever wanted," Jake tells me.

"What is it that you've always wanted?" I ask.

Jake turns around to face the vignettes. He gestures to them, gazing at them with an affectionate smile on his face.

"This," he says warmly. Like he's talking about a family. My blood is ice.

"To kill people?" I ask. "Innocent people, who have done absolutely nothing to wrong you? Why would you want that?"

The smile fades as he looks at me. "No. No, no. That's not it. This is an evolution, a discovery. What you don't know is this isn't all of them. No one else knows that. There are others. Scattered in fields and woods, floating in the water. Across five states, there are others. I started with them for the sheer purpose of elimination."

"What were you eliminating?" I ask. I look around the room and back at him. "It was all a lie, wasn't it? Everything you told me. All those stories were lies. That's what this is about."

Jake gives a short, mirthless laugh and walks over to the edge of the Christmas scene. He stares at the older man.

"My family was horrible. My father was a cruel, abusive alcoholic raised by a cruel, abusive alcoholic. Most of the time, he wasn't even home. He stayed at the bar and crawled his way up to the apartment at night."

"I went to the cemetery. There are no graves for your mother or any siblings. Are they real?"

"Oh, they're real. They aren't buried there. I don't know where they are. My mother preferred my sister. She was the only thing that mattered. She got everything she wanted, including every existing drop of my mother's love. There was nothing left for the rest of us. My brother was distant and cold. He stayed away most of the time. We grew up here."

He looks around like he's gazing up at the entire house. "This was my home. No one knew that, of course. Nobody in town realized people still lived all the way out here. Few people in town even knew my siblings existed, and only Cole Barnes ever met my mother. They knew me because my father dragged me to the bar to put me to work by the time I was old enough to wash a dish."

"What happened to them?" I ask.

Jake leaves the Christmas scene and walks over to the dinner table. He runs his fingers along the hair of the woman, and my body shudders.

"The only solace I had when I was young was my grandmother." He looks up at me with a smile. "She was very real."

I nod. As much as everything inside me wants to lash out, I'm staying in control. Keeping Jake calm is the only way I can hope to stay alive another minute, another hour, and find out what I need to know. Building his trust back up will be what gets me out of here.

CHAPTER THIRTY-FOUR

I t sinks in there are no elderly corpses in the room. No women over slightly older middle age. Just the men and women, the young men and women, and the girl with the baby. Jake's mother and father. His sister and brother. And someone else. But no grandmother. He didn't need to create her because she was real.

"I know. The quilt in the cabin. My favorite one. She made that, didn't she? It has fabric in it from the dress she was wearing in the picture of Easter morning."

"Yes. But that wasn't Easter. We never celebrated any holidays as a family. At least, not my parents and siblings. My grandmother would try to do things for me when I got shoved with her. I spent as much time with her as I possibly could, and when I was lucky, my parents would just leave me with her for days at a time."

"Why did no one in town mention to me the cabin I'm staying in belongs to your family?" I ask.

"Because they don't know. My mother was my grandmother's only child. She loved her, but she also knew the type of person she really was. She saw that my mother only truly cared about my sister and didn't want anything to do with her sons, especially me. Pretty quickly, it became obvious any acknowledgement of me or affection toward me meant my mother took me away, and my grandmother didn't see me for a while. I was always in worse condition the next time she saw me. So, she stopped talking about me. Stopped asking about me or showing any sign of caring about me. Until my mother would leave. Then she showered me with love, fed me as much as I could eat, and encouraged me to play. I never got any of that any other time. Whenever my parents would show up to get me, I pretended to be miserable. If they stayed for dinner, my sister sat at the table with my mother and grandmother while my father put me downstairs with the dog. He barked if I got near the door. They didn't want me running out and going into town. But the better I got at acting like my grandmother's house was hell, the more time I got there."

"But then your grandmother died," I guess.

Jake nods.

"When I lost her, everything was taken away. What I thought was a bad life was nothing compared to the way things got after that. It got worse and worse until finally, everything shattered. My brother walked away, and we never heard from him again. One day I came home from school, and my mother and sister were gone. They had just packed up everything and left, abandoning me here with my father and nothing else."

"If you went to school, how did nobody know what was going on? How did nobody know where you lived or the type of family you had?" I ask.

"This town has secrets, Emma. And it keeps them for others. People believe what they're told and close their minds off to everything else. It means I don't have to confront things I don't want to think about, and they can protect what they don't want other people to know about themselves."

"The entire town failed you," I frown. Even if he did horrific things, I still have to keep up appearances that I care about him. "Someone should have protected you."

"But they didn't. After my mother left with my sister, my father just got drunker and angrier. More often than not, I was the one running the bar because he just couldn't do it. He died when I was nineteen. I inherited the bar, and I've been living my life ever since."

He's had his back to me as he speaks, but now he turns and looks over his shoulder with a hint of a smile. "Do you really believe it was that simple?"

I shake my head. "No."

"Good. You're catching on." He turns back to the dinner scene, then moves over to the board game, leaning down to clean up the pieces scattered across the floor by the ornament I threw. "The first time I killed someone, it was a man I watched get drunk at the bar and then hit his wife. It brought up all the memories of everything I went through with my family. I hated the idea of anyone else hurting their family the way mine did each other. I held him back as his wife jumped in the car and drove away, then let him stumble down the street, making sure people saw him leave. Then I went around the opposite side of the building and down the alley so I could meet him a few blocks down. When they found him, they called it a mugging. That started my habit."

"You became a vigilante."

"In a way. I told you, it was about elimination. I eliminated those people who hurt others and were perpetuating families that were toxic and destructive. I hated the idea of any other child having to go through what I did, or more being born into paths that would just lead them to being the same type of people as the parents who came before them. Each killing cauterized the wound. I stopped it before it could happen. But after a while, I realized I wasn't really doing myself any good with it. I wasn't moving forward in my life. Killing those people was still me having to give something up, still doing what was right for other people rather than what was right for me. So, two years ago, I decided to change that."

He looks me straight in the eye.

"I never had a happy home or a happy family. I never got to make any of the memories children are supposed to make. If you ever look through all the photo albums in my house, you'd see a lot of pictures of my grandmother, my sister, some of my father. But there are only a few of me. They are all at my grandmother's house, and she hid them away so my mother would never find them and know she took them. I found them in the cabin years after she died, and my mother didn't step forward to claim the property. I wanted to take the quilt with me, too, but something told me to leave it. It's like still having her there."

"What happened to these people?" I ask. "Why them?"

"It wasn't about them. Not really. I'll be the first to admit most of these people did absolutely nothing to justify what happened to them. Unfortunately, sacrifices sometimes have to be made, and after a life-time of sacrifice, it was time for me to be the one who benefitted. I deserve memories of a good family. I wanted stories to tell and things to laugh about. So, I set out to create them for myself. I found people who reminded me of my family members at different ages, or what I wished they would look like. Then I brought them here and created the memories I always wanted. I told you once that archery was my thing. Along with that came preserving animals. I don't do either one of them anymore, but I was able to use those skills to preserve these people as much as I could. This way, I can keep them. They can be my family, and I can share these memories with them."

I'm somewhere between my heart breaking and passing out. Jake is settling down, sliding into the calm complacency I want him to be in so I can convince him to open the door. But there's still more for me to know. If I have to be down here, I need to get every bit of informa-tion out of him I possibly can.

"What about your father's bones? Why did you dig up his body and hide them at his best friend's house?" I ask.

"I didn't want to keep my father's body. He was the worst of the memories I had as a child. I wanted to completely obliterate him and replace them with others. So, that's what I did. I found men who exemplified everything I would have wanted in a father and put them in his place. But that didn't fully release me from everything he put me through. There were others who still needed to answer for what they had done. Including Cole Barnes. He really was my father's best friend. They were friends nearly their entire lives. He did my family a lot of harm. What little harmony we may have ever had, he was at the heart of destroying it. My father discovered he had been having an affair with my mother, and it put him completely over the edge. My father took it all out on me. He needed to pay for what he did. I dug up my father and put the bones with Barnes to remind him of what he did to give him a little bit of hell, knowing it was all catching up with him. I wanted him to fear being arrested. Going to prison. If you hadn't interfered, I was going to make sure there was much more he went through. He deserves every bit of it."

It's clear to me now why Jake was ostracized from his family. Why his father despised him, and his mother wanted nothing to do with him. He wasn't his father's child. He was the product of his mother's affair with her husband's best friend. Every moment of Jake's life was a reminder of her betrayal and the further breakdown of their family.

A feeling deep in my gut pulls me away from the door and closer to the center of the room.

"Jake?" He turns to face me, and I look toward the only scene that doesn't make sense to me. He walks toward the young woman cradling the baby in the rocking chair. "Who is she?"

"What could have been. My wife. Melanie was so much more beautiful, but this woman had a laugh that sounded so much like hers I couldn't resist her." His voice grows emotional as he strokes his fingertips down along the side of the woman's face. "My wife was everything to me. When I found her, it was like my life finally started. I woke up. The world was new and wonderful. It didn't matter how my father acted or what was going on with anyone else. If I got to see her, it made everything better. I knew her a week when I knew I wanted to marry her. We were high school sweethearts. We got married the day she turned eighteen. It was the happiest day of my life. I know everyone says that about their wedding day, but it was true. I saw my future. I saw a life ahead of me. She was going to be the start of the family I never had and so desperately wanted to give to my own children."

"But she got hit by a drunk driver," I say.

Jake shakes his head. "No. In a way, I suppose that's true, but that's not what happened."

"What do you mean?" I ask.

"I already crafted the type of life I wanted, the world I imagined, and the family I wanted to be in. I told you the stories I told myself a thousand times. I was almost starting to truly believe it. So, I told you a story about her, too."

"What really happened to her, Jake?"

"My father." The breath catches in my throat, and I swallow it down painfully. Jake looks at me with hardened eyes, and tears slide unchecked down his cheeks. "He was obsessed with her. He wanted her from the second he met her, and I did everything I could to protect her. Everything. But he went after her. It was like everything else in his life; it didn't matter who he hurt or what he had to do. If he wanted something, he was going to get it, and that included my wife. We were married three months when he showed up at our house and smashed me over the head with his gun. He tried to rape her while I was on the ground. I attacked him and told her to run. Melanie escaped, but he hit me again and got away from me. Before I could stop him, he got in the car and went after her. He ran her down in the middle of the road."

"Jake, I'm so sorry."

Despite all I see around me, the pain and sympathy are real.

"She was my hope for my future. My dream. She had just found out she was pregnant with our first baby. And he took it all away from me. He had to be punished. I could have ripped him limb from limb with my bare hands in that very moment, but it wouldn't have done me any good. It would have been satisfying right then, but it would also have meant living out the rest of my life in prison. My father would have won. He always saw me as a failure and a disappointment, a representation of everything wrong in his life, and it probably would have amused him from beyond the grave to see me put away. So, I bided my time. I didn't tell the police what I knew about Melanie's death. I wanted my own justice. For the next several months, I slowly tormented my father, making him believe at any moment he would be arrested. Replacing his alcohol with colored water and extracts, so he slipped into delirium. I tortured him. When the time was right, I started to slowly poison him. I didn't want his death to be dramatic and cause a lot of attention. Something slow, painful, and horrific that could be explained away as a sick old man who destroyed his body was perfect. When he did, I got everything he had, everything he never wanted to be mine. I buried him close to Melanie so I could always turn my back on my father when I went to visit my wife, and for all eternity, he would have to relive what he had done."

CHAPTER THIRTY-FIVE

"So, your father was actually the first person you murdered," I point out. "Not that man from the bar."

He smiles. "I guess you're right. I just don't think of killing my father as murder. I prefer to think of it as I carried out his execution. But it was that first death that taught me I was capable of killing. I was good at it and could use it to get what I wanted. I didn't think about that for a long time after, but the night I saw that man in the bar, it all came back to me. Killing him was as natural as breathing." He looks at me with an expression of treacherous tenderness in his eyes. "You could have been my future, Emma. You are the only person who has gotten my attention since my wife. You could have given me the life I wanted. But then I found out who you really are."

My stomach sinks.

"What do you mean?" I ask.

"You know exactly what I mean, Emma *Griffin*. It wasn't hard to figure out you are more than just someone looking for a new start to her life. I can understand a fascination with crime, but I saw something in you, something I've never seen in anyone. Other than me."

"I'm nothing like you," I say.

"Oh, but you are. You know exactly what you want. You go after it, no matter who's standing in your way. And when you think you know what's right, you will do anything to stand up for it. You protect what matters to you, and you fight fiercely against anything that may threaten it. You are exactly like me," he says. "But you're also like everyone else. You're a liar, pretending to be someone you're not. And you were catching on to me. It wouldn't be long until you realized your theory was unraveling, and everything was leading you right to me."

"I came here to find you because I was worried about you," I tell him.

"I know you did," he whispers, walking up to me and putting his hand on the back of my head. He pulls me close and kisses me in the middle of the forehead. "I know."

With one swift punch to his gut, I send him to the ground and jump down on him with my knee direct in the center of his chest. I incapacitate him long enough for me to reach into his pocket and take out the key to the door. Another stomp in the middle of his stomach keeps him down. I spin on my heel, running to the door to unlock it.

He's already back on his feet as I wrench the door open and run up the stairs. I don't even risk looking back as I scramble up, hoping beyond anything that the door slams shut on him. But I hear him grunt and his hand catch it before it does. I silently curse my luck and lunge for the top of the stairs.

He's pulled the wardrobe almost back into place. I have to squeeze myself through the gap. I don't have time to reach into my pocket and pull out my phone, so I run blindly through the dark, dank basement in the direction I hope will lead me to the steps. I can hear him behind me, getting closer as he screams my name.

"Emma!"

It echoes around the walls, doubling back on itself.

"Emma!"

Finally, my feet hit the bottom step, and I trip forward, landing on my face on the rough, unfinished wood. I scramble up the stairs on my hands and knees, finally pulling myself up when I get to the door. Outside, the sun has set, and the house is filled with gloom and shadows. Jake's footsteps have gotten even closer. I feel his hand clutch the back of my shirt. Whipping around, I smash my forearm into his face, sending him tumbling back over an armchair.

Bursting out of the house, I run for the woods. His footsteps fall heavy on the wooden steps leading down from the porch. I hope for the darkness to conceal me, for the moonlight to not betray me. Once in the trees, I try to find the path with the least branches, trying to keep my feet quiet. I know now it was him following me in the woods that night. He pursued me almost silently, watching me as I moved along this very path and then back toward the cabin. He knows how I navigate the trees. He knows how I move about these woods.

Abandoning the path, I head in the opposite direction, kind of hoping it brings me somewhere I can find help or at least a place where I can hide until daylight. Exhausted and out of breath, I drop down behind a fallen tree. Pressing my back to the damp bark, I struggle to fill my lungs with air without making noise. I stay there as long as I can spare before standing up.

As soon as I turn around, something hits me in the side of the head.

I come out of a groggy stupor, being dragged across the ground. I writhe and fight to get my feet under me. I try to stand. I scream, but it's useless.

No one is anywhere around here. No one will hear me. Just like no one heard Cristela. No one heard any of them.

Jake says nothing as he pulls me back through the woods. He has me in a tight, complicated grip that keeps me from getting loose. My back aches from the angle it's bent at as he drags me, but when I loosen up completely, I feel like I'm choking.

Finally, we're back to the house, and he pulls me up to my feet but doesn't release me. I'm standing with my back to him, my arms twisted around behind me. He tucks one hand around the front of my throat and kisses my cheek.

"You're not going anywhere, Emma. Like I said, you could have been my future. We could have had such an incredible life together. If you had only just done what you were supposed to do."

"If you already knew who I am, why did you let it go this far? Why didn't you just confront me before? Why did you keep going with this ridiculous plan?"

"There was a part of me that still hoped so much it could happen. You might suspect me and were catching on to me, but if I could prove it was LaRoche like you had believed all along, all that would go away. Just like with every other lie you lived before it was me, you could put it behind you. If I could prove to you that you were right all along, and someone else was responsible, I could keep you, and we could have such a beautiful life. But you came here. You didn't come here looking for me because you thought I was still alive out of some miracle. You came here looking for me because you knew. I was not convincing you of anything else."

"I told you. I came because I was worried about you."

"Please don't lie to me, Emma. It's going to make it so much harder for me to come up with a beautiful memory of us if those are the last words I hear from you."

"A memory?"

"Yes. I'll create a wonderful memory for us to have. I just don't know what it will be yet. I think that we should enjoy some special bonding time together first. I want to get to know you a little better before I really decide what to create with you. Come on. There's something I want to show you."

Jake forces me up the steps and into one of the rooms on the top floor of the farmhouse. Unlike the other rooms, this one looks well maintained and taken care of. Like it's been used regularly for years. It's clean and is furnished with modern furniture, candles strewn across the top of the windowsill and the surface of the table. Heavy drape hanging from the window and elaborate bedding accentuates a massive bed in the middle of the room.

"This is my room," he says. "It was my parents' room when I was growing up. Which, of course, means it was my mother's room most of the time. We were never allowed in here. And now it's mine. Do you like it?"

I don't answer him, and he shuts the door, locking it. He moves around the room, lighting all the candles like he's trying to create a romantic atmosphere for us. He tells me to make myself comfortable, and I choose one of the overstuffed chairs positioned across from the bed.

I sit there for the next few hours, listening to Jake tell me actual stories of his childhood. Time stretches forever. My panic rises as he replaces each of the lies he's told me with a real recollection. Actual glimpse into what he dealt with. He starts by pacing around the room, then sits across from me, almost close enough that our knees touch. Every so often, he gestures, and I jump, and he reaches forward to touch my leg and soothe me.

After a while, he suddenly jumps up and goes to the bureau, pulling out a bottle of liquor. He doesn't sit down in between drinks, and soon he's slurring, his movements slowed. The more he drinks, the more animated his stories become, and the deeper he delves into the horrors he experienced.

Finally, the bottle is almost empty, and it seems so is he. Jake's head falls back against the chair, and his eyes droop, then close. I watch him sleep for a few minutes, hoping beyond hope that he is actually unconscious. When I'm finally assured, I stand and cross the room as quickly as I can.

I get to the door and try the handle before I remember he locked it. I tiptoe back to the chairs, trying to reach into his pocket and pull out the key. He starts and grabs my wrist, glaring at me with reddened eyes filled with fury.

"Maybe I don't actually have time to get to know you," he growls at me. "You just can't leave well enough alone, can you?"

I don't have any more time to waste. I have to do something, or I won't survive to get out of here. I'm not going to be able to get through the door, which means there's only one option left. I need something to distract him and get him to release me. I compulsively grab the bottle of liquor from the floor and splash what's left across the heavy curtains hanging on the window just beside the chairs. His hand loosens from my wrist in a startled response to my move. I take advantage of the opportunity and lunge for the candles on a nearby table. I toss them onto the curtains, and they immediately ignite.

Flames eat through the tapestries in a matter of seconds and crawl up to the ceiling and walls. Flecks of paint from the ceiling and droplets of fire come down, igniting the bed. Within just a few breaths, the room fills with thick, acrid smoke.

I can barely see through the red and orange. Jake is screaming, stumbling for the curtain to try to pull the fragments down. I dart toward him, shoving him with both hands. His body smashes through the glass and drops through the window. The air from outside creates a backdraft, and the flames roar around me. Pain licks up my back. I have only a fraction of a second to climb through the window. Outside is a steeply pitched roof. Digging my feet down onto the shingles, I move sideways as fast as I can, headed for the flat roof over the front porch.

Suddenly Jake's head appears out of the side of the roof. He caught himself when I pushed him, and now he scrambles back up onto the roof to confront me. He runs toward me, and we clash, clutching at each other. The struggle quickly brings us down. I feel the burn of melted tar on my skin and a scrape of the gutter on my back as we both tumble off the roof and onto the ground. Our eyes lock on one another as we fall, and then everything goes dark.

CHAPTER THIRTY-SIX

I don't know how long passes before I wake up. The lights are so bright I cringe, and somewhere around me, a voice hisses at someone to turn the lights down.

I know that voice. It's Bellamy.

It takes a few seconds for me to process the beeps, sharp smells, and cold air. When I do, I realize I'm in a hospital bed. Everything hurts. My entire body aches, and it feels like if I lift my head up off the pillow, it might split in half. But at least I still have a body to hurt. At least I'm still alive to feel that pain.

I stop myself for a long moment. Am I dead? Is this the light flashing before my eyes before it's snuffed out? My mind is a fog. I don't know what's going on.

Bellamy takes my hand. The fog clears. And when I finally get my eyes all the way open, I see her smiling down at me. Tracks of tears mark her makeup, but she's still beautiful.

"You're the only person I know who can look so good when they're crying," I tell her.

I know my voice sounds weak and scratchy, but she still laughs through the new tears falling from her eyes.

"You do, too," she says.

"No, I don't. My mascara comes off, and I look like I'm melting," I say. I can't believe it. I'm alive. I'm not dead in a basement. Not burned in a house fire. I'm safe and joking with Bellamy right now.

This isn't a dream, right?

"Then we'll just have to not let you have as many reasons to cry," Eric adds, coming up to the side of my bed.

"That's always kind of the goal, isn't it?" I chuckle weakly. I look between them. "How are you both here? Did the hospital call you?"

"No. You did," Eric explains.

"What?" I ask, trying to pull myself up. I wince in pain. Definitely not a dream.

Bellamy reaches down and adjusts the bed, helping me prop up the pillows behind me so I can still rest back on them.

"Well, not a call, exactly. But you did email me. Next time I'd appreciate a little bit of a heads up when you're going to send me pictures like that."

"How did you get that email? I didn't have any service in the basement," I point out.

"You must have gotten it at some point because it came through. It was the middle of the night, so I didn't get it until a few hours later. I'm sorry," he says.

"You got it, that's all the matters. I took all those pictures and attached them to an email to you when I first got down into the sub-basement, but there was no service. I was locked down there for hours. The service must have kicked back in and sent the queued email when I escaped and ran out into the woods," I explain.

"You escaped?" Bellamy asks.

"Briefly. But he found me and knocked me out so he could drag me back into the house. I put up as much of a fight as I could."

"You can't blame yourself," Eric says. "This is a man who has killed at least fifteen people."

"More than that," I say, recounting the story Jake told me of the vigilante murders.

"Holy shit," he gasps. "You got out of the hands of a man who has killed much bigger, much stronger people. And because you did, that email got sent. The timing was apparently perfect. The field team you requested was consulting with the local police, literally the moment I called. I described what I saw and tracked your phone to the closest it would place you. The police chief knew immediately where I was talking about. They got to the house just in time to see it go up in flames and the two of you fall off the roof."

"What happened to Jake?" I ask.

Both Eric and Bellamy stiffen, but I don't care. He's still a human being. One who has been tortured and tormented in a way none of us will ever understand.

"He survived the fall. We peeled the two of you out of some overgrown hedges. You got the better of it. The way he fell made him hit a rock wall and then land in the bushes. He's not doing well, but they expect him to recover. As of now, there's a war going on over who gets their hands on him first," Eric explains. "I think the FBI is coming out on top. Considering one of our own cracked the case."

"You make me sound like I should be wearing a fedora and chewing tobacco," I mutter, my head still throbbing. "How is Creagan taking it?"

"Right now, he's in the thick of it all. He led the team into the house and found all the bodies. They've been linking them to all the missing persons cases. Some of them are a bit trickier than others."

"Why?" I ask.

Bellamy and Eric exchange glances. He looks worried about her, and she releases my hand, grabbing a bucket from beside me.

"I'll go get you some ice chips," she says.

"I'm not giving birth, Bellamy," I call weakly after her, but she doesn't turn back.

"Some of the bodies weren't complete. A few of them have parts from others stitched onto them. The theory until we can get more out of Jake is that the original parts were damaged in some way, so he replaced them," Eric explains.

I remember the bodies that didn't look exactly right and realize it was because they were pieced together. I shudder.

"So, they have to find out who those parts belong to," I muse.

Eric nods. "It will probably take a good while. There are a lot of missing persons cases floating around in the surrounding areas, and this might wrap up quite a few of them. At this point, it's pretty much a mess, and everyone is just starting to unravel it all. You're going to be a lot of help in that."

I nod, acknowledging that I'm only at the beginning of all this, but wishing I never had to think about it again. I'm glad it's over, at least this part of it, but this isn't like any other case I've ever worked on. I'm not going to be able to just put it behind me and move on it like I've been able to before. This is something I will always carry with me.

"How could I not know?" I whisper.

"Emma, don't do that to yourself," Eric says.

"No, but how? This is my career, my entire life. The entire reason I was sent to Feathered Nest was because of this case. It was my job to figure out what was going on because no one else was able to. And I managed to, on the very first day I was there, attach myself to the man who did it. And I couldn't even tell. I was so wrapped up in the theory I had; I couldn't see what was really happening."

"He wasn't going to let you see what was really happening. He's been fooling people for years. Well before all this started. You know that. You can't blame yourself for not immediately looking at him and knowing it was him. If it was that easy, none of us would have jobs."

"But I shouldn't have let myself get close to him to start with. I should have been focusing on my job and not... whatever that was."

"You've been through a lot in the last few months. No one blames you for wanting to find comfort in somebody. And you managed to get through this not only alive but with all the evidence we are ever going to need to make sure Jake never hurts anyone ever again."

"What about all the people he already hurt?" I ask.

"You can't make that go away. You can't go back in time and save them. But you did give them their voices back. You gave their families the ability to bury their loved ones and know what happened to them. And you prevented anyone else from having to feel that because of him."

"I want to petition to have the courts change his wife's death certificate to murder," I say.

"Alright," Eric nods. "But why?"

"Because she deserves her voice and to have her story told, too."

Bellamy comes back into the room with a bucket of ice and a can of ginger ale. She fills a plastic cup with the ice and pours the sparkling drink down over it. It passes over my lips as one of the most delicious tastes I've ever had. I realize it must be almost forty-eight hours since I took a drink. That explains the IV in my arm, pumping fluids into me. I'm aware of my friends talking, but I can't pay attention to the words they're saying. My mind is still swimming, my brain fogs up again, and finally, my eyes close.

When I wake up again, Eric and Bellamy are sitting across the room, talking quietly as they eat from Chinese takeout containers.

"Did you order me egg drop soup?" I croak.

Bellamy smiles and carries a container over to the bed, handing it to me along with a deep spoon.

"I still don't think that's the best thing for her right now," Eric frowns.

"The doctor didn't say she couldn't have it," Bellamy points out.

"Did the doctor say she *could* have it?" Eric asks.

"Technicality."

I smile and take a few bites of the soup. I want to think about anything but Jake and the case, but it seems like there isn't anything else to think about.

"Have they found Jake's mother, brother, and sister?" I ask.

"You should try to rest. There's going to be plenty of time for you to think about this when you get out," Bellamy says, but I shake my head.

"No. The sooner this all gets resolved, the better. I'm not going to stop working just because I fell off a burning roof. Did they find them? They're going to need to be a part of the investigation. They need to be around to corroborate the stories he told about his father and explain themselves and their role in his childhood. They can give insight into his mindset and experiences that no one else can."

"They've traced his mother and sister. Both of them are coming in within the next couple of days. They're still looking for his brother. There doesn't seem to be any trace of him in years, but that doesn't mean much. He very easily could have changed his identity and moved to another country or just fallen off the grid. But we'll keep looking for him. If nothing else, I think it's probably a good idea for everybody who's ever come in contact with Jake to be accounted for," Eric says.

"They need to run a DNA test on Cole Barnes. I think he's Jake's father," I say.

I know I'm going to come in contact with Jake again in the near future. I'll also probably encounter his mother and sister. I don't know how to feel about any of it. Part of me has compassion for them. I can see how all this will horrify his mother and sister. It will be incredibly hard for them. This is something they'll have to live with for the rest of their lives, knowing they contributed to Jake's complete breakdown and to tremendous losses of life.

But at the same time, they put Jake through hell. They let the man he thought was his father mistreat him, and they abandoned him when he was far too young to have to go through all that alone. They are, at the very least, partly to blame for this. Not that they made him do it, or it's an excuse, but they are most definitely a contributing factor. I will have no hesitation telling them that. They need to understand what they did and the damage it caused.

But I also know after everything, Jake doesn't really deserve much of my compassion. He knew exactly what he was doing. That will have to sit alongside all the other feelings I ever had for him, and I will live with it, dealing with it every day as I move forward.

EPILOGUE

Bellamy and Eric offered to clean all of my stuff out of the cabin, so I didn't have to go there again, but I didn't take them up on it. I felt like I needed to come here again to try to get some sort of conclusion and closure to everything I experienced in Feathered Nest. I don't know if that's really possible. Part of me will linger here, and there won't ever really be any closure. But coming back here and being able to put the finishing moments on the job gets me closer.

My bags are packed, and I carry them out of the bedroom and into the living room. I've already cleaned out the kitchen and tucked away all the dishes I used. The furnace hums along smoothly, keeping the space warm. Clancy will be by later to deactivate it, putting it to sleep until the next time somebody comes to visit.

I have a feeling it won't be long. As soon as the story of what happened here spreads, people will flock to stay in the cabin on the lake and explore the woods. They crave the mystery. People like that bring me back to my theory of the atmosphere being stained by crime. Maybe they can see it and feel it in a way other people can't. They flock to them to remember those spaces and never let them forget.

All that's left is packing up the remaining papers I have. Most of my notes and pictures are with Creagan to be used in the investigation, but I still have some of the original clippings and papers I brought with me. They'll go home with me and get tucked away into a case file, then put on a shelf in my house just like all my other cases. I never look through those books, but they're there. One day long after my time with the bureau is done and I retire, maybe I'll take them down and flip through them, remembering these days. I can share them with my children and hopefully inspire some of the same pride as my father always did in me.

I hear a knock on my door just as I'm slipping the last of the papers into my satchel. I look back over my shoulder and see Eric at the door.

"You ready?" he asks.

"I think so," I nod. "Actually, can you bring these to the car? I need just one more minute."

"Sure."

He takes the bags and walks out of the cabin, closing the door behind him. I wait until his steps leave the porch and walk back into the bedroom. Opening the top drawer of the dresser, I reach in and pull out the thimble. I tuck it into my pocket, draw in one more breath, and walk away, leaving the bed perfectly made and spread with the crazy quilt.

Eric looks over at me when I climb into the passenger seat.

"Are you okay?" he asks.

"Yep," I tell him, reaching behind me to get my seatbelt. I wince at the pain that radiates through me at the twisting motion. "Mostly. Did they already come for the car?"

"Yeah. They towed it over to the police station to use as evidence. I can't believe you drove around with that glass in your back seat."

"I can't believe I'm actually going to miss that thing."

He laughs and turns the engine over. We pull away from the cabin and down the long driveway. Bellamy has already gone home, and I can imagine she's at work filling my freezer with whatever she comes up with, so I have meals to warm up during my time off.

I told Creagan I was going to take the vacation I haven't taken in the last three years, and he didn't argue. But I'm not planning on staying home for all of it. As a reward for the success of this job, he turned the other way when Eric slipped me a bit of information they found about Greg's disappearance. I plan on following up on it as soon as I'm feeling back to normal.

"How long are you planning on staying in Maine?" Eric asks.

"As long as I need to. It depends on what I can find while I'm there," I shrug.

"And then?"

"And then, I don't know. Creagan still won't let me be a part of the investigation, and I think his goodwill towards me is only going to last but so long. I'm not sure how much interference he's going to tolerate. I might just have to pass along anything I find out to you and hope for more."

"Somehow, I don't think that's actually what you're going to do," he smiles.

"We'll see."

"And if nothing pans out? Are you going to go visit Florida?"

He knows how much my heart longs for the state. The water parks. The burn of the concrete on my feet. I could definitely use some time to let my bones thaw from this miserable weather.

But I reach into the pocket of my hooded sweatshirt and pull out the printed picture inside. Looking down at the image of my parents, young and smiling, my father's skin touched with gold; I focus on the vaguely familiar face between them.

"How do you feel about Iowa?"

THE END

My dear reader,
I hope that my book has brought you enjoyment and in its own way that it also brought a lot of thrills to your life.

If you can take a moment out of your very busy day to leave me a review, I would appreciate that enormously.

Your reviews allow me to get the validation I need to keep doing what I love and continue to pursue my love of writing.

It also helps me tremendously as a new writer just starting out.

It is always a challenging journey to start something new.

Being an indie author is no exception.

Your review doesn't have to be long, but however short or long you want.

Just a moment of your time is all that is needed.

When you leave me a review, know that I am forever thankful to YOU.

Again, thank you for reading my novel.

Look forward for my next one!

I promise always to do my best to bring you thrilling adventures.

Yours,

A.J. Rivers

P.S. If, for some reason, you didn't like this book or found typos or other errors, please let me know personally. I do my best to read and respond to every email at aj@riversthrillers.com

THE GIRL THAT VANISHED (SNEAK PEEK)

Check Out Emma Griffin FBI Mystery Book 2 Now.

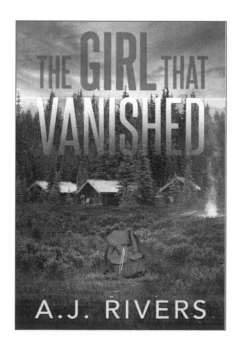

Ring...Ring...

One call from her past was all it took to change everything.

A ten-year-old girl has vanished on her way home from camp.
And things took a turn for the worse when another child, a child that Emma knows, goes missing.

Disappearances, death, and tragedies has followed Emma Griffin throughout her childhood.
Her obsession with finding out the truth behind her past was what led her to join the FBI.

It's been months since the horror of Feather Nest.
After the shocking revelation of the last case, FBI agent Emma Griffin decides to take a much-needed vacation.
But a phone call from Sheriff Sam Johnson, a man from her past, completely derails her plans.
A young girl has disappeared, and another child has gone missing.
With the number count slowly climbing.
Emma must now put her plans on hold, go back to her hometown and face some ghosts from her past.
When a mysterious package appears on her birthday.
Emma can't shake the feeling that someone is monitoring her every movement.
Someone is getting too close for comfort.
The question is who?

In the close-knit town of Sherwood, the truth is never as it seems.

Order your copy now!

Type the link below in your internet browser now to join my mailing list and get your free copy of Edge Of The Woods.

https://dl.bookfunnel.com/ze03jzd3e4

ALSO BY A.J. RIVERS

Made in the USA
Monee, IL
15 April 2020